Praise for Tara Ta...

"One of the skills that has served Quinn best...has been her ability to explore edgier subjects."
—*Publishers Weekly*

"One of the most powerful Superromances I have had the privilege to review."
—*WordWeaving* on *Nothing Sacred*

"Quinn writes touching stories about real people that transcend plot type or genre."
—*All About Romance*

"Quinn explores relationships thoroughly.... Her vividly drawn characters are sure to win readers' hearts."
—*Romance Communications*

"Quinn's latest contemporary romance offers readers an irresistible combination of realistically complex characters and a nail-bitingly suspenseful plot. Powerful, passionate and poignant, *Hidden* is deeply satisfying."
—*Booklist*

"*Somebody's Baby* is an exceptional tale of real-life people who are not perfect, feel heartache, make mistakes and have to find their inner strength.... *Somebody's Baby* easily goes on my keeper shelf."
—*The Romance Reader Reviews*

Where the Road Ends is "an intense, emotionally compelling story."
—*Booklist*

Dear Reader,

Most of us, when we were children, spent a lot of time playing. As we grew up and responsibilities presented themselves, the child inside us was slowly buried. For some, the burial was complete and we forgot how to play at all. For many of the rest of us, playtime was minimal. We not only lost the "fun" that filled the majority of our waking hours, but we lost the ability to believe in things we couldn't explain, to assume we'd be loved just because we existed, to wish for something with any expectation of receiving it.

A Child's Wish is the story of a woman who didn't lose that ability to listen to her heart, who didn't lose the ability to believe in the things she couldn't explain. It's also the story of a child whose greatest wish, and her attempts to achieve it, could cost her her life. And it's the story of a man who trusts only what he can explain with his head, not his heart.

A Child's Wish feels, in part, like my own autobiography. While all the events are pure fiction, the catharsis, the coming of age, by all three of the story's major players touched me personally. This story gave me hope and joy; it gave me not only the reminder, but the license, to play. I hope you can find the freedom to believe what your heart tells you, no matter where it leads—even if it goes against the crowd. I wish you all joy in life. I'm off to play now....

Tara Taylor Quinn

P.S. I love to hear from readers. You can reach me at P.O. Box 133584, Mesa, Arizona 85216 or through my Web site, www.tarataylorquinn.com.

A CHILD'S WISH
Tara Taylor Quinn

TORONTO • NEW YORK • LONDON
AMSTERDAM • PARIS • SYDNEY • HAMBURG
STOCKHOLM • ATHENS • TOKYO • MILAN • MADRID
PRAGUE • WARSAW • BUDAPEST • AUCKLAND

ISBN 0-373-71350-9

A CHILD'S WISH

Copyright © 2006 by Tara Taylor Quinn.

Printed in U.S.A.

Books by Tara Taylor Quinn

HARLEQUIN SUPERROMANCE

HARLEQUIN SINGLE TITLE

*Shelter Valley Stories

MIRA BOOKS

For Kevin, Rachel, Mom and Sherry,
the daily recipients of my intensity, who hang around
in spite of me. You are the culmination of my deepest wishes
and I am grateful for you every single day.

Acknowledgment

Many thanks to Maricopa County Sheriff's Office Deputy
David Parra for his generous contribution to the technical
aspects of this book. And for the kindness, respect and
humor with which he handled my ignorance.

CHAPTER ONE

"Ms. FOSTER, are you alone?" Startled as the loud-speaker sounded in her third-grade classroom during her Thursday-afternoon planning period, Meredith glanced up from the sloppily scrawled math problem she'd been trying to decipher.

"Yes, Mr. Shepherd." She used the formality, just as she always did when anyone else was around—or could possibly be around.

"Could you come down to my office?" The principal's inner sanctum—the only place in the building where one could be guaranteed an uninterrupted meeting.

Meredith dropped the purple pen she'd been using to grade papers.

"Yes, Mr. Shepherd. I'll be right there."

The beautiful March day had just taken a nosedive. She was in trouble again.

"YOU'RE THE BEST teacher I've ever had, Meredith. Year after year, your students average higher scores than any other students in the district on both national and local aptitude tests."

"I know." Hands clasped in her lap, one thumb

rubbing the opposite palm, Meredith added, "Thank you."

"You're also the teacher who brings me the most parental phone calls."

She occupied one of the two wooden armchairs in front of the scarred but spotless desk while the principal, dressed in casual slacks, cotton shirt and tie, stood at the window behind it.

"I know."

"Those parents pay my salary."

"I know."

"And yours."

She nodded, pulling her hair in the process as her waist-length ponytail got caught in the corner of the chair's arm.

"Some of them make up the school board and the superintendent who oversee us."

It must be bad.

"They are the community that—"

"Mark, I get the picture," Meredith interrupted. "Mr. Barnett called." She was only guessing, but it didn't take a psychic to figure it out.

"He got me at home last night—during dinner."

"I'm sorry." For what, she wasn't sure. Causing him aggravation, certainly. Interrupting his dinner, of course. But for telling the boy's divorced mother that she suspected Tommy's father was emotionally abusing him— no.

"You not only created grief that we didn't need, your conversation with Tommy's mother yesterday afternoon resulted in a nasty fight between the boy's parents."

Unfortunate, to be sure.

"Which should be avoided at the cost of an eight-year-old boy's safety?" She shifted and felt a sting as the back of her leg stuck to the wood. If she'd ever learned to tuck her skirt beneath her when she sat, as her mother had urged her to do for most of her life, that wouldn't have happened. Instead, the long folds of colorful cotton flowed around her.

"You're a third-grade teacher, Meredith, not the school counselor. Your job includes speaking to parents about scholastic concerns, reading problems, poor test scores or a lack of attention in class—not about unproved suspicions of suicidal tendencies."

"So I should just let a kid kill himself or rip himself to pieces considering it? I should let his monster of a father continue to tear him down until he eventually believes there's no point in being alive?"

"He's eight years old!"

"A very mature eight years old."

"There's a protocol for these things. Professionals who are in place to help if you suspect trouble. People who are trained to deal with sensitive issues, with families and life tragedies."

"I've talked to Jean twice. She talked to Tommy and said she didn't think there was any need to call in the boy's parents—or to speak with him again unless something else came up."

"Jean's been with us for four years. She has almost a decade of child psychology training and is highly respected in her field."

That might be. But Jean Saunders lived completely in her head. If it wasn't logical, if it didn't fit a predetermined pattern, it didn't exist. "She's missing something with this one."

"What did she say?"

"That he's suffering from the usual apprehensions, guilt and insecurity of an only child pulled apart by divorce. That at most, his parents are using him to get at each other. Which they are."

"Meredith…" The name was drawn out in warning. "You have no way of *knowing* that."

She didn't respond to his comment. There was no point. Mark wouldn't listen.

"Tommy is considering suicide," she said softly, instead. "His father has convinced him that he's not a stable child and that he is the sole cause of his parents' divorce."

His father was rich, powerful and the current district attorney.

Mark's eyes narrowed. "Has he said as much to you?"

"No."

"But you overheard him talking to someone else? One of the kids?"

"No."

He stood behind her and began to pace. "I'm guessing he didn't write a paper on the topic."

"He's only in third grade. We're working on learning cursive script, nouns and verbs, not creative writing."

Mark settled against the edge of the desk, directly in front of Meredith. She wished he wouldn't do that. His closeness made this all much harder. And it was hard enough already.

This was one of those days when she found it a

tempting idea to turn her back on Mark Shepherd, walk right past his secretary in the outer office on the other side of the thick mahogany door and out of this Bartlesville, Oklahoma, school forever.

But she didn't know what she'd do if she couldn't teach. And there was Tommy—and others like him—to consider.

"I'll call Mr. Barnett and apologize," she said, glancing up at the man she might have dated if they hadn't been working together, if sexual relations between colleagues at the same school hadn't been against district policy—and if he'd ever asked. "And then I'll call Mrs. Barnett and tell her I was out of line and to disregard what I said."

"You know as well as I do that she won't. The suspicion has been planted."

Meredith stood, which made her just inches short of her boss's six feet, allowing her to meet him eye to mouth. Frank, her ex-fiancé, was Mark's height. It had been one of the few things she'd ended up still liking about him.

"I hope for Tommy's sake that she won't ignore it," she said to him, standing her ground. "I hope she gets him into counseling and away from his father eventually."

"All of which you absolutely are not going to say to her."

No. Because she couldn't do any good for anyone if she was out of work and away from the children she knew she was here to help. But it would be hard.

"He did it to her, too," she said, facing him, the chair at the back of her legs. "That's why it was so easy for her to believe that he was doing it to their son."

"Let me guess, she didn't tell you that. You just know."

"No." She shook her head, the colorful earrings dangling. "She told me."

"TOUGH DAY AT WORK?" Susan Gardner slowly ran her fingers through Mark's hair, back and forth. He loved it when she did that.

"Hmm," he said, his eyes half closed as he lounged beside her on the couch. He'd listened to Kelsey's bedtime prayers an hour ago, checked to make sure that her cat was curled up beside her and was only now starting to relax.

"I really admire your ability to spend your entire day with kids and not go crazy," she said. "I wouldn't have the patience."

"I could never spend my days looking down people's throats and up their noses," he responded, grinning.

She chuckled, as he'd meant her to. "I do not spend my days looking up people's noses," she said, tugging gently on a strand of his hair. "I only do that once or twice a week. Now if you want to talk about peering into ears…"

He didn't. Not really, though he greatly respected her ability. He spent his days refereeing, while Susan, an ear, nose and throat specialist, spent hers healing.

"Kelsey seemed awfully subdued tonight."

Susan was being kind.

"She was rude," he said, frustrated with his nine-year-old daughter. She'd always had such a big heart, her awareness of those around her advanced for her age.

Lately, however, there were moments when she was a person he didn't even know.

"She doesn't like me."

"It's not you...." Mark turned his head, taking in the beauty of the woman beside him. Susan's hair was short, dark, sassy. Her eyes big and luminous. Nothing like the long red-gold hair and soft green eyes of the woman who'd made his day ten times more difficult than it had needed to be.

He liked short, dark and sassy.

"Kelsey's not used to sharing me."

"We've been dating for almost six months."

"But she had me to herself for almost three years before that."

Her hand trailed down the side of his face to his neck. "I might believe that, if you two didn't still have three nights a week alone," she said and shook her head. "I'm not that great with children. I like them, I just don't know how to relate to them. Put me in an operating room and I'm calm and confident, but leave me alone with a child who's not a patient and I'm completely out of my element. I don't know what to say."

"You just talk to them," Mark explained, touched by her earnestness. "They're people like everyone else, only shorter."

"They don't think like adults."

"So, you were a kid once. Think back to that."

She sighed, resting her head against his shoulder. "I don't ever remember being a kid. My folks had me on the fast track before I was five."

Her parents were older; he'd met them several times. And she'd been something of a child prodigy. She was four years younger than he was and she'd been in medical school when he'd still been an undergraduate in college. She hadn't had many chances to make friends her own age. He knew all this. He'd just never considered the possibility that her unusual upbringing might have robbed her of childhood thoughts as well as everything else.

"We'll work on it," he told her, reminding himself to think of some ways to do that. Tomorrow.

Tonight his mind was tired and his body was restless. He slid an arm around Susan, enjoying the slender shapeliness of her athletic body. She came to him eagerly, raising her mouth for his kiss.

They wouldn't sleep together tonight. Mark never had sex in his house when Kelsey was home. But he needed to—tonight more than many other nights.

Her lips opened and he slid his tongue inside, finding the rhythm that had become familiar to them over the months, relishing her response. Until he reminded himself that he had to stop.

"Being a parent's tough sometimes," he said with a groan.

"Did you get a sitter for tomorrow night?" Susan's whisper was hoarse and not quite even.

She'd invited him to her place for grilled steak—and a couple of hours in her bed.

"Not yet." Mark's mood dropped as the day—the week—came back to him. "It's the spring dance," he said. "But I have one more person to try."

"If you can't find anyone else, I'm sure Meredith would do it."

"No." Mark regretted his tone the second he'd responded. Regretted, too, that being friends with people at work wasn't against policy—unlike dating. It would be a damned fine reason to keep Meredith Foster out of his life a whole lot more.

Susan leaned back to look at him. "Uh-oh."

He didn't say anything. He couldn't. Meredith Foster was Susan's best friend. Meredith had introduced them to each other.

"What'd she do?" Susan asked, her eyes serious, concerned, but with a hint of a smile on lips still wet from his kisses.

With as few words as possible, he told her. And wasn't at all pleased when Susan sat back after a moment and said softly, "She's probably right, you know."

"No, I don't know." He was tired. Cantankerous. He'd been cussed out a second time by Larry Barnett that afternoon. His daughter was being snippy. He needed to make love. Meredith Foster was his scapegoat.

"How many times have you called her into your office over the past four years?"

Mark sank down on the couch, his feet on the floor straight out in front of him, his head resting against the cushion. "I have no idea. Too many."

The lights were low, and soft new-age jazz played in the background. He should be relaxed.

"And how many times has she been wrong?"

"Every one of them. She steps outside her position, she apologizes and life goes on. Until it happens again. She's a damn good teacher, Suze, I'd hate to lose her, but she butted heads with a powerful man this time and I don't know how long I can keep explaining things away."

"I mean about the kids, Mark," Susan said, her voice filled with compassion—whether for him or her friend, he wasn't sure. Knowing Susan, it was probably a bit of both. "How often has she been wrong about the kids?"

In a way, he resented her generosity. Meredith Foster deserved anger tonight, not compassion.

"She's good with the kids, no one's arguing about that."

Susan straightened up on the edge of the couch, facing him. "How many times have her predictions turned out to be true?"

"I honestly couldn't tell you," he said. "The point is irrelevant. Anyone can guess and be right fifty percent of the time."

"I'd bet my retirement fund that her percentage is closer to eighty or ninety than fifty."

He highly doubted it—but he couldn't prove either of them right without a hell of a lot more work than he had time for. Meredith Foster was stepping outside the boundaries of her position and she could cost both of them their jobs. If she'd wanted to psychoanalyze, she should have gone into psychology.

"What about Amber McDonald?"

"Who?" He opened an eye to glance at Susan. Other than her current choice of topic, she was good company. He was glad she was there.

"That little girl two years ago. She was being sexually abused by a family friend and no one suspected anything until Meredith came forward."

She was Amber Walker now. Her mother had remarried and moved the child to a different state. Last he'd

heard, she'd joined Girl Scouts and was starting to socialize a bit.

"Amber must have told her something," he said.

"Testimony revealed that she'd been threatened and
manipulated so completely that she couldn't even tell
the police, her mother or counselors about it—not even
after the guy was arrested."

He'd forgotten that. It had been a minute detail
compared to the anguish everyone—including Mark—
had experienced over the incident. That event had
branded within him a fierce need to protect his daughter.
He'd carefully screened the four teenage girls who were
permitted to sit with Kelsey. And at no time, under any
circumstances, were these girls to have anyone over
when they were in his home. If there was an emergency,
the police were to be called. Followed by him.

"Meredith *felt* it, Mark," Susan said, her brow
creased. "I know it's hard to grasp, this gift of hers, but
that doesn't make it any less real."

He stared at her, not sure what to say. He'd suspected
that Susan put credence in Meredith Foster's fantasies,
but she'd never before actually come out and said so.
They'd managed to avoid conversation on the subject
until now.

He respected her right to believe whatever she
believed. She just wasn't going to convince him. It
wasn't logical.

"Has she ever known stuff about you without first
being told?" he asked. He was somewhat curious to
hear the answer, but he also hoped to show her the hole
in her theory. Meredith and Susan had been friends
since they were fifteen years old—having met at a

church youth function and found common ground in their non-traditional lives.

"All the time."

Mark's eyes opened wide at her response. Susan was a medical doctor, for God's sake. A scientist.

"Ten minutes after Bud died, Meredith was at my door. I was still in shock, hadn't called anyone yet, and there she was."

"You said she stopped by often during the last days of your husband's fight with leukemia."

"She did. But she always called first to see if Bud was awake. She didn't want to impinge on what little time we had left together."

"So maybe she was in the area."

Susan shook her head. "She *knew,* Mark. She didn't knock, she just used the extra key, came in and found me on the bed beside him sobbing…."

Mark's throat tightened as Susan's eyes filled with tears. He could see her need to believe—he hurt for the anguish she'd been through, and cared enough to let the rest go.

Pulling her against him he held her while she cried, rubbing her back, wanting to do whatever he could to ease a grief that he understood would be with her always. Three and a half years had passed since Barbie had walked out on him and Kelsey, and the ache still throbbed as intensely as ever during the dark hours.

"THESE ARE BAD MEN."

Kelsey Shepherd leaned over on the stained couch to whisper to her mother. Two scary-looking old guys had come in from the garage door and they were putting something in the refrigerator. Kelsey thought they were gross.

Dad would kill her if he knew she was there with them.

Smiling, Barbie was shaking her head. "They're fine," she whispered back quickly and Kelsey stared at her. Was her mom okay? Even after all these times seeing her, she couldn't get used to the short, choppy hair and no makeup and sloppy clothes. She remembered her mom being beautiful.

Of course, maybe that was just kid stuff.

"Don, sweetie, come on over and meet Kelsey," Mom said. She squeezed Kelsey's hand so hard her fingernails cut into Kelsey. "Kelsey, this is Don."

The bigger of the two men, the one with the beard that mostly covered his mouth and made it so you couldn't tell if he was smiling or getting ready to spit, came over, his big boots making a lot of noise on the tile floor, which, as far as Kelsey could tell, covered the whole house.

"Hi there!" he said, rubbing Kelsey's head. She wanted to jerk away but she was afraid to upset her mom. Her mom wasn't doing so good today. She was in one of those moods where she could be happy and then all of a sudden cranky.

"Hi," she finally said, leaning into her mother.

"So your mom here tells me you're in fourth grade." Another squeeze of her hand. "Uh-huh."

"You like your teacher?"

I'd like it if you'd go away. "She's okay."

"You get good grades?"

"Uh-huh."

Did Mom really live with this guy? When she could have Daddy?

"I'll bet you have lots of friends, a pretty girl like you."

Kelsey felt creepy. She wanted to leave.

Her mother's nails bit into her hand again, reminding Kelsey that she hadn't answered.

"Uh-huh." If she didn't love her mother so much, she'd never come back to this place, for sure. She hoped Mom wouldn't make her. She liked driving around in the car more—even if it was old and rusty and had ripped seats and a bad smell.

"Cool." Don smacked his lips, leaned down and gave her mother a wet, messy kiss that lasted so long she could smell that he stank. He slid a finger through the hole in the thigh of her mom's jeans. Just when Kelsey was going to jump up and leave, Don stood and went out the garage door. Kelsey listened for a car, hoping he was leaving, but there was only quiet.

Mom let go of Kelsey's hand and gave her a hug and a soft kiss like she used to do at bedtime. Kelsey almost had to wipe it off. She didn't want any spit from that awful guy on her, anywhere.

"You remember that 'fluffy puppy' book we used to read?" her mom asked, like she'd read her mind or something.

"Yeah." Kelsey still had it.

"Remember how the cover was all stained and torn?"

"Yeah." She liked it that way.

"The story was still the best, huh?"

What was even better was that her mom remembered. And was talking like those days were important to her, too. "Yeah."

"Well, that's how Don and his friend James are. They're kind of rough-looking on the outside sometimes, but inside they're the best."

Oh. Well, she hadn't looked at the puppy book in a long time. It was probably covered up with her puke and stuff.

"He has yellow teeth." The hand running through her hair stopped.

"Coffee stained is all. Don's a truck driver and has to stay awake all night sometimes."

"Daddy drinks coffee."

Her mother didn't say anything. She never seemed to listen when Kelsey mentioned Daddy, but Kelsey kept trying anyway. Her mom put both arms around her, pulling her close and Kelsey forgot all about her dad. If only she could come home from school every day and have her mom there waiting with a hug—the way Josie's mom waited for them.

"James has a daughter your age," her mom said, and Kelsey didn't feel as good. If all Mom was going to talk about was those men, then Kelsey shouldn't have come. Didn't she realize that Kelsey'd be grounded for a year if she was caught here? Daddy thought she was at Josie's house, which she would be in time for him to come pick her up.

"Last month, James stayed up all night sewing trim on a dance costume his daughter needed for a competition she was in."

Kelsey nodded. A dad who sewed. That was cool. But one who looked all dirty and long-haired and tattooed like James?

She wanted to ask if his daughter had tattoos, too, but she was afraid that Mom would switch back to being cranky again. Even as old as Kelsey was now, that part of her mom still scared her.

CHAPTER TWO

"HI, MS. FOSTER, come on in. Daddy said you were coming. Can we do some more of that yarn stuff like we did last time?"

Meredith grinned at the petite little girl with long, straight dark hair. Her face was often solemn, but right now she was smiling profusely. "Hi, Kelse," Meredith said, stepping through Mark Shepherd's front door, a denim bag over her shoulder. "Yes, I brought plastic canvas and yarn. I thought we'd make a butterfly bank for your room—how's that sound?"

"Cool! I got that new comforter, too," the child said, closing and locking the door before skipping ahead in front of Meredith. "You know the purple and pink one with butterflies?"

"I remember," Meredith said, completely comfortable with Kelsey. If only her father were already gone and Meredith wouldn't have to suffer through even a few minutes in his company.

"You want to see it?"

Did she want to run the risk of running into Mark in the bedroom hallway?

"I do, but can I put this down first?" She slid her bag down her arm.

"Oh." Kelsey's expression was momentarily blank as she glanced at the bag. "Sure. I forgot. Sorry."

"No need to apologize, honey." Even before she'd had Kelsey in class the year before, Meredith had adored this child. She was sensitive and aware and far more responsible than most kids her age. Meredith missed seeing her every day.

Heading for the kitchen where they'd sit at the table and work on their project with the little TV mounted beneath a cupboard playing one of the Doris Day movies she'd brought, Meredith set her bag down and waited. Once Mark was on his way, the tension would be gone.

"I love your jeans," Kelsey said, plopping onto one of the wooden kitchen chairs. "I wanted some with beads like that, only instead of flowers they had butterflies, but Daddy said all that stuff would come off in the wash anyway."

Oh, great. She was already in the doghouse with this man and now she either had to lie and say that the jeans fell apart when she washed them, or she would have to tell his daughter he was wrong about that. She bent to pet the calico cat that was weaving itself in and out between her legs.

"Are you and Daddy fighting again?" Kelsey's pert nose wrinkled as she glanced over at Meredith.

"Why would you ask that?"

"You are, aren't you?" Kelsey frowned. "He said Susan asked you to come over tonight and usually *he* asks, and since he sees you at school and all, it's not like he couldn't get ahold of you. I figured that meant you were fighting again."

As the cat wandered off to investigate something more interesting, Meredith dropped down opposite Kelsey, hating the tightness she was feeling just beneath her rib cage. It meant she wasn't relaxed—and it was uncomfortable. "Your father and I don't fight."

"Well, *you* don't maybe. I don't think you'd ever have a fight with anyone. But he sure gets mad at you."

So much for keeping things between teacher and principal.

"Do the other kids at school know that, or are you extra smart?"

"I think it's just me, 'cause I live with him," Kelsey said, her adult-sounding assurances so touching.

"Well…" Meredith took a deep breath and sent up a quick request for assistance, please. "Sometimes I get a little carried away when I try to help, and your dad doesn't want me to lose my job."

"How could you? He's your boss."

"Yes, but the school board is *his* boss and if they told him to fire me, he'd have to do it."

"Are they going to tell him that?"

"No, sweetie, they aren't," Meredith said, with a cheerful smile, crossing her fingers. "Your dad just worries a lot sometimes."

"I do not worry."

Swinging around, Meredith stood up and saw Mark in the doorway behind her. His snug-fitting jeans and long-sleeved white shirt distracted her for a moment— but only for a moment.

"You worry all the time," she told him. "About everything."

"I get concerned, with legitimate cause. I do not

worry." He said the words firmly, with a completely straight face.

Meredith burst out laughing. Kelsey's worried stare settled on her father, until Mark slowly smiled.

Thank goodness. He was finished being angry with her. This time.

"I'm out of here, pumpkin," he said, resting his hand on his daughter's head.

She nodded.

"Bedtime is ten tonight, since Meredith is here and it's not a school night."

"Thanks."

"Don't answer the…"

"Door." Kelsey turned around to grin at her father. "We know the rules, Daddy," she said with only a hint of condescension.

"Then give me a hug so I can get lost, as you two are obviously eager to have me do."

Meredith's throat grew tight as she watched Kelsey jump up and throw her arms around her father's trim waist. Mark held on for a long moment and then let her go, glancing over at Meredith.

"I don't know how late I'll be."

She didn't want to think about why—it was kind of embarrassing—but at the same time she was glad to know that Susan was intimately involved. Her best friend was slowly but surely coming back to life.

"Tell Suze I said hi and I love her."

With a nod, Mark was gone.

An hour later, the muscles beneath Meredith's rib cage still had not relaxed.

"You feeling okay?" she asked Kelsey. Tongue

peeping out one side of her mouth, the girl was intent on following the pattern of squares and colors that Meredith had placed on the table in front of her.

"Fine," Kelsey said, her needle going through the plastic canvas with quiet deliberation.

Meredith had assumed that as soon as Mark left she'd relax. She'd been fine before she arrived. So what was making her tense? Her own internal radar? Someone else's?

The fact that Mark and Susan were doing what adults do when they're alone together—while she spent her Friday evening stitching butterflies with a fourth grader?

"You and Josie getting along okay?" The girls might be suffering from too much togetherness, now that Mark had agreed to let Kelsey go to Josie's every day after school in exchange for summer care for Kelsey's friend.

"Yep. We're best friends now."

Meredith's yarn knotted. She hated it when that happened. "You used too long a piece," Kelsey said, glancing over and then looking back at her own work.

"I know. I make a better teacher than a doer." She dropped the needle and canvas on the table. "You want a snack?"

"Ice cream?"

"Of course. What weird flavors did your dad buy this week?"

"Butterfinger and rocky road."

Grabbing three bowls and two spoons, Meredith pulled open the drawer where Mark kept his ice cream scoop. "So what'll it be for you, young lady?" she asked, scooping a bit of vanilla into the first bowl for Gilda, the cat, who was purring at Meredith's ankle.

"What are you having?" Kelsey asked without looking up.

"I guess I'll try Butterfinger. I've never had it before."

"Then that's what I'll have, too."

"DO YOU THINK judging a book by its cover is the same as knowing about people?"

It was five minutes to ten and Meredith was tucking Kelsey into her white-painted canopy bed, pulling up the new comforter. Though it'd been in the fifties all week, the temperature was supposed to drop down to near freezing that night.

"What do you mean?" Meredith asked, sitting on the side of the bed, careful not to disturb Gilda, who'd already curled up and was sleeping soundly. She tried to ignore the tightness in her stomach—too much ice cream, she told herself.

"If a book looks bad that doesn't mean the story inside is bad. So if people look bad, should we still think of them as good?"

Meredith forced herself to focus carefully on the nine-year-old's questions and ignore the increasing pain in her gut.

"That's not a yes or no question, sweetie," she said. "No, you shouldn't judge people just by how they look, but people put out messages about themselves— messages you need to learn to read as you go out into the world and deal with strangers." The words rolled off her tongue without conscious thought.

Kelsey nodded, but her eyes were full of confusion.

"Say, for instance, you see someone who has wild clothes on. That wouldn't mean that the person doesn't have a good heart. It might just mean that he or she has artistic taste."

"What if they have tattoos?"

A few years ago the question might instantly have been a cause for concern. "Lots of people have tattoos these days," Meredith replied. "It's kind of the in thing for college students, and lots of moms are getting little ones on their ankles and other places. And you've seen girls at the mall with them on their lower backs, haven't you?"

The girl nodded, her hair falling around her shoulders.

"It's more accepted now, so people are changing their opinions about tattoos and a lot of quite regular people are getting them."

"They might be good people?"

"Right."

"And say, maybe, someone was greasy and dirty looking... It could be that he was just working in the garage, huh?"

"Could be. But unless you know that he was in a garage, I'd be careful there. Someone who doesn't have good hygiene might be wonderful inside, but it might also be a sign that he or she is down on his luck—which could make him desperate. Or it might mean he has no respect for the human body, in which case you don't want to go anywhere near him."

Kelsey's features relaxed, but Meredith's stomach didn't.

"Okay?" Meredith asked.

Kelsey nodded, sliding down until the covers were up to her chin.

"You have some stranger bothering you?" Meredith had to ask.

"No."

"You sure?"

"Yeah. I just heard someone talking about judging people and it didn't really make sense to me, is all."

Thank God for that. Kelsey Shepherd had already been through enough in her young life. And so had her dad.

AT TEN AFTER TWELVE Meredith heard Mark's automatic garage door start to open. She yanked on her ankle-length hikers, tied the laces and grabbed her bag, which was packed and waiting. And then she reached for the remote control and turned off the TV.

"Hi," Mark said, coming in and dropping his keys on the brass plate on the counter.

"Hi." Meredith looked at the keys rather than at Mark. If his hair was mussed or he had that satisfied look in his eyes, she'd die of embarrassment.

"I know it's late, but you got a minute?"

Her gaze darted to his. "Sure." Her stomach was still uncomfortable, but she'd lain down after Kelsey went to bed and it was better than it had been before.

"In the living room?"

Odd, but…okay.

The first time she'd ever been in Mark's living room, three years ago for a retirement party for one of the teachers, she'd been impressed with the simple, elegant gold, brown, maroon and green decor. The room had the feeling of a cozy fall day, right down to the coasters on the plain oak coffee table. Rather than choosing the love seat or the sofa, Meredith chose the autumn-colored wing-back armchair. It only sat one. No awkwardness there.

"What's up?"

"I need your help with Kelsey."

Meredith's stomach tensed again. "What's wrong?" The little girl had been happy enough that night.

"Nothing, when she's with you." Mark's words weren't quite resentful, but his frustration was evident.

"She's not okay with you?"

"Yeah." He shook his head. "She doesn't seem to like Susan and I don't get it. Susan's kind and gentle and she wants so badly to be Kelsey's friend."

Settling back into the chair, allowing her bag to slide down her arm and onto the floor, Meredith nodded. "I know she does."

"I'm sure it's just because Kelsey resents having to share me, but I have no idea what to do about it. I make certain that she and I still have at least three nights a week alone and on at least another two, she's included in whatever plans Susan and I make."

If only more parents tried that hard. "So what do you want from me?"

She could take Kelsey to her house to spend the night, or even a weekend now and then, but that wasn't going to solve the problem.

"To see what you think. I couldn't talk to you about this at school, of course, and most of the time you're around, it's with either Susan or Kelsey there."

Thank goodness for that. She wasn't sure how long

she and Mark could last without fighting, if they spent
much time together by themselves. She had a tendency
to piss him off.

"I guess I was hoping, since Kelsey seems to adore
you, that you'd be able to talk to her or something. Or
maybe have some insights as to what I might do."

Meredith wasn't sure what to say. Susan was her
closest friend—a lot of times in her life she'd been
Meredith's only friend. She would be loyal to Susan
until death. So would it be disloyal to talk about her
behind her back if she was attempting to help Susan get
what she'd said she wanted?

Waiting until she felt calm inside, until she felt the
doubts fall away, to be replaced by the certainty that
she'd learned long ago to trust, Meredith let the quiet
of the room settle around her.

And then with more confidence, she said, "Susan
never learned how to interact with kids."

Yes, it was okay to say that. "She wants to be
Kelsey's friend but she has no inner direction, nothing
instinctual, not even a memory to draw on to tell her
how to be a friend to someone that age. Which makes
her feel awkward and insecure, and so she forces things.
Kids can tell when people aren't being natural with
them and they respond with a defensiveness that's
mostly unconscious."

That was how it felt. Pretty much.

Mark thought for a minute, hands rubbing slowly
against each other. They were nice hands. Big. De-
pendable-looking. Meredith had seen them gently
wipe away tears, tenderly hold shoulders, sign papers
and applaud success.

"I understand," he said at last. "But I still have no idea what to do about it."

"I'm not sure, either," she said. "Except to keep doing what you're doing. The more they're around each other, the more Kelsey's going to be able to see that Susan's a good person and perhaps start to trust her a bit. And the more Susan will learn what a nine-year-old kid's about and start to relax, which will help Kelsey trust her."

And...

No. Meredith refused to acknowledge her inner "awareness." So what if she'd been shown a picture, a flash only, of her and Kelsey together. Then together again somewhere else. That didn't mean it was real. Or even if it was, that she had to take heed of it.

And...

"And I think that it might help if, instead of always calling teenagers to sit with her—girls who are trustworthy and will keep her safe, mind you, but kids who don't really see Kelsey as anything more than a chance to earn a few extra bucks—you call me. Or let me take her to my place for a night. That way she won't feel like a castoff."

Her life's purpose was to help kids. She knew that. Any kids. Anywhere. Any way she could. It wasn't so much a choice as a conviction that she wouldn't be happy any other way. Helping kids completed her.

"I can't ask you to do that. You have a life."

"You aren't asking. I'm offering. And it's up to me how I spend my life."

"Why would you give up your weekend for me? I'm not even that nice to you."

"You're not un-nice to me." She should have left the television on. Of course, that would be out in the kitchen, which wouldn't offer much distraction in here. "Besides, I'm not doing it for you. I'm doing it for Kelsey and Susan."

He nodded. And relaxed. And when she realized she knew that, her own tension grew. She didn't want to know any more about him than anyone else knew. Especially when all she experienced were random feelings without explanation and minus a name tag so she couldn't even be sure of the source. But someone in this room had just relaxed, and it wasn't her.

"I'll think about it," he said. "Thank you."

Time to go. Meredith grabbed her bag as she stood, moving as quickly as she could for the door without looking as if she was running. He was right beside her, reaching for the doorknob—and not opening it.

Meredith didn't like the way his tired, yet…something…look made her feel. All edgy and, oh, maybe…she didn't know what. Just more. Was it him? Her? Both?

"In all the months I've been seeing Susan, I've never once heard of you out on a date," he said.

"So?"

"I'm surprised. You're a beautiful woman…."

And thirty-one. Her clock was ticking—slowly, granted, but still ticking.

Yet, if he thought she was beautiful…

"Thanks."

She moved toward the door. It didn't open. His hand was solidly on the handle. Hell, it was solid, period. Reassuring. Capable. She'd never thought much about men's hands before.

"Why don't you?"

Meredith's first priority was to get out of there. She needed space. Peace.

"I find that my life's happier that way."

"Are you gay?"

In today's world it was a reasonable question. "Does it matter?"

"No!" He stepped back. "Of course not." And then… "Are you?"

She debated her answer. If she'd been gay, this intense awareness of him would never be an issue; never be discovered or even suspected.

"No, unfortunately, I'm not," she said.

"Unfortunately?"

Yeah, she'd stepped right into that one.

Meredith shrugged, catching her hair in the strap of her bag. As she reached up to pull it out and slid her hand into the beaded back pocket of her jeans, she decided to tell him. Maybe then she could escape and go home. Where she was safe.

"It would've saved me a lot of heartache."

"How so?"

"I was engaged." It wasn't something she talked about. And out of respect for her, Susan wouldn't have told Mark, either. "Frank was kind and smart, witty, good-looking. Motivated. He got along well with his family. And with my mother. I trusted him."

She stopped, her chest tightening as she fought the memories.

"He had an affair," Mark said softly, his eyes darkening. "What an idiot." He leaned back against the door.

"No, he didn't," Meredith said. "I wish he had. It

would've been a lot easier to deal with, because that would have been his problem, his weakness and not mine."

"So what happened?" Mark folded his arms across chest.

Solid chest. Strong. Reliable. Firm.

"He didn't show up at the wedding." A woman's worst nightmare. Or at least hers. And it had come true.

Sometimes she still couldn't believe it had really happened. Surely that whole part of her life had merely been one of those nightmares that seemed so real you had a hard time distinguishing fact from fiction.

"The church was full. My mother had spent far too many thousands of dollars on flowers and food and photography and a band and invitations. I was there in my dress, my friends all around me in theirs..."

"Damn!"

Mmm-hmm.

"I waited not one hour but two," she said with a twisted grin. As soon as she could actually laugh when she told this story, it would no longer have the power to hurt her. Maybe three lifetimes from now.

Which was why she never told anyone. Susan knew, but then she'd been the woman in the soft purple maid-of-honor gown, holding Meredith up as she walked sobbing from the church.

People who'd known her then knew. They'd all been there. Witnesses.

"Did you ever find out why?" Mark didn't touch her, but she thought he wanted to. Or maybe it was just that she wanted him to. Wanted a man to find her worth the effort.

She nodded, and stood with her chin held high. "There was a letter for me taped to the front door of our apartment. He'd moved all his stuff out while I was at the church waiting—"

"Cold bastard!"

Meredith smiled a little at the interruption, nodding. She never should have started this, and now she was having to force herself to breathe.

"What did it say?"

"That as much as he loved me, he couldn't handle a lifetime of living with me. I'm too much."

"What does *that* mean?"

"You need to ask?" she said, staring up at him. "You're right there with him, Mark. I'm too intense. I feel too much. And when I experience certain sensations, I act. Even if the situation is one I should probably walk away from. But you know what?" She was feeling a little better. "I'm never going to walk away, not from any of it. I can't. I am what I am. I'm intense, just as my fiancé said. I feel everything around me, and I'm glad about that. I can't imagine life without the depth, without the magic that accompanies the pain." She was on a roll. Perhaps she should do this more often. She could stand on street corners and tell everyone her story.

"I like me." She finally said it. And stood there shocked. She'd never said that before; never consciously thought about it. She'd never known it.

But it was true.

Life was good.

CHAPTER THREE

"HEY, DADDY."

Mark glanced up from the bathroom sink on Monday morning to meet his daughter's sweet brown eyes in the mirror. She was wearing hip-hugger jeans that were getting a little too short, along with hiking shoes and a beige long-sleeved sweater. She'd pulled her hair into a ponytail that was decidedly crooked. His heart caught—how he loved this kid. "Hey, Kelse."

She boosted herself onto the second sink, watching as her father scraped another row of shaving cream from his cheek.

"I fed Gilda."

"Good girl. Thanks," he said, while he rinsed the razor. "What do you want for breakfast? Cream of wheat or pancakes?"

She scrunched her chin for a moment. "There's more dishes from pancakes, so cream of wheat."

Mark stopped, razor halfway to his face, and grinned at her. "What do the dishes matter?" he asked. "You don't do them alone."

"I know." Her voice was light. Her gaze followed his hand from sink to face and back again—just as it had done most of the mornings of her life. This ritual was one of the best parts of his day.

Before Kelsey, Mark used to shave in the nude. Since his daughter's birth, however, he'd always had slacks waiting by the shower so he'd be ready to run if she called.

"I forgot to tell you, Lucy's mom called and invited you over to play with Lucy after school Friday. I can pick you up on my way home, or you can spend the night and I can get you Saturday morning."

"No, thank you." The heel of Kelsey's shoe kicked lightly against the cupboard as she swung her leg. Mark considered telling her to stop. But the wood was dark enough that scuffs wouldn't show. And anyway, what showed could be cleaned.

"What?" he asked when he realized what she'd said, all thoughts of wood and scuff marks leaving his mind. "You love going to Lucy's! And you haven't seen her in a couple of weeks."

Lucy and Kelsey had gone through preschool and kindergarten together before the other girl's family had moved across town.

"I know. I just don't want to this Friday, Daddy." Those soft, dark eyes glanced up at him. "Do I have to?"

"No, Kelse, of course you don't. But can you tell me why you don't want to?" He dried his razor and put it back inside the cabinet. "Did something happen the last time you were there?"

"No."

"Did you and Lucy have a fight?"

"No."

"Was her mom or dad mean to you?"

"No."

Something wasn't right. "Then what?"

She shrugged. "Nothing. I just don't want to."

Short of calling his daughter a liar, which wouldn't get the desired results anyway, Mark was going to have to leave it at that.

He didn't like it.

"Turn around, sweetie. Let's fix that ponytail," he said, tugging gently on the beige-and-blue holder she'd chosen and sliding it down the silky length of her hair. Her mother's hair.

"I'll call Lucy's mom first thing this morning," he said, compelled at least to try one more time. "If you're sure that's what you really want."

She nodded, helping him create another crooked ponytail.

"HELLO?"

"Hi, Mom. It's me." Meredith held the cell phone against her ear with one shoulder while she unwrapped a granola bar, which—with a glass of Diet Coke—would be her breakfast.

"Meri, hi!"

Meredith's mood sank. Too much exuberance. She'd been right to follow her impulse to call. Something *was* wrong.

She had to leave in five minutes if she was going to get to class before her kids started to arrive. And with third-graders, that was always a good idea.

"I was feeling a little uneasy about you this morning," she said, holding her unwrapped breakfast in one hand as she put down her drink long enough to haul her school bag up onto her shoulder. The big green M&M emblazoned on the black patent leather was facing out.

"I went out to go to bridge club last night and my tire was flat," she said. Evelyn Foster, a retired scientist and executive from Phillip's Petroleum, lived in a nice condominium in Florida in an active-living adult community.

"Did you call road service?" Drink back in hand, Meredith headed for the door. "You got that extended warranty."

"I know. I called and they're coming out first thing this morning."

Hmm. Then…

"Nope, I still feel uneasy. Come on, Mom, I'm late. Tell me what's wrong."

Evelyn chuckled. "You know how hard it is having a kid you can't keep things from?" she asked.

Meredith's tension eased, but only slightly. "Your kid's all grown up, Mom. You don't need to hide things. Come on, what gives?"

She was in her car—a Mustang convertible, which she never drove with the top down.

"I'm sure it's nothing," Evelyn said, drawing out the words in a way that told her they were a lie. "I have to go in for a liver biopsy in the morning."

Her tires squealed and Meredith stopped fifty feet short of the sign at the end of her block. "What?" A quick, automatic glance in the mirror assured her no one was behind her on the dead-end street.

"I had my annual physical last week and the blood work raised a few questions."

"What's the worst case scenario?"

"Cancer, cirrhosis of the liver, maybe hepatitis…."

Meredith dropped her granola bar onto the car's

console next to her drink. Stared out the windshield, registering nothing—focusing. Feeling.

Her widowed mother. Alone in Florida—except for the many friends she'd made. Kind. Sixty-one. Active.

Alive. Very alive.

Meredith nodded. She stared again, barely aware of a horn honking behind her, a car speeding around her.

And then, blinking, she picked up her granola bar, stepped on the gas and turned onto the road that would take her to school.

"It's going to be okay, Mom," she said.

"It is?"

She found it hard to listen to the fear in her mother's voice. All her life Evelyn had been Meredith's strength. Sometimes her only strength. Meredith didn't want to think about her mother getting older. Failing.

"Yes," she told her, grinning over her own relief as much as for the relief she felt for her mom.

"What is it?"

"I don't know," Meredith told her, eating half the bar in two bites. "But you feel fine to me."

"You're sure?"

"Yep."

"Well, I knew it wasn't serious," Evelyn said brusquely. Then she added, "I love you, Meri."

"I love you, too, Mom."

"Be safe."

"You, too."

Meredith clicked the phone shut and took a long swig of soda. She was tired and the day had hardly begun.

"SUSAN INVITED US over to her house for dinner tonight. You want to go?" Mark had been working up to the question most of the morning and now they were almost at school.

His daughter, ponytail centered on her head after a third try, turned away. "No."

He could barely hear the words aimed at the passenger window, but her slumped posture said enough and his mood slipped a notch.

"How come? She's going to make chicken alfredo. You loved her alfredo, remember?"

"I just don't wanna."

"But Monday night's our night to have dinner with Susan."

"It's your night, not mine," Kelsey said. "I never said I wanted to."

This was going from bad to worse.

"Talk to me, Kelse," Mark said, taking the long way to school. "Why don't you like Susan? Do you resent the time I spend with her?"

"No."

"Then what? Is it that she's not your mom?"

"No!" The derision in the child's tone put that one to rest.

Mark pulled onto the shoulder of the country road he'd chosen, put the car in Park. "Then what?"

His question garnered no response. Not even a shake of the head. But he had plenty of time to analyze the perfection of the ponytail his daughter was showing him.

"Why don't you like her?" he asked again. He couldn't deal with what he didn't know.

"I do like her."

Really? "Then why are you so quiet around her?"

The hardness in the eyes that turned to face him shocked Mark. He'd had no idea his daughter was capable of such strong negative emotion. "She treats me like I'm an alien from Mars."

"No, she doesn't," he said, and then wished he'd bitten his tongue instead. "I'm sorry. I didn't mean to discount your feelings."

Kelsey showed no reaction other than to stare out the windshield at blacktop, gravel and emptiness.

"Susan's not very good with kids," Mark said. "But only because she's never been around them and not because she doesn't like them. She never had a chance to be a kid herself. But she likes you, Kelse. She wants to get to know you, to be your friend."

"No, she doesn't."

Don't argue perspective, his schooling taught him. It was a lose-lose approach. "Why do you think that?"

"I dunno." Hard not to argue, when the opposing side gave illogical answers.

"You don't have a problem with Ms. Foster— Meredith," he said, in response to his daughter's knowing glare. Meredith had been at their house the previous Thanksgiving for dinner, helping Susan with the meal. She'd granted the child the right to call her by her first name, since Kelsey had graduated from her class months before. As long as she could remember not to do it at school.

"So?" Kelsey said, sliding down in the seat as she crossed her arms over her chest. When had his precocious pal turned into a drama queen?

"She and Susan are best friends."

"So?"

Well, he didn't know. That was the point of this conversation. He thought. But obviously Kelsey didn't think so. Until the past few months, they'd had no problem communicating. What had changed?

Not him. At least he didn't think so.

"You never talk to Susan." He tried a different approach, glancing at his watch. In fifteen minutes they were going to be late.

Good thing he was the boss. Because he was willing to miss the whole damn day if that was what it took to reach an understanding with Kelsey again.

"She never talks to me."

This was getting more frustrating by the second.

"But you don't wait for Meredith to talk to you."

The child's eloquent answer to that was a shrug.

He could make her clean her room. He could make her brush her teeth. He could make her do her homework. But he couldn't make her share her confidences.

"What do you two talk about?" he asked, without much hope of enlightenment.

Kelsey sighed. "I'm growing up, Daddy. Girls have stuff."

Stuff. Uh-huh. For the first time since his daughter's birth, Mark felt completely incapable of caring for her.

"What kind of stuff?"

"You know," she said, having a stare down with him. "Girl stuff."

He almost choked. Did girls start that stuff at nine? He'd thought he had more time….

And then he caught the uncertainty in Kelsey's innocent gaze. The child was out of her league.

At least they still had something in common.

"You don't want to tell me."

"Nope."

"Is everything okay?"

She glanced over at him and then away. "Sure, why wouldn't it be?"

He had no idea.

"Have you ever tried to talk to Susan about some of this 'stuff'?"

Kelsey's silence said far too much.

Watching her for another minute, thinking over everything he knew about child development and patterns of behavior, Mark figured it was best to cut his losses for the moment. He pulled back onto the road and drove the rest of the way to school in silence.

And the first thing he did when he arrived was phone Lucy's mom to say that Kelsey wouldn't be coming on Friday, after all. Then he called Susan and cancelled dinner that night. As always, she was understanding.

MEREDITH STOOD AT THE DOOR to her classroom, dressed in a red turtleneck sweater and a black cotton shift that featured a colorful shoe print. She'd opted for hose and pumps in honor of a new week, and her gold shoe earrings, necklace and charm bracelet completed the day's ensemble. Smiling, looking forward to Monday morning, she welcomed each student as the kids slowly filed in, shouted greetings at classmates, put backpacks in lockers, took their seats or a place at one of the computers against the far wall or stopped to chat with a friend.

"Good morning, Erin. How was your weekend?" Meredith asked a tiny red-head who, though the smallest in the class, had proven to be one of the most rambunctious. If there was trouble, Erin usually found it.

Innocently, but completely.

"Boorrringgg," Erin sang, knocking her backpack into Jeremy Larson as she passed on her way to her locker.

"Hey!" Jeremy shoved back.

"Hold it!" Meredith's voice stopped all movement in the classroom. "Jeremy, what's the first rule of this classroom?"

The boy turned red and looked down. Then he mumbled.

"Excuse me?" Meredith asked, aware of the eyes turned in her direction, but focusing only on the boy.

"Don't hit." He refused to look at her.

That wasn't it, exactly. "And?"

"Don't be mad."

That wasn't it, either, not exactly. But he was close.

"Do you think Erin bumped into you on purpose?"

Jeremy shifted from foot to foot, his chin tucked down on his chest. He was one of the kids who caused her the greatest concern. He had far too much pent-up anger. But she had no idea why. He came from a good family—lots of siblings, support, closeness. She'd taught an older sister and a brother of his, so far. Knew both of his parents well enough to be completely comfortable with them.

"I didn't," Erin blurted out, as Jeremy remained silent.

"Jeremy?" Meredith said again, smiling as another couple of students shuffled in, eyes wide at the silence so early on a Monday morning. "Do you think she did it on purpose?"

"No."

"Good. Erin? Do you have anything to say?"

"I didn't do it on purpose."

Meredith bit back a smile. "You already said that. What else?"

"I'm sorry." The boisterous little girl spoke so softly she could barely be heard. But because of the earliness of the day and because of the kids still coming in, Meredith chose to accept the apology, thin as it was. She watched long enough to see that the kids were separated by half the room and then turned back to the door.

"Macy! How long have you been standing there?"

Mark's secretary, Macy Leonard, was one of Meredith's heroes. Calm and unflappable, the plump fiftyish woman exuded good nature.

Usually.

"What's wrong?" Meredith asked more softly, reaching the other woman's side.

"You've been summoned." Her voice was low, serious. Concern shadowed her soft blue eyes.

With a quick look up at the loudspeaker directly over her head Meredith said, "I didn't hear anything."

Macy shook her head, her short gray curls stiff with spray. "He sent me. I'm supposed to stay with the kids."

Her chest tightened. "He wants me to come right now?" Before she'd called roll or set the kids to work?

Macy nodded.

"Why?" Meredith asked, attempting to quell the nerves in her stomach. "What's wrong?"

Shaking her head, the older woman gave Meredith's hand a brief squeeze. "I don't know, honey, but judging by the look on his face when he came from his office it's probably best not to keep him waiting."

"I used to think he was such a happy guy," Meredith said softly, a bad attempt to make light of the situation. Better that than let her nerves have their way. That was never good.

With a quick clap of her hands, Meredith called her class to their seats, told them that Macy was in charge and moved after-lunch reading to first thing in the morning.

She'd never been called to Mark's office twice in one month. Never two school days in a row.

She'd phoned both of the Barnetts as she'd promised to. And she hadn't spoken to a single parent—or student, for that matter—since she'd gone home on Friday.

Hurrying down the hallway she tried her best not to fret, not to make a big deal out of something that would probably be nothing.

But she couldn't for the life of her figure out what would require an early Monday morning summons. As a rule, a teacher never left her classroom if there were students in it, unless there was an emergency. The kids always took precedence over administrative business.

Had she talked to any other parents recently? Said anything that could have backfired and caused friction? She didn't think so. Couldn't remember if she had.

So who was missing that morning? She turned the

corner, mentally checking her roster, praying there'd been no accidents or emergency surgeries over the weekend—nothing that she'd have to prepare her students to face.

Other than Tommy Barnett, she was pretty sure everyone had arrived before she'd left the room. And Tommy was always five to ten minutes late.

Mark was standing behind his desk, staring out the big metal-framed window that took up most of one wall. The lush green trees that Bartlesville was known for were in full spring bloom, but Meredith was pretty sure, judging by the tense way Mark was holding his shoulders and neck, that he wasn't finding any joy in their beauty.

"Did you see the editorial section in the *Republic* this morning?" He spoke with his back to her.

"No." Her heart started beating heavily, blood pounding so hard she could almost feel its passage. Had there been an accident?

Mark's silence was excruciating. "I don't get the newspaper…. I don't watch the news, either," she said inanely, in case he thought maybe she'd heard about whatever it was they had to discuss. "Too depressing."

Mark shook his head, sighed loudly and turned. She couldn't decipher the look in his eyes, but she knew he wasn't pleased.

And if she wasn't mistaken, he was more angry than sad and the unkind sentiment was directed at her.

At least, unlike Larry Barnett, he wasn't lashing out. Yet.

He reached for the Bartlesville morning paper and tossed it in her direction.

"Read it."

CHAPTER FOUR

REPUBLIC EDITORIAL
FAMILIES AT RISK
Local Teacher Sticks Her Nose Where It Doesn't Belong

Washington County district attorney Larry Barnett got the shock of his life Thursday evening when his ex-wife called to say she had to speak with him on a matter of urgent business regarding their eight-year-old son, Thomas. This "urgent business" was a message from Tommy's teacher saying that recently elected, highly respected Barnett was abusing his son—and all on the basis of some kind of hunch!! In a society that is becoming obsessed with its own shadows, why would we put in our classrooms, in charge of our impressionable young children, women who send out alarms without a trace of proof? And to make matters worse, according to Barnett, the teacher in question had made the damaging statement after referring the boy to his school counselor, who sent him back with a clean report. Lincoln Elementary School principal Mark Shepherd assured Barnett that he had the situation in hand, after which an apology was forthcoming. An apology? For scaring a single mother half to death? For falsely accusing a father of hurting his own son? I say fire the woman immediately!

HOPING THE TREMBLING in her lower lip wasn't visible, Meredith glanced up. "He didn't waste any time, did he?"

It was only an editorial.

"That's all you have to say?" His words were soft, far too controlled. She'd never seen Mark so angry.

"Bo Reynolds is always trying to scare up trouble about something." Even Meredith, who rarely saw the paper, had heard of him. "Everyone knows you have to take him with a grain of salt."

"I've had more than forty calls already this morning," Mark said, still by the window and facing her now, arms behind his back.

She had a feeling they were being forcibly held there for her protection. He'd sooner have his hands around her throat. She stood up.

"From whom?" she asked, pretending a calm she couldn't even remember how to feel.

"Parents who wanted to make sure their third-grader was not in the same class as Tommy Barnett."

Sweat oozed out her pores. "How many of them were?"

"One."

Out of four third-grade classes, roughly 120 students, with forty calls, only one had been from her group?

"My parents know me and trust me." Other than the obvious exception.

Mark dropped his arms, sighed. "I suspect you're right," he said with some hesitation. He leaned on his desk with his palms down, bringing his face closer to hers, his eyes deadly serious.

"It has to stop, Meredith."

She said nothing.

"I mean it."

"I know."

"Not one more time," he warned. "Please."

Meredith withstood his scrutiny even when that hard glint returned to his eyes. He stood up and said, "I don't want to have to fire you."

"I know." But he would if he had to. Still, the threat wasn't going to stop her feelings, wasn't going to stop the knowing. And she wasn't going to stand by and silently watch children suffer, if she thought she could help them.

Of course, if she wasn't around, she'd be useless to them.

She was just going to have to get a whole lot better at figuring out how to act on those situations that "occurred" to her without her being told about them.

"Can I go back to my class now?" she asked. "Mrs. Brewer is here for music this morning and we're second on her list."

"Yes." Mark waved a hand at her. "Go."

She didn't wait for any niceties, didn't intend to say another word. But at the door she turned.

"Mark?"

"Yeah?"

"Who was the one?"

She wasn't surprised when all she received in reply was a frustrated stare.

Tommy Barnett didn't show up late for school on Monday. He didn't show up at all. But his mother did, late in the afternoon, avoiding Mark's gaze as she withdrew her son from Lincoln Elementary School.

"I'm sorry," she told Mark, sitting in his office, filling out papers on a clipboard she rested on her lap. The obviously expensive gray pantsuit she was wearing, the jewelry, makeup and well-tended hair didn't seem to give her any confidence at all.

"Don't worry about it," Mark told her. "I completely understand." He sat behind his desk, an authority figure who lacked the power to change a situation that had arisen under his care. Or even to explain it. "We're the ones who are sorry," he continued. "We let Tommy down—and we let you and his father down, as well."

Ruth Barnett glanced up then, her eyes wide and luminous. "You didn't let Tommy down," she said softly. "He loved it here and he particularly loved Ms. Foster. His second-grade teacher told us she suspected he was dyslexic. This year, after just six months with Ms. Foster, he's reading up to his grade level and beyond. Something had been holding him back, but it wasn't dyslexia. I hope you know what a gem you have in her."

Such a passionate speech from this woman startled Mark. But then, women had a tendency to do that more often than not.

His relief was less easy to accept. He was Meredith Foster's boss, nothing more. If he had to fire her, he would.

"She's very consistent with her classroom results," he said now, choosing his words carefully.

Pen held poised above the plastic clipboard, Ruth studied him. "My ex-husband insisted that Tommy change schools," she said, naming a private institution across town. "Larry Barnett is a powerful man."

Mark nodded.

"He won't let this drop."

It was confirmation he'd rather not have had.

"With your support, Ms. Foster might be able to keep her job." Mark didn't miss the plea in her voice or in her eyes.

"What she did was completely inappropriate." He said what his job required him to say.

"What she did could very well save my son's life."

It was Mark's turn to study her. "You're saying there's truth to her claim?"

The woman began to write again—rapidly. "I'm not saying that."

"Then what?"

"Nothing, really."

"If you know something you have to speak up, ma'am—if not to me, then to someone else. The authorities. You could be Tommy's only hope."

"I'm very well aware of my son's safety requirements, Mr. Shepherd."

She was a frightened woman, afraid of her ex-husband's power.

On the other hand, if Tommy denied the abuse and his school counselor saw no evidence of it, and if his mother knew nothing, what was the flack all about?

One woman's intuition.

It was pure craziness.

"If, as you say, your husband's pursuing this, then it would help Ms. Foster a great deal if you went public with how you feel about her."

She was writing so fast he didn't see how she could possibly have read the questions. "It's best if I stay out of this."

Best for whom? Tommy? Not if he was being mistreated. Best for her, then?

"Are you keeping Tommy away from his father? Or at least having supervised visits?"

A bitter chuckle was her first response. "You obviously aren't familiar with my husband," she said. "If I tried to keep the two of them apart he'd find a way to take Tommy away from me completely."

"The courts wouldn't agree to that. Not without compelling reasons…."

"The 'courts' is one judge, when it comes down to that." She spoke quietly, but not without cynicism. "Whatever judge is assigned to the case…. And with Larry's contacts, you can bet he'd be assigned a judge who would be sympathetic."

Mark was well aware this kind of thing happened. On television. In big towns. In other people's lives. "Then why hasn't he done that—gone to court already?"

"It wouldn't be convenient," she said simply. "Larry likes to play. Being responsible for a child 24/7 would hamper his freedom. And taking a child away from his mother might lose him some votes. Still… If there's any possibility of people believing the truth of Ms. Foster's claims, he'd get full custody simply to show that he has the stellar reputation to do so. It would shut up his critics. If he has any."

Barnett had the woman sufficiently boxed in. There would be no help from her.

Assuming they needed help.

Assuming Mark had any intention of supporting Meredith Foster.

Or was Mrs. Barnett just bitter and slightly off the mark and her husband was to be pitied and taken seriously? If Mark had to put money on it, he'd probably choose the latter scenario.

"So if Barnett continues to have access to Tommy, how did Ms. Foster's statement have any bearing on the boy's welfare?"

"It put Larry on notice."

Eyes narrowed, he watched her carefully for signs of dishonesty—shifting eyes, nervous twitches, lack of focus. There were none. She made that statement as if it were a given, as if Barnett had a reason to be on notice.

"Is Larry Barnett abusing his son?"

"Not that I know of."

Mark tossed down his pen, frustrated with the entire mess. No one knew anything and yet a student had just been yanked from school, Mark's reputation had been smeared in the local paper and Meredith Foster could lose her job.

"Do you believe he is?"

"I hope not."

"But there's a possibility."

She stood. "I really must go," she said, laying the clipboard on the edge of his desk. "Tommy won't want to wait for me to pick him up after his first day in a new school."

Mark rose from his chair and walked her to the door. "Did Barnett ever hit you, Ruth?" His use of her first name was calculated, but he justified his attempted manipulation with the thought that it was for a good cause.

"No, of course not. Now I really have to leave."

"Will you give me a call if anything changes?"

She nodded and was gone.

"MORE WINE?"

Meredith hesitated as her friend held the half-empty bottle of expensive Riesling over her glass. "I shouldn't," she said. In the morning, she'd have a roomful of feisty eight-year-olds to face. "But okay."

Susan topped up her own glass next. "Thanks for coming, by the way. I'd already made the pasta this morning, and you know how I am about eating it fresh."

"Hey, I'm the one who benefited here," Meredith said, relaxing for the first time that day. "I can't believe you aren't upset with Mark for leaving you in the lurch at the last minute."

Susan shrugged. "It was up to Kelsey, and based on our track record chances were good that she'd say no."

"But you made the pasta anyway."

"There's always hope." Susan grinned.

Toying with her butter knife, Meredith said, "You feel more conflicted than nonchalant here, woman."

"And it's eerie how you see right through me."

"I've known you a long time."

"About as long as I've known you, and you can be falling apart inside but I won't know it until it actually shows on the outside."

The knife slipped from Meredith's hand. "I'm sorry."

"Oh, don't be!" Susan's talented, steady fingers closed over Meredith's, drawing her gaze downward first and then to Susan's eyes. "I need you, Mer. I rely on you to understand me when I can't see myself—to find me in the muck and pull me out."

"I'm not a magician. Nor am I always right."

"Of course not. You aren't always tuned in, either. I love you for all kinds of different things, but this gift you have…I want you to know that I realize how important it is. I believe with all my heart that it's as real as you are."

Meredith's eyes rimmed with tears she didn't even try to hide. It'd been a long few days filled with far too much emotion, leaving little time for the familiar routines of life. Everyday events she needed in order to keep everything in perspective.

"So tell me what's going on with you," she said a moment later. "Is there a problem with Mark?"

"No." Susan sounded sure, but her eyes were clouded. "He's a great guy," she continued. "Warm, considerate, patient, funny. Sexy as hell…."

Meredith reached for the butter knife again, twirling the little handle back and forth between her fingers. It wasn't that she was prudish, but she didn't need to hear about Mark and Susan doing…it. Didn't need to think about Mark in that way.

Because it was too easy to picture?

Please, no, don't let it be that.

"So what's the problem?" she asked, pulling her mind firmly back to the conversation. "He's sexy, but you aren't turned on by him?"

Why the hell had she said *that?*

"Oh, no, I am!" Susan grinned. "Every single time he kisses me I want to go to bed with him."

Now, Meredith desperately wanted to change the subject. And if that was odd, considering that she and Susan had been best friends when they'd lost their virginity and had always spoken openly with each other about intimate topics, she wasn't about to ask herself why.

She had too many other things to worry over at the moment.

"The problem is the rest of the time," Susan said, her voice dropping. "I look forward to seeing Mark and I want to spend as much time with him as I can, but I don't feel…I don't know…like I've arrived yet. Does that make sense?"

"Yeah." Meredith wished she could take that lost look from Susan's eyes, the feeling from her heart. "You aren't trusting in a future."

Susan's eyes were moist as she glanced up—wet and fearful. "What if I never do, Mer? I mean, how can I? I know firsthand that there are no guarantees, that nothing lasts forever. That you can get up one morning, shower and have breakfast as you always do, go to work, looking forward to the day, the evening ahead, the weekend to come, and by afternoon, with one phone call, all hope of a future is wiped away."

"Bud's future is gone, but yours isn't. It's just changed. And as long as you're alive, that future is a guarantee. When you're dead, it's gone—but then so are you."

Trite words, maybe. But Meredith felt the truth of them clear to her core. "It's up to you to put the promise back in your future, Susan. Or not to, in which case you're right and you'll never have it again."

"I mentioned Bud the other night, when I was with Mark."

"And?"

"I started to cry."

"And Mark was good to you, wasn't he?"

"Yeah." Susan's gaze lightened as she smiled softly. "He was."

"Tommy Barnett transferred schools today."

"Shit."

The two women were still sitting at the table, nursing their wine. It had been weeks since they'd spent this much time together. Meredith hadn't realized how much she'd missed it. Susan was one of the few people with whom she felt completely safe—with whom she didn't have to hide or filter her natural reactions, her thoughts.

"Mark threatened to fire me if there are any more 'episodes.'" She said the word as if it were nasty and needed to be hidden.

"He's blind as a bat on this one, but he has a good heart."

"I know." Meredith nodded. "Otherwise I'd never have trusted him with you."

Susan sat back, wineglass in hand, slowly sipping. "I just wish I got along better with Kelsey."

Meredith did, too. She was missing something there. They all were. In her spare time, when she thought about it, it was driving her crazy. "She'll come around," was the best she could manage to offer.

"Do you really think so?"

Oh, no. Susan was giving her that look: she wanted complete truth.

"I think it's possible," Meredith said slowly, trying her best to differentiate between what she thought and what she felt—to separate it all from the depression that had been threatening to descend ever since she'd been summoned to Mark's office the previous Friday.

Susan nodded. "I'll do whatever it takes."

Because Mark meant that much to her. Which was exactly what Meredith wanted for her.

So why did the thought make her melancholy when it should have brought her joy? Was her own situation pulling her that far down?

If so, she was going to have to do something to change that. Immediately.

"You want to go for ice cream?"

"A banana pie creamie?"

The first time they'd shared that concoction from a local ice cream carry-out chain, they'd been in college.

"We could take one to Mark." If she came bearing a delight to feed his ice-cream fetish, maybe he wouldn't dislike her so much.

"Kelsey loves cookie dough," Susan said.

"There you go! You're already learning how to please her." Meredith began to clear the table, and with Susan's help they made short work of the dishes. "All it takes is paying attention to the little things and Kelsey'll come around," Meredith assured her friend as they drove across town in Susan's silver BMW. She hoped she was right and that it would really be that easy. "Kelsey's like anyone else," she added. "She just needs to know that she matters."

"Did Mark tell you she refused to go see her best friend from across town today? He'd made arrangements with the girl's mother and had to call and cancel that, too."

"Mark and I weren't exactly on speaking terms today," Meredith said slowly, thinking about Kelsey. "Did she and Lucy have a fight?"

"Apparently not."

Meredith looked at the houses they passed, noting the lights on in living rooms, kitchens, bedrooms, wondering about the darkened ones. So many people, so many lives saturated with hope and fear and love and regret; so many emotions. Trapping her.

"I told Mark I'd be happy to keep Kelsey overnight any weekend the two of you want some time alone," she said slowly, deciphering her feelings as she spoke. "Maybe we should do it this weekend. Think you can come up with a plan to entice him?"

Susan pulled to a stop at the corner. "You want some time alone with her."

"I enjoy Kelsey."

"You're worried about her and you want to see if you can figure anything out."

Meredith didn't answer. She had no idea if there was anything wrong with Kelsey Shepherd other than the usual little-girl jealousy that came with the territory when a single dad started dating. She had no idea if there was any real justification for this feeling that she should be paying special attention to Kelsey right now. She had no idea if she was being overemotional, reacting to the trauma of the past several days, or if she was getting intuitive guidance.

"I'll make it happen," Susan said, her foot back on the gas.

CHAPTER FIVE

"I THINK I WANT HER, Don."

Barbie Shepherd lay naked in her lover's arms, hoping he wasn't going to get all bossy and manly—and hoping he'd stay in bed with her until she fell asleep. She hated nights. The dark, the loneliness....

"Want who?"

"Kelsey."

Every time she'd thought about the idea in the four days since her daughter had last been here, a good feeling had come over her. Now that Kelsey had met Don—and more importantly, now that he'd met her—she couldn't be happy without being a real mom again.

"You want her to live here with us, you mean?" His voice was soft, kind of hoarse, like it got right before they had sex. Or right afterward.

He had to leave soon, on a run to Colorado. She toyed with his nipple. "Uh-huh."

"I'm okay with that."

"Really?" she asked. "You mean it?"

"Sure." Don leaned over, licked her breast, his beard tickling her. Then he sat up, reaching for the cigarettes that were never farther away than the nightstand. She watched the amber flicker of the lighter's flame, saw the cigarette catch and glow as Don inhaled deeply. Took her own drag when he handed it to her and lit a second one for himself.

"I'm her mother. I have rights."

"Of course, you do." The end of the cigarette disappeared between his whiskers and Barbie told herself he was a good-looking man. Especially in the semidarkness, when you couldn't see his teeth.

"You're the one who carried her around in your body," he said now, running a finger lightly from her breasts down and over her belly. "You went through labor, gave birth to her…"

"Breast-fed her and raised her for the first five and half years of her life…"

"She's an asset," he continued. "*Your* asset."

Yeah. Kelsey was someone who had to love her, no matter what.

"Kids are good for lots of things," Don went on, letting the ash grow dangerously long before flicking it into the ashtray. "She can help you out around here."

She hadn't thought of that. Kelsey had still been too young to be of much use when Barbie had left. Not that she'd minded. She'd liked taking care of her. Still…

"So, what do I do?" she asked now, straddling his stomach as she leaned over to flick off her ashes.

Crushing the remains of his cigarette in the ashtray, Don grabbed her butt. "Get a lawyer."

She took one last drag and ditched her cigarette. "Can we afford that?"

"You can get one for free." This was the best news yet—she'd thought the legal part would be the most difficult. "State has to appoint one for you."

Barbie slid down the roundness of his belly until she rested at the top of his thighs. "You sure about that?"

"Yep."

Then he moved and she couldn't think about Kelsey or being a mother anymore. Don wasn't like Mark in bed. He had lots of tricks, kept her guessing, and as usual she gave herself over to whatever he had in mind. It always ended in orgasm and those moments were glorious.

MEREDITH APPROACHED her Mustang in the deserted parking lot an hour after school let out. It was only Wednesday afternoon and already she was worn out—longing for the weekend, forty-eight hours of anonymity, hot baths, good books and little responsibility.

Her students, whether picking up on her own tension or bringing it from home, had been restless as well, talking too much, too loudly, focusing only in short spurts. And that afternoon during art class Erin had tripped near Meredith's desk, and now Meredith had a patch of red poster paint staining the white silk blouse she'd worn with her black slacks and white-and-black pumps.

Black-and-white jewelry, black-and-white leather satchel. She'd been hoping for a black-and-white kind of day—and had ended up splattered in red.

"Ms. Foster, could we have a word with you?"

Glancing up sharply, Meredith stopped. She'd noted the van in the parking lot, of course. Enough to be aware that it was there. Not enough to have noticed the Tulsa local-news logo on the side or the two people who had just emerged from it.

"We'd just like to ask a couple of questions."

She walked past them to her car.

"We're interested in the editorial that ran in Monday's *Republic*. I understand that the newspaper didn't contact you. Is that correct?"

She looked at the brunette, who was her age, at least, dressed in jeans and a white sweater, and wondered if she liked her job. The hefty, bearded cameraman behind her she ignored completely.

"We've got some good tape from Mr. Barnett," the woman said, her eyes showing something akin to sympathy. "My producer was ready to run with it, but I insisted that you deserved to have your side told, as well."

Keys in hand, Meredith stood there another second, assessing. Granted, her senses weren't honed at the moment, but she believed the other woman was sincere.

The brunette dropped her mic at her side. "He was pretty brutal," she said. "I'd like to hear what you have to say."

Meredith glanced back at the school. Mark would kill her if she said anything.

And if she didn't? She'd be crucified.

Who'd stick up for her? Ruth Barnett? Hardly. The woman was a classic battered woman, so intimidated by her jerk of an ex-husband that she'd still lie just because he told her to. And that left—who? Her boss? Fat chance.

"What do you want to know?" She regretted the words even as she said them. There would be hell to pay. And at the same time, she felt better. She'd done nothing wrong, had nothing to be ashamed of. Unlike Larry Barnett.

"Did you tell Mr. Barnett's wife that he was abusing his son?"

Meredith glanced at the school one more time. This was her last chance to walk away.

But for what? To let that man take everything from her, without even trying to defend herself?

"You can't blame people for what they're going to think, if you don't give them another perspective," the other woman said, her gaze compassionate.

"I told her I suspected his father was inflicting some pretty severe emotional abuse."

"You suspect," the woman said, moving nearer with her microphone as the cameraman closed in behind her. Meredith was trapped between her still-locked car door and what suddenly felt like two vultures. The school was behind her—a perfect backdrop.

"You have no proof," the woman prompted gently, after a long pause.

"No."

"What made you suspect?" The question was more curiosity than accusation. She was receiving a fair chance to be heard. Which was more than she'd expected following Mark's pronouncement Monday night over ice cream. Ruth Barnett had said her ex-husband was not going to let this go away.

Give me strength, she asked her unseen source of guidance—as she'd already done uncountable times over the past week.

"Tommy was a student in my class. I listened to him, as I listen to all of my students."

The reporter's eyes narrowed. "So Tommy told you?" she asked, perhaps seeing a larger story brewing. If it was found that the D.A. actually was abusing his son, she'd have a much bigger audience for a longer period of time.

"No." Meredith hated to disappoint her. She sighed, searching for the best words. "But every time fathers were mentioned, or Tommy mentioned his father, I sensed that there was great turmoil. But no physical danger—at least not yet."

"You sensed."

Meredith nodded.

"As in how? You just thought about it and reached this conclusion?"

That was how Mark saw the situation. And probably the majority of Bartlesville, as well. Meredith was tempted just to leave them to it. In the end, it might be far less painful than to have everyone think she was some kind of quack.

But if she didn't stand up for herself, who would? How could anyone even have a chance of choosing to believe her, to understand, to support her, if she didn't speak out?

And if she allowed herself to be lied about, allowed her credibility to be crushed beneath Larry Barnett's expensively shod foot, how would she ever do any good in this world?

A vision of Tommy Barnett's innocent young face appeared before her.

"I get feelings," she said. "I tune in, focus deeply and I can feel what other people are feeling. Sometimes."

"So you're saying you're psychic."

"No." She didn't believe there were special people who were granted the right to know everything about someone else, both past and future. "I don't get grand messages," she said. "I'm not told secrets, nor can I predict anything that's going to happen in the future—no more than you can predict your own future. I can just feel what they're feeling. Sometimes."

She wasn't some kind of weirdo. She didn't run around town invading people's privacy.

"What am I feeling?"

"I don't know." She didn't want to know. She wanted to go home. Perhaps cry. Call her mom. Take a hot bath.

"What's he feeling?"

"I don't—" Meredith glanced at the cameraman, let her guard down without meaning to. "Good," she said, head slightly tilted as she eyed him with warning. "Not nice, but good. Self-satisfied. I'd guess he's having inappropriate thoughts about something or someone and feeling good about them."

The camera slipped, was righted…and Meredith met the man's eyes. She didn't know if she'd been the target of his thoughts and she didn't know if they'd been sexual in nature or just mean-spirited, but she knew she'd caught him.

And he knew it, too.

The reporter chuckled uneasily. "Uh, you ever think about working with the police?"

The woman believed her.

"No." Meredith smiled straight into the camera. "I'm a teacher, not a cop. And I'm nothing special.

"Everyone has the ability to do what I do," she explained, paraphrasing what she'd read in the books that had finally made her abilities make sense. "My senses are heightened in this area, but we can all—with focus—tune in to other people's energy. Their emotions."

Except that in her case, sometimes she couldn't turn off the feelings.

"Wow," the woman said. "I'd like to hear more about this, but unfortunately we're out of time. This is Angela Liddy for KNLD news." She clicked off the wireless microphone and nodded to her cameraman, who lowered his equipment and turned back toward the van.

"Thanks," she said to Meredith. "I don't know what good it'll do, but I'm glad we got both sides."

Meredith hoped she'd be glad, too, already regretting what she'd done. "When will it air?"

"Tonight, if I get back in time," she said. "If not, then it'll start tomorrow morning."

Unlocking her car, Meredith dropped her bag on the floor behind the driver's seat.

"I probably shouldn't tell you this," Angela Liddy said, speaking softly as she paused beside the car. "But you should know that Larry Barnett is determined to see you lose your job."

Yeah, Meredith had gathered that much. "It'll take more than my speaking with his wife to make that happen," she said. "I have rights."

"And he has power," the reporter said. "I'd be careful if I were you."

Careful. What did that mean—not talking to reporters? Okay, she'd screwed up that one. And otherwise she was just living her life, going to work, coming home, watching the game-show network while she graded papers. What could she do that would be any more careful than that?

Not feel, not be herself?

How the hell did one do that?

MARK CAUGHT the news Wednesday night, lying in bed alone with the television on, attempting to fall asleep. Heart sinking when he heard the intro to the coming stories. Remote control in hand, he raised the volume another couple of notches.

She'd done a damned interview? Bad enough that Barnett was spreading this all over the media, but did Meredith have to feed the frenzy? Did she have no sense at all?

One thing was for certain: she was making him mad. Furious. He was going to have to fire her, just to keep from wringing her neck. Murder one wouldn't sit well on him.

By now, Mark was standing at the footboard, waiting through the commercial, impatient as hell. He'd done all he could for her and she just wouldn't listen. There was nothing more he could do. He couldn't help, couldn't save her job.

"Welcome back, ladies and gentlemen," the newscaster said. "We went to Bartlesville today, where they have a psychic in town…or do they?"

He bowed his head, couldn't watch. Barnett's interview came first and the man was impressive—the sort of lawyer who could probably convince a jury to set a six-time sex offender free if he wanted to. And here he was merely attempting to demolish the credibility of one relatively harmless third-grade schoolteacher.

"It pains me to say this, but I believe Meredith Foster needs psychiatric attention," Barnett said, his voice seemingly filled with compassion. "I mean her no harm, but she can't be trusted with our children...."

Hogwash. Bullshit. Mark paced to the window, back and forth. Barnett told of other incidents in which Meredith had spoken to parents concerning their children, making her sound like a certifiable lunatic.

How had the man unearthed all this stuff?

Mark had told Meredith so many times to stop. He'd warned her that something like this could happen.

But had she listened to him?

No.

And if she had, would Amber Walker still be alive today—or would she be dead?

Barnett was citing some statistic about the number of people in psychiatric wards and prison who believed themselves to have psychic abilities. Mark was shocked at the percentage.

And then Meredith was there, standing with the solid bricks of Lincoln Elementary School at her back, giving thoughtful and intelligent responses to an off-camera reporter.

Thoughtful and intelligent. Which he knew her to be.

But she was wrong about Tommy Barnett. Wrong to speak out based on hunches. Misguided to believe she could see inside people and know when they needed help. All the same, she was smart—and kind.

And...

He reached for the phone and for his laptop computer, looking up a number and then dialing.

"Hello?" She sounded wide awake.

"You give a damn fine interview."

"Mark?"

Only then did he realize that he was standing in his bedroom late at night wearing nothing but a pair of thin cotton pajama bottoms.

"I'm sorry," he said immediately, glancing at the clock. "I forgot it was so late."

"It's only ten," she told him. "I'm still up."

"Did you see the news?"

"No."

"You were on it."

"I know."

"And you didn't watch?"

"I never watch the news."

"Ah, right, too depressing." He flipped off the set and walked over to gaze out at his backyard.

The grass needed to be cut.

Perhaps he should get Kelsey a pool this summer. She'd been asking for one for years. Maybe that would make her happy again.

Happy with him.

"And I most particularly wouldn't want to see Larry Barnett eat me up and spit me out," Meredith said, her voice welcome in his darkness. "What purpose would that serve?"

None. At least none that was productive. But most people would've watched anyway. He would have.

He didn't answer, figuring her question had been rhetorical.

"Well, did he?" she asked.

"Eat you up? Yeah," he said softly, offended all over

again as he thought about the interview. It hadn't been so much what Barnett had said—some of it Mark would have had to verify, had he been asked. It had been the *way* he'd said it, making Meredith sound like some kind of freak. "But before he could spit you out, there you were, sounding so…sane."

"Yes, well, that's me," she chuckled. "Sane as they come."

Fifteen minutes ago he'd been ready to fire her. "You take everything in stride, don't you?"

"I try to."

"I try, too, but you seem to be much better at it than I am. What's your secret?"

"I live alone," she quipped. "I hide a lot."

"Really."

She paused and Mark wondered if he'd been too transparent, said too much and allowed her to figure out that at the moment he admired her a lot. Personally.

He hoped not. He had to hang up. Should never have called.

"I just know that there are only certain things I can control in this life," she said softly after a moment. "I try to focus on those and let go of the rest. It's that 'rest' that drives us all crazy—and we're never going to be able to change it anyway."

He needed to think about that.

"And while we're so busy fretting about stuff we have no control over, we miss opportunities to make choices that will direct the things we actually *can* change."

"Are you always philosophical late at night?" he asked, afraid of what he couldn't control at the moment; afraid she might know that he wanted the conversation to continue, that her voice sounded good to him. That even while he didn't believe in her so-called abilities, he trusted her logical insights. And that right now, with his daughter seemingly slipping away from him, she was a safety net.

"It's not that late. And I'm philosophical all the time, Mark," she said, laughing at him again—or at herself. "But I normally spare those around me and keep my torture to myself."

He needed to call Susan. Immediately. Before his thoughts took him into territory that would only prove his own instability. There were a few things he admired about Meredith Foster, that was all. He didn't want to stay on the phone with her—or think about how she looked late at night in her own home. That was none of his business.

His focus had to remain on the choices she made that he didn't agree with. And to make certain that she didn't continue to make them at work.

Susan had been doing rounds at the hospital tonight. Perhaps she was still awake and would be willing to drive over for a glass of wine.

"Well, I apologize again for calling so late," he said, back beside his nightstand, poised to drop the phone in its cradle. "I just wanted to tell you you'd done a good job." Not that he expected anything she said to have noticeable effect on Larry Barnett.

"Hey, don't apologize. I appreciate the comment, especially coming from you."

Mark smiled—it was nice pleasing someone. Even if that someone was a general pain in the ass. Go figure.

He'd tell Susan about it when he called her.

"Okay, then, see you tomorrow."

"Okay, good night—"

She clicked off before Mark could say the "sleep well" that was on the tip of his tongue.

Pushing buttons rapidly, he waited for Susan to pick up. Lesson to self: never call your teachers late at night. They morphed into something weird after eight o'clock. Or maybe *he* did….

CHAPTER SIX

"Psst, Kelsey!"

Kelsey glanced at Josie as the two of them walked through the playground, taking a shortcut to Josie's house after school on Thursday.

"I thought you were only going on Fridays," blond pigtailed Josie said, glancing toward the bushes on the far side of the baseball diamond.

"I am," Kelsey answered, also glancing at the shrubbery from which another call would be forthcoming if she didn't change course. It wasn't that she didn't want to see her mom; she did. But she felt bad ditching Josie.

And she couldn't get that Don guy out of her head.

"We were going to play The Sims."

Josie was close to Kelsey's size, just a little taller. Even if she told Josie about her mom's boyfriend, the two of them together wouldn't be enough to keep her safe if that man tried to hurt her or anything.

"I know," she said, trying to think about the computer game with its own world, where she built a family and even got to be the mom if she wanted. Or a kid with a good mom who lived in the same house with the dad and took care of the kids like Josie's mom did.

"Psst. Kelllseeey!"

"Just tell her you'll see her tomorrow," Josie said. "I already told my mom we were going to swing and stuff before we come home tomorrow."

And that was something else. She kept having to make Josie lie to her mom about Kelsey having the secret job helping a teacher after school on Fridays to earn money for a new saw for her dad for Father's Day. Kelsey had dropped his old one and broken it one day when Josie had been over to play, so her mom knew all about it. She had no idea what she was going to do after Father's Day, if Josie's mom ever said anything to Daddy about his new saw.

But it would be summer by then and maybe they'd all forget.

"Kelllllsssssseeeeey." Mom's whisper was so loud it practically had spit in it.

Kelsey didn't really know what to do. "I'm afraid to tell her no," she said to Josie, stopping to stare at the bits of color she could see behind the bush. Her mom was wearing red and blue today. She must be in a good mood. "What if it hurts her feelings and she doesn't come back?"

"Yeah." Josie's face got all scrunched, the way it did whenever they had a problem to figure out. "I forgot she gets upset so easy. Okay," she said, sighing. "You better go."

With a quick hug to her best friend, Kelsey ran off. "Tell your mom I was helping Jennifer with a math problem. I'll be there by four-thirty," she called, using yet another excuse on the list. It was getting harder and harder to make up new ones.

"'Kay," Josie called, walking slowly in the opposite direction.

Kelsey tried not to wish that she could go with her.

"CAN I SPEAK with you a minute, Ms. Foster?"

Turning from the blackboard where she was writing the next day's date and the cafeteria lunch menu, Meredith smiled at the woman standing in the doorway of her classroom.

She pulled her short red tunic jacket down over her navy slacks. "Ms. Hamilton, of course, please come in."

Bonnie Hamilton, mother of eight-year-old Eric, had helped out in the classroom during all the holiday parties. She'd made some killer sugar cookies for Valentine's Day.

"I'm sorry to bother you after school. I know you must be tired, but Eric has Cubs on Thursdays and I wanted a chance to speak with you in private." Bonnie Hamilton looked closer to sixteen than twenty-seven in her tight-fitting jeans, sweater and cowboy boots, with her long blond hair hanging loose.

"No problem," Meredith said, pulling an adult-sized chair away from the multipurpose table along the computer wall and motioning for the other woman to do the same. She hoped she wasn't walking into more trouble. "I'm here for at least an hour after class most afternoons, just for this reason," she told her visitor.

Eric's dad, a farmer who'd married a woman half his age, obviously adored his wife as much as she adored him. People enjoyed just being around them.

Meredith smiled now, trying and failing to think of any problems Eric had been having. Either in school or out.

Not that she was looking for trouble.

She'd practically held her breath all the way to school that morning and had taught with half an ear on the loudspeaker in her room, expecting a summons—trouble resulting from the previous night's news show. But though the day had prompted plenty of remarks from her colleagues who'd seen her on the news and needed to tell her about it, she hadn't seen or heard from Mark all day.

And most of the feedback had been positive—or at least teasing in a friendly manner.

"What's up?" she prompted, as Bonnie appeared to be content to sit quietly until it was time for her to pick up her son.

"Well, it's just that… I don't quite know how to say this."

The woman's gaze lowered and Meredith's stomach sank. If Eric's dad was going to insist on pulling him out of her class, others would follow. She'd already lost one student this week. Many more and she'd be done, without Mark having to fire her.

"I've found that it's best just to get it out," she said, preparing herself to be kind, supportive. To focus on what was best for Eric.

Bonnie glanced up, her blue eyes wide and filled with fear, but also with anticipation. "I need your help."

That didn't sound bad—unless she had to help convince Roy Hamilton to keep his son in her class. "What can I do?"

"I need to know whether or not to have another baby."

Meredith sat back. "Excuse me?"

"I need you to go wherever you go to find out stuff about people and tell me if I should have another baby," Bonnie said, her eyes begging Meredith even more than her words had done. "I wouldn't ask but I'm at my wit's end, Ms. Foster. I want a baby so badly it's on my mind practically all the time. I see other women with babies and I feel cheated. I think about never being pregnant again, never feeling those little feet and hands sliding around inside me, never breast-feeding…"

"What does your doctor say?" Meredith asked, even though what she wanted to do was grab her bag and go home.

Bonnie blinked. "Nothing. Why?"

"I assumed, since there's some question about this, that you'd been in consultation with your doctor."

"Oh!" Bonnie shook her head. "No. I'm sure I'm fine there," she said. "It's Roy. He says he's too old to go through all of that again. But he's only forty-five, Ms. Foster, and I just know that once he held our baby in his arms he'd be just as thrilled as I would be."

"Bonnie," Meredith said, feeling older than both Hamiltons at the moment. "I'm your son's third-grade teacher, not a counselor. I can't possibly give you advice in this situation."

And then Meredith stopped herself—before she did just that. Not because she could feel anything. She wasn't tuned in to Bonnie, didn't intend to tune in, *couldn't* tune in right now. But because the answer just appeared to be so obvious.

"But you have to!" The young woman leaned closer, touching Meredith's leg. "I saw you on the news last night and I knew, right then, that you were on TV for a reason. It was a message to me to come to you for my answer. See, I'm all out of pills, so if I'm going to do this, now would be the time."

Moving her leg out of the other woman's reach, Meredith focused on staying in her chair and getting through this calmly, rather than giving in to the sense of profound discomfort that was pushing at her.

"What does your husband say?"

"I'm not telling him." Bonnie flopped back against the seat, her hands clasped tightly in her lap. "He'd say no for sure. That's the point, Ms. Foster. I need to know whether or not I should just quit taking the pills and let him think it was an accident. Because I can tell you, I'm not going to be happy with him for the rest of my life if he robs me of this chance."

The young woman needed counseling. Or at least she needed to grow up a bit.

"I know you can do this for me, Ms. Foster. Just take a quick peek and tell me what you see."

And if I don't? Do I have another angry person out to get me?

"It's not that I don't want to help you," Meredith said slowly, breathing deeply, pulling her ponytail over one shoulder. "It's just that I *can't*. I'm not a psychic and I have no way of knowing what your future holds."

"But you said last night…"

"That sometimes—only sometimes—I can feel what other people are currently feeling."

For the most part. But she didn't need to go into that.

"Then 'feel' Roy," the woman said quickly. "Tell me if he'll divorce me if he ever finds out I tricked him."

Meredith paused, tired, unsure how to extricate

herself without damaging future relations with the mother of her student. And then she realized that she simply had to live as she always did, true to what she knew, regardless of the consequence. "I can't, Bonnie. I'm sorry, but I can't trespass on your husband's privacy that way."

She'd promised herself long ago that she wasn't going to intrude at will. She'd take things as they were given to her. Period. She wasn't even sure she had the ability to do that anymore.

The woman's shoulders dropped and all sparkle left her eyes. "I don't understand," she said. "I was so sure you were my answer."

Your answer is no, Meredith wanted to say. *Dishonesty, trickery, is seldom the best choice.*

"I wish I could help."

Bonnie stood. "Well, thanks anyway."

Meredith nodded from her seat, too weary to get up and walk Eric's mother to the door. She was just as exhausted half an hour later when she arrived home to find twelve messages on her machine from people she'd never heard of, all with similar requests. Oh, not about babies, but with pleas to help them with some decision—job, marriage, children—as if she were their last resort.

Twelve messages, because that was all her machine would take.

Meredith didn't feel like a teacher at that moment. Or a daughter. Or a friend. She felt like a freak.

ON FRIDAY AFTERNOON, Mark wandered down to Meredith's classroom—timing his visit to coincide with her planning period. He stood unnoticed in the doorway for a full minute, watching as she stapled colorful artwork of varying degrees of proficiency onto the bulletin board. The assignment must have been spring—he guessed by the colors—and he could tell one thing for sure. At Lincoln Elementary, students had a vast array of opinions, vivid imaginations and different ways of expressing themselves.

Not bad.

Nor were Meredith's legs. Long, slender. Exposed by the short denim skirt she was wearing with a long-sleeved yellow blouse that was a perfect backdrop for the cascade of red-gold hair she'd left loose.

"Oh, Mr. Shepherd. I didn't see you there." She came down off her toes and turned, smoothing her skirt.

And Mark gave his libido a mental shake. He was alive, human, he was going to notice women. Had been doing so quite regularly since puberty.

Just not this woman.

"I should've said something." Not that. It indicated that he'd been there long enough to have spoken up.

"I was just hanging these," she said, not quite meeting his eyes as she pointed to the papers lining the wall. "Is there a problem?"

He hated the hunted look in her eyes—even knowing that she had, at least in part, brought it on herself. "Not really," he replied, still standing in the doorway. "I wanted to let you know that while we've received a few calls as a result of the news show two days ago, they've almost all been calls of support."

"Thank you." There was little sign of emotion on her face, as if she'd closed herself off from him. Was she that way with everyone? He tried to picture her with Kelsey or Susan.

"How about you? Did you get any response?" he asked.

"Some," she said, folding her arms in front of her. "People here commented, but I think more because they'd seen me on TV than because of anything I said."

"You've worked here a long time. They know you—and respect you."

As he did. But as her boss, he was in a more precarious position. He couldn't let her go around breaking rules, upsetting parents, regardless of her motivation.

"So all else was quiet?"

"Pretty much."

Not entirely. He wondered what that meant. Wanted to push, but knew her well enough to be certain that it wouldn't do any good.

"I, uh, also…" He stepped into the room completely and shut the door behind him. "I wanted to make sure that you're okay with the plans for this weekend. It's not too late to change them, if you decide you don't want Kelsey spending the night." She stood in the front of the bulletin board, looking beautiful—and somewhat defenseless surrounded by the artwork of eight-year-olds. "If something's come up that you'd rather do…"

Policy allowed them to socialize outside school, as long as they didn't date. But that didn't mean he should take her time for granted.

"There's nothing I can think of that I'd rather do than spend tonight with Kelsey," she told him, her voice strong and clear.

Mark rocked back on his heels, sliding his hands into

the pockets of his slacks, trying not to feel quite so pleased and…relieved…at her response.

"She's looking forward to it," he said, not ready to turn around and leave this room, which thanks to Meredith Foster was as much a safe haven as it was a place of learning. "And I am grateful."

"I understand." She smiled. "You and Susan deserve some time away—and alone. I hope you guys have a great evening."

So did he. But that wasn't what he meant. "I'm grateful to have someone who shares my enthusiasm for time spent with my daughter," he remarked, though he supposed it would have been better to keep his honesty to himself.

"Susan loves being with her."

"Susan loves her," he corrected. "And she wants very much to get along with her. But Kelsey makes it a little difficult for Susan to be comfortable doing that. I wouldn't feel all that enthusiastic about it myself, if all I knew of Kelsey was what I see when Susan's around."

"That'll change."

"I know that." He was counting on it. "But in the meantime, it's good to have someone else out there who cares about her and whom Kelsey responds to."

She nodded, smiled. A real smile that reached her eyes. And reached him. "I can't imagine how tough it is being a single dad to a little girl."

He shrugged. Grinned. "Sometimes it's not hard at all." Then he grew serious again. "And sometimes, more so lately, it's like walking around in an unfamiliar, pitch-black room. You never know when you're about to take a misstep, what you're going to crash into or when you might fall."

"Sounds like teaching." She came closer, leaned against one of the students' desks, legs crossed in front of her, hands propped on the wood behind her. "Was her mother active in raising her at the beginning?"

Funny how, because he had a child, his personal life wasn't so personal.

"Very," he told Meredith. "Kelsey was pretty much her entire life. She never left her with a sitter or even sent her to preschool. Which is part of the reason it was such a shock when she abandoned us."

"Susan says she didn't even try to get partial custody."

"Nope." He shook his head, thrown momentarily back to the time of disbelief and confusion that had consumed him those first months after Barbie's departure. "She never tried to see her again."

"Odd for a women who cared so much."

Yeah, well, Barbie had had problems. "Anyway, I just wanted to ask…" He started again. "If Kelsey says anything that suggests I'm not doing something I should be, please let me know."

"Mark, you're a good father," she told him easily. "I doubt that she's going to say anything beyond which boy Josie thinks is cute, which usually means she does, too, or how badly she wants something you won't buy for her. But if she does, you'll hear about it."

He nodded, frowning. "I'm not asking you to betray her confidences."

"Hey," she interrupted. "I'm a teacher, remember? I know the fine line we tread when we're caring for other people's children—and earning and deserving the trust of the children, too. If Kelsey tells me she has a crush on someone, I'm keeping that to myself. If she tells me something you need to know to keep her safe, healthy and happy, that goes straight to you. Her welfare comes first. Always."

He should go. He had what he'd come for, for the most part.

"And…uh…with, you know, female stuff." He cocked his head and tried for nonchalance.

"What about it?"

"She gave me some speech earlier this week about growing up and talking 'girl stuff.' I just… If she asks, you're okay to answer her?"

Meredith burst out laughing. And somehow Mark was smiling, too.

"Are you asking me if I know the answers, Shepherd?"

"No, of course not," he assured her quickly. Then added, "Well, maybe. Which is entirely ludicrous considering the fact that you spend your days with thirty curious children."

"Third-graders aren't all that interested in reproduction," she told him. "And I don't think Kelsey is, either. It's a bit early for her to want to know. But if she does, I think I can remember what my mother told me, even though that was a really long time ago."

If her tone of voice hadn't made it perfectly clear that she was teasing him, her ear-to-ear grin did. He was trying to be sensitive, responsible, and she was making fun of him. He should probably take offense.

"It's okay, Mark," she said softly, before he could decide how to respond. "If Kelsey asks about her body,

I'll answer her—and I'll tell you what I told her. I know we purposely leave these things to parents at this age, and then to health class after that, but I'm comfortable speaking with her if the need arises."

"Thank you." His gaze couldn't leave hers.

"You're welcome."

Voices in the hall startled him. Meredith glanced toward the door just as it flew open and a flock of energetic eight-year-olds came pouring in from their reading class, filling the room with so much noise he could almost convince himself that a very dangerous moment had not just taken place there.

Almost, but not quite.

"KELSEY?" Barbie stared out the car window at trees covered with spring blossoms, believing in happiness. She adored these times, when life held promise. When she could feel so good. Kelsey snuggled against her, seeming as happy as she was just to be close. Nothing else had ever felt quite as wonderful as having her little girl's weight against her.

"Yeah?" Her daughter's eyes weren't as easy to read as they'd been when she was five. Or two. But still, as Kelsey tilted her head back to look up, she could see love in the little girl's eyes.

"I'm sorry about yesterday," she said. "I'm sorry I called you away from your friend."

"It's okay," Kelsey said. "I get to be with her every day."

God, that sounded good. Like Kelsey wanted to be with *her* every day, too.

"I'm sorry I was grouchy."

"I'm sorry I didn't want to go to your house, Mom. I will next week, I promise."

"It's okay, honey. You just don't know Don, yet, but when you do, you'll see that he's the best. He'll treat you like a queen."

She hoped. He was good to her. Understood her. Put up with her even when she was down, without making her feel like a failure. No one had ever done that before.

Except Kelsey.

"I'm thinking about seeing a lawyer," she said now, her stomach a little tense as she took this chance. What if Kelsey didn't want to be with her? Barbie could probably still get visitation rights. She was her mother, after all, and had never abused her or done anything to hurt her. Don said she'd have no trouble proving it.

But if Kelsey didn't want her…

"What for?"

"What would you think about you and me being together, legally?"

Kelsey pulled back, her sweet expression concerned but not appalled. "What about Daddy?"

Barbie almost lost it then, had to count to ten and think about the trees to keep from snapping at her daughter. The thought of Mark Shepherd still did that to her. The man shouldn't have given up on her. All of this was his fault.

But Don said she wouldn't have him if Mark hadn't let her go and he was right about that. Remembering that she'd much rather be with Don allowed her to continue.

"You'll still live with him, too, of course," she said. The man was an elementary school principal. And he'd cared for Kelsey when Barbie had fallen apart. They'd never take Kelsey away from him completely.

"But I'd get to see you for real?" Kelsey asked, hope lighting her big, dark eyes.

"Yep." Barbie's heart sped up and a sense of almost euphoric well-being replaced the queasy feeling in her stomach.

"No more hiding?"

"Nope."

"And Daddy would let me?"

"That's the point of the lawyer, honey. It'll all get worked out so that everyone is satisfied."

Or at least Mark would have to pretend to be satisfied.

"Really?" Her daughter's doubt tore at Barbie, making her more determined than ever to come through for Kelsey again. Just as she had every single minute for the first five years of her life.

"Really."

Her arms barely caught the little girl as she threw herself against Barbie—a feeling that was so good she could hardly bear to experience it.

"Oh, Mommy," Kelsey breathed against her. "I'd love that. I would really, really love that."

"Then we'll make it happen."

And Mark Shepherd be damned.

CHAPTER SEVEN

MEREDITH SAT behind the steering wheel of her Mustang, driving calmly. The top was down, and although she knew that she'd never put her top down if this weren't a dream, she also noticed and enjoyed the breeze against her heated face, her heated body. Why was she so hot? It was March. She shouldn't be hot. The entire car was hot, almost burning up, but she couldn't stop to find out why, to help herself. She was being pulled along by speeding traffic that moved faster and faster, the curves on the road becoming sharper. Someone was in the car with her. Her mother. She needed help. Meredith reached out a hand but couldn't reach her. She was right there next to her, and still she couldn't reach her. Her hand flew back to the wheel as another curve suddenly appeared. She skated the side of the road, gravel flying, overcompensated and the car tilted slightly as her tires started up the walled embankment on the other side and then returned to the road.

Past the curve she glanced over at her mother, and a child was there, needing help. The child laughed at her hand, which couldn't reach... And waited for her to figure it out. Meredith didn't know what she was supposed to figure out. She meant to ask, but another *curve was upon her. More speed. Faster. She was dizzy, could hardly breathe. She was going to crash. Braced herself and knew the absolute horror of imminent death. But first there was a van ahead, on the side of the road. While her car still sped along with her at the wheel, Meredith was somehow also beside the van, staring in the passenger window. Her father was there—alive again. He needed her to help him. She was the only one. He called out to her. His seat was going to explode any second and he couldn't get out. Meredith got the door open, saw the unfastened seat belt…and fastened it. But the sound of it clicking closed wasn't the sound of a seat belt. It was the lock on her hotel room door—opening. She stood on the inside, staring as it opened as far as the safety chain would allow. There was another open door in front of her, leading into a room that connected with hers. She knew the people in that room; was there with them. A child stood in the doorway and she tried to speak to him, telling him to call an adult male who was in the bathroom shaving. The child called out, but the adult didn't hear.*

Fingers slid beneath the hotel room door, and Meredith thought about the bills that normally entered hotel rooms that way. She tried to speak with the child again, but the child couldn't hear her. He just stood there, glancing into his room as if watching television. Big male fingers appeared around the side of her door, pushing by the chain until a full hand was in her room. The fingers were going to break the chain. She screamed for the adult in the adjoining room, but no sound came out. Her throat was numb, wouldn't move

*to make sound. As the lock started to give she screamed
again and again, straining her throat until it was
raw....*

DARKNESS WAS A RELIEF. Meredith slowly came to an
awareness that she was alive. In her bed. In her house.
Safe and secure. But she felt neither safe nor secure.
Dread filled her, turning her inside out, chafing as it
continued to course through her veins. Her heart was
beating so hard she could feel it—and hear its rapid
rhythm in her ears. Her pillow and the back of her
gown were soaked with sweat. Hot and cold at the
same time, she lay there, opening her eyes and then—
fearing the world around her—closing them.

Her interior world, containing that hand, her father
careening to her death, was no comfort. Her eyes
snapped open again.

She had to figure out what it meant. There would be
no peace until she knew. Was her soul sending her a
message? That could explain some of the dream, but
what unresolved issues could she have about her father?
He'd been a stern man, but good to her. He'd died of
kidney failure ten years ago.

So had she been, in her relaxed state of sleep, open
to someone else's torture? Or had it just been a crazy
nightmare?

"Meredith?" The small voice startled her, and she
gasped. And then she remembered that she wasn't
alone.

Glancing toward the open door in the moonlight,
she could make out the shadow of her pajama-clad
houseguest.

"Kelsey! Come in. What's wrong, sweetie?" She sat up, turning over her pillow before she propped it and its mate behind her, then patting the top of her down comforter. "Did you have a bad dream?"

The little girl shook her head. "I don't think so," she said. "I can't remember. I just woke up scared and thought I heard you choking."

"Yeah, I just woke myself up," Meredith said, finding a grin and hoping it would precipitate a lightening of the tension inside. "Guess I need a drink." Reaching for the water bottle she always kept beside her bed, she took a long swallow as Kelsey crawled in beside her.

"It's dark and kind of creepy in that other room by myself. Can I stay here with you?" she asked, her feet already beneath the covers.

"Of course." Meredith capped the bottle, resisting the urge to pull the little girl into her arms and promise that things that go bump in the night would never harm her.

Because she knew better.

"When I was a little girl I used to have really scary dreams sometimes," Meredith said now, sliding back under the covers herself. "I wasn't allowed to sleep in my parents' bed, but I'd sneak into their room and lie down on the floor by my mother's side and fall asleep. I can still remember the feeling of that shag carpet under my cheek."

Kelsey turned her head toward Meredith, her eyes mere dots in the darkness. "Did you have brothers and sisters?"

"Nope," Meredith stared at the ceiling and then

turned back to the child. "I was an only child, just like you."

"Did your mother ever know you were sleeping there?" Kelsey's childish voice was precious to her, like peace in a turbulent world, solace in the dark of the night.

"I didn't think so at the time," she said, smiling. "I didn't really sleep all that much because I knew I had to sneak back into my room before she woke up." The memory was bittersweet. She'd spent much of her childhood afraid. And had rarely understood why. "Several years ago she told me she'd known I was there," she added now.

"She had?"

"Mmm-hmm. But she didn't say anything because she knew my dad would've made me go back to my own room. He was a stickler for rules."

"And she wanted you there." Kelsey's voice was filled with reverence.

"Yeah." Evelyn Foster had been her champion her entire life. It had just taken her a while to figure that out.

"Girls need moms."

The simple statement instantly put Meredith on alert. "Of course they do," she said, opening her mind to Kelsey completely and waiting to see what she might perceive. "And because moms are important, the world provides us with all kinds of ways to get them," she continued slowly.

"Like with lawyers?"

Wishing that the moonlight was brighter and not behind the little girl, Meredith asked, "Why would you say that?"

"I saw a commercial on TV."

Kelsey wasn't lying. Meredith could feel her sincerity. And something more. But what? She tried to slow down her thinking, to empty out and feel only the little girl beside her, but the residual effects of her dream were still on her mind.

"For adoptions, you mean?"

"I dunno. It just said giving kids the parents they need." She mimicked the last part.

"Well, that's one way to do it. But girls who don't have moms of their own living with them sometimes unofficially adopt their friends' mothers."

"Like Josie's mom."

"Yeah."

"But she's Josie's, not mine, and it's not the same. She yells at Josie and teases her, but she's always really nice to me."

Out of the mouths of the children we thought we needed to teach...

"So adopt a mom of your own." Maybe not the best thing to say, but it felt right. Susan was there, ready and willing.

And Meredith had agreed to try and guide the two of them together.

"Like you?"

Meredith's heart ached with the need to slide her arms around Kelsey. "Or someone else," she said, knowing that to push too much would lose Susan this chance.

Kelsey turned onto her back, her small features facing the ceiling. "I want you for my special friend, Meredith, and I don't mean to hurt your feelings but you aren't a mom."

Of course not. And it didn't hurt. Not really. It was what she wanted.

"You never had a kid," she went on.

Neither had Susan.

"A lot of women who don't or can't have children adopt kids and are wonderful parents."

"But you aren't family. Moms have to be family."

Turning on her side, Meredith watched the little girl's placid face beneath the moon's glow. "You've given this a lot of thought, huh?"

"Uh-huh." Kelsey nodded.

Because of her father dating Susan? Were they closer than they thought to winning the little girl's approval?

"And what conclusions have you drawn?"

Kelsey turned her head, her tangled hair haloed around her. "I want a mom of my own more than just about anything."

Meredith's heart overflowed with longing. Kelsey's longing. "I know you do, sweetie."

"And you know something else?" The child's voice dropped to a whisper.

"What?"

"Promise me you won't tell my dad yet?"

Oh, God. What now? Get Kelsey's confidence, to keep her safe and happy? Be honest and tell the child she couldn't make that promise without knowing what she was going to say? Listen and keep her mouth shut regardless of what she'd promised Mark?

She finally came up with, "As long as what you're about to tell me isn't illegal or going to hurt you, I think I can make that promise."

"I've been wishing for a mom and asking for a mom in my prayers every single night since I can remember, which is a really long time. And that means I might get one soon."

Meredith's melancholy smile was lost in the darkness. Susan and Mark were almost home free. She was relieved, grateful, honestly happy for her friends. And uneasy at the same time.

Life for someone like Meredith was never entirely easy.

CLIMBING THE STEPS to Meredith's vintage three-bedroom home, Mark tossed his keys and caught them again, grinning. Life had its ups and downs and nothing was going to be perfect, but still there was enough good to keep a man happy.

Ignoring the old-fashioned doorbell, he pulled open the screen and rapped his knuckles against the solid wood. Meredith's house might be old, but it looked great—freshly painted white siding and black shutters, smooth floorboards on the porch, even the windows and screens were clean and in good repair. This was one woman who didn't need a man to take care of her.

She was also a woman who wasn't opening her door. He knocked again, glanced toward the windows on each side of the house. Had they gone out for break-fast? Her garage door was closed, so he had no way of knowing if her car was here or not.

One more knock and Mark was ready to sit it out on the porch. They hadn't set a specific time for him to be there....

The door opened a crack and through the darkness

beyond he saw some strands of hair covering most of the face peering out at him. "Yes?"

And then, before he could say a word, "Oh, my God. Mark! What are you doing here?"

The door remained closed except for the original inch.

"Susan got called to the hospital," he said. "And since Kelsey never sleeps past seven on Saturdays, I thought I'd spare you…."

"What time is it?"

He couldn't help grinning, although he suspected it might make her mad. "Nine."

"Did you say *nine?*"

"Uh-huh." The woman was cute first thing in the morning. And he'd only seen an inch of her.

"I haven't slept this late since college," she muttered, sounding confused. "Hold on. I'll go wake Kelsey."

"She's probably parked in front of your television," he told her. "She's good about amusing herself quietly on the rare occasions I get to sleep in."

"She's still asleep," his unusual babysitter told him.

"You probably just didn't hear—"

"Mark! Would you please stop being so cheerful and chatty?" So the woman had a temper in the morning, too. Why didn't that surprise him?

"I know she's still asleep, because she's in my bed. She woke up in the middle of the night and we were up for a while."

His grin faded. "Was something wrong? Is she sick? You should've called."

"Everything's fine." Her voice was back to its usual calm, if perhaps a bit tired-sounding. "I had a coughing fit that woke her up and then she couldn't get back to sleep. Probably because she was in a strange house."

His heart settling back into a more normal pace, Mark had a vision of his daughter in Meredith's bed. Which led him to thoughts of Meredith in Meredith's bed.

A place he absolutely did not belong. "So, is everything okay with her? Anything I need to know?"

"Nothing," Meredith said, and he wished she'd pull open the damn door so he could see her.

And then, remembering she'd just come from bed, revised that thought.

"But I don't think she's as averse to Susan as you think," she added, pulling his attention firmly back to the life at hand—and the satisfaction he'd felt this morning. "We talked about girls needing mothers."

He narrowed his eyes, needing a better read of her expression than he was getting.

"Did she bring that up or did you?"

"She did."

He shook his head, glad that the road was clearing for him and sad at the same time that he had to hear this from someone else. He and Kelsey seemed to be growing further and further apart. "She and I never mention the subject," he admitted. "After her mother left, Kelsey was understandably devastated. She'd break down and cry anytime I mentioned Barbie. Naturally, I stopped. She's never said anything to me about it."

"Knowing Kelsey, I'd guess she doesn't want to hurt your feelings."

That sounded like Kelsey. And made good sense. He didn't kid himself that Kelsey had done or would do an instant turnaround and suddenly love Susan dearly, but if she wasn't averse to the idea of a new mother…

He glanced up, getting ahead of himself and yet finding no reason to hold back on the idea that had fallen into place for him that morning. "If you really think Kelsey could be ready, that pretty much solidifies my plan to ask Susan to marry me."

The door fell open another couple of inches, although Meredith's expression was still lost to him. "You're going to propose?" Her initial, half-asleep reaction was followed by a more enthusiastic, "That's wonderful!"

"You think she'll accept?" He was a bit nervous about that, and he couldn't imagine anything better than marrying Susan. She was perfect for him. Practical, logical, beautiful. And equally important, Susan wasn't prone to inexplicable emotional outbursts as Barbie had been.

"I don't know." Meredith's hesitation gave him pause until she added, "I hope so."

He hoped so, too. Except that, if he married Susan, Meredith would be around for the rest of his life.

Mark worried about that particular notion on and off for the rest of the day.

"So, HOW'D IT GO with Kelsey?" Susan's breathless question came about fifteen minutes into her Sunday morning hike with Meredith. Before that, Meredith had hogged the conversation, telling Susan about her mother's mixed-up lab report and perfectly healthy liver.

She'd also shared her sadness for the other woman, the

stranger whose perfectly healthy report was now going to be retracted and replaced by something more serious.

"You think it's life-threatening?" Susan had asked as they'd arrived at the state park. They'd taken the longer of the two routes they normally hiked. It was early enough that they still had it to themselves.

Meredith's only reply had been a shrug, but she suspected, considering the heaviness she still felt, that this other woman's illness was terminal.

"Earth to Mer," Susan said now with affectionate exasperation. "About Kelsey?"

"I didn't get much," she told her friend. "She really felt happy, or at least peaceful. As though she was satisfied with the way things were going."

Susan stopped, turned right where the path got steep and Meredith's tennis shoe skidded on a loose stone in the dirt. "How sure are you that you were feeling her feelings?"

"About seventy percent."

They'd long ago determined that anything over sixty on Meredith's confidence scale had at least some truth to it. She pulled her ponytail away from her sweaty neck and secured it on top of her head with a clip pulled from the pocket of her denim jacket.

"And that was last night while I was out with her father," Susan said, resuming the climb.

"Yep."

"Did she mention me?"

"We didn't talk about you specifically," Meredith said carefully, hating the fact that her friend felt such a lack of confidence in this area. It was so unlike her.

"So she could've just been happy to be with you."

"Suze," Meredith said, taking the few long steps that would put her in touching distance of her best friend. She set a hand on Susan's shoulder, turned her around and looked her straight in the eye. "You're going to blow this if you worry too much. Just be you, pay attention to her and don't fake it."

"How sure are you that'll work?" Susan's softly spoken question showed a vulnerability that few people knew existed.

And Meredith wished she had a better answer. "Fifty percent."

"You think it, but you don't feel anything at all one way or the other," Susan translated.

Meredith nodded and Susan went back to climbing.

"HERE, BARBIE, have some." Barbie rolled her head sideways on the couch to put her lips to the pipe Don was holding out. She took a long drag, held her breath and then slowly exhaled. And waited for it to work. She hadn't moved from the couch since she got up that morning—hadn't even showered. She just didn't have the energy. Was afraid to try.

Don sat down beside her and she showed her gratitude with a smile. She'd heard James leave a few minutes before, and had hoped that meant she wouldn't be left to sit here alone with her torment.

"You going to tell me what's got you down?"

She hadn't planned to.

But the good feeling was all gone, leaving her with nothing. "I don't qualify for free legal aid," she told him. "You make too much money."

"But we aren't hitched," he told her. "It's for low income."

"Only for some services. I gave her up without a fight, so I don't qualify."

She might as well die. She'd had the best of life. There wasn't anything else to look forward to.

Don reached under her T-shirt and found a nipple. She didn't really care. He could play with it if he wanted to. She wasn't going to get turned on.

He held the pipe to her mouth again and she inhaled. His thumb rubbed back and forth. Nothing.

She thought about driving over to the elementary school, but it was Sunday afternoon. No one would be there. Besides, she was afraid to get in her car alone. She might wreck it and then she'd have to spend the night in jail, and that was one place Barbie knew she'd never survive.

Don pulled her away from the couch, lifted her shirt, exposing her skin to the cool air in the room and then set her back. She glanced down at her breasts, took another toke from the pipe and watched as he suckled her. She kind of liked how that looked, being touched. And the way he pulled on her nipples sent tiny shards of feeling lower down.

But then she remembered what she'd learned from the lawyer's office and she pulled her shirt down.

Don didn't even frown. He just took another deep toke and sat back.

"It'll be good for us to have her around," he said, almost to himself, but she knew he was really talking to her. "Give us respectability."

That sounded nice.

"Hire a lawyer, Barbie. Just make sure you find the cheapest one you can."

She lifted her head. "You mean it?" The elation that shot through her was such a relief it made her cry.

Don nodded, and grinned.

And with that she climbed on top of him.

CHAPTER EIGHT

ON TUESDAY AFTER WORK Meredith came home, collected the mail—and frowned as she saw the letter with an unfamiliar return address. Sensing that her life was about to take a hard turn, she slowly slid open the envelope. It was from an upscale law firm in Tulsa. She read the letter once, carefully slid it back into its envelope and put it away in the drawer of the desk in her spare bedroom—apart from the bills waiting to be paid.

Wrapping imaginary arms around herself, pretending she was stepping into a great big "bubble" made up of cotton and coolness, she poured a glass of wine, drew a hot bath and soaked until bedtime.

THE PHONE WOKE HER at six-thirty the next morning.

"Get dressed. I'm on my way over."

"Mark?" Her vision was blurry and she could hardly see through reddened eyes. She'd cried for some time after she'd finished her wine the night before.

"Susan's coming here to stay with Kelsey and take her to school."

She sat up, trying to ignore the thickness in her head. She knew better than to drink wine on a school night.

"What's going on?" She forced a normal tone into her speech, though the effort cost her.

"You don't take the newspaper."

And that had never been a reason for her boss to visit her at home before seven in the morning. He wouldn't say any more, just gave her ten minutes to make herself decent.

She used up five of them filling the coffeepot to the brim, turning it on and waiting for the first cup to drip before she put the pot back under the filter to catch the rest. If it took her more than the five minutes she had left to shower, Mark Shepherd was going to have to wait.

MARK'S EXPRESSION WAS GRIM when Meredith opened the door to him in a calf-length jumper patterned with hearts and flowers. She didn't think the two minutes she'd made him wait at her front door was cause enough for his obvious upset.

"Can I get you some coffee?" She was on her third cup already and had a scalded tongue to show for her haste. But at least her head wasn't quite so foggy.

"Please." Dressed in dark brown slacks and a white-and-brown striped Oxford shirt, he followed her to the kitchen, a folded copy of the *Republic* clutched in one hand. His sandy hair was still damp at the ends.

"How do you take it?" She reached for the least girly mug she could find. It was purple and beige with green vines, but at least there were no hearts or flowers on it.

"Black, no sugar."

Straight up. Her kind of coffee.

She poured, and then carried his coffee and hers to the table. Sat down. And then there were no more niceties to distract her.

Ignoring the coffee, Mark opened the paper. "Read it and then we'll talk."

Eyes purposely averted, Meredith said, "Can't you just tell me what it says?" Obviously the news wasn't good, otherwise a phone call would have sufficed. Whatever this was about, it would be easier to take with a middle man there to dilute the negative energy.

"It's a full story this time, rather than an editorial."

Barnett strikes again. She'd known he would, of course.

"They interviewed him, and also quoted from your aired interview."

"Let me guess. They twisted what I said."

"The words sound odd when taken out of context."

She sipped her coffee. Wrapped her fingers around her mug, comforted by the warmth. She concentrated on that. And on the comfort of her yellow kitchen, the familiarity of the flowered utensils hanging on the wall. The softly woven amber, yellow and orange placemats.

"That's not the worst of it," Mark said, his words clipped. "Apparently you got a letter?"

She froze.

"You might have mentioned it."

"I just got it. Last night after work." *Dear Ms. Foster.* She'd read it twice and now had the whole damn thing memorized. But then, it wasn't very long. *I am writing on behalf of my client, Lawrence P. Barnett, JD, to request that you resign from your position at Lincoln Elementary school immediately. My client feels that*

*such an action on your part would help to restore faith
lost in him by those in the community who are aware
of your accusations regarding Mr. Barnett's treatment
of his son. If you choose not to comply with this request,
we will be forced to pursue the restoration of my client's
reputation by other means. Sincerely...*

"So it's true." Mark sighed. Sat back with his arms
crossed over his chest. His hands, which were so gentle,
capable and strong, were tucked in on either side where
she couldn't see them.

"What does the paper say about it?"

He glanced at her, his dark eyes showing compassion for the first time that morning. "That he asked for
your resignation."

"Does it also say that he threatened further action if
I don't do as he demands?"

"He did?" Mark sat forward. "Do you mind if I see
the letter?"

Of course she did. It was humiliating, difficult even to
touch. She retrieved it anyway, handing it to him, envelope
and all. And rinsed out the coffeepot while he read.

"This is definitely a threat."

"I know." Drying her hands, she came back over to
sit with him.

"And it's telling that the paper doesn't mention that."

"Probably."

He folded the letter, returned it to the envelope and
met her gaze. "I don't like threats."

"Me, neither." She tried for a grin. "Especially when
they're aimed my way."

He glanced down and then, with his head still
lowered, looked up at her. "What do you intend to do?"

He wasn't going to like it. "Nothing." She'd done all there was to do. "I have a contract, Mark. I can't be fired without proper—and documented—justification, a hearing by the school board and a chance to defend myself. If I'm made to leave I can sue the school district, and at this point I'd win hands down."

"He's not giving up, Meredith."

"I know that."

"And you think it's good for the school—the kids—to draw this out?"

Meredith had to focus in order to breathe. Deep breaths, slowly, in and then out. Tension was normal to her. If she let it take control, however, she'd make poor decisions.

"There are many things at stake here." She started speaking slowly, after she'd collected her thoughts. "My reputation is one of them, but not the most important factor. Since it's an easy place to start, however, I'll begin there. Resigning now would be tantamount to an admission of guilt. And what would that do to my chances of getting another teaching position?"

He said nothing, his thumb tapping against the rim of his mug. He appeared to be engrossed with the action.

"Would you hire someone who came to you with a forced resignation on her record?"

She took his silence for a no.

"Second, and neither is this the most important thing, it's just plain wrong to let a bully win."

"This isn't the school playground."

"Third…you know what he's doing, don't you?"

He glanced at her, his eyes narrowed. "Why don't you tell me?"

Why don't you just support me? The impression came—and went. Mark was Mark. He believed what he could see. And the fact that he was there, sitting in her kitchen at seven in the morning, *was* his way of showing support. He was there even though he thought what she'd done was wrong.

"All this ruckus, Mark… Do you think he'd be spending so much time and energy on one school-teacher, if he didn't have something to hide? Think about it. He moved his kid to another school, so Tommy's not going to be affected by me. Why does he care—for the other kids? Has Larry Barnett ever shown one iota of concern for the children in this community? He says it's to protect his reputation, but *he* was the one who made the whole thing public! If he'd kept his big mouth shut, no one would've known about this except Ruth Barnett, you and me."

"And anyone his wife might have told. She believed you. He was afraid she might pursue an investigation," Mark said slowly, as though following a new thought.

"And what would that matter, if he wasn't guilty? It would've been done quietly, and then—assuming nothing was found—the issue would've disappeared and as he'd done all through the process of their divorce, he'd have claimed that she was emotionally overwrought. It's his M.O. Make everyone else look bad in order to look good himself. It's always the other guy who's messing up because it couldn't possibly be him. After all, he's the district attorney."

Meredith stopped, a bit embarrassed by her evident bitterness. She'd assumed she had a better handle on herself. On the whole Barnett situation. After all, she'd drowned him in half a bottle of wine.

"If I'm guilty of wrongdoing, so much so that I end up losing my job, he looks innocent. He's an injured victim, deserving of sympathy and support."

"What exactly are you saying here?" Mark asked, sitting forward, forearms on the table.

"He's abusing his son, Mark. I'm certain of it."

He shook his head. "You have no proof of that, Meredith. You can't keep making potentially slanderous statements without any proof."

"I'm telling you, not the *Republic*."

She needed his help if she was going to be able to have the time to fight this. She had to keep her job.

"If I resign, the episode will go away and Barnett will continue to harm his son. The next article we see on this topic could be about Tommy's suicide. Or his murder."

Mark said nothing.

"I have a fourth reason."

Mark's lips quirked, almost as if he was holding back a smile. "I'm not surprised."

"I'm a good teacher, Mark. And I have the test scores to prove that. How does it help the kids if I leave so close to the end of the year? Chances are good they'll end up with subs over the next two months until school is out."

He nodded and she took her first easy breath. She could do this, if Mark was behind her.

And not just because he had her job in his hands.

"There's going to be a scandal, I get that," she acknowledged. "But there'd be a scandal either way.

We'll just have to do what we can to minimize it, where the kids are concerned."

"And how do you suggest we do that?"

She was leaning forward. And so was he. His face was close, his gaze connected with hers. And when she felt herself being drawn even closer Meredith stood, taking her cup to the sink.

What in the hell was the matter with her? The man was practically engaged to her best friend. And he was her boss. How could she forget that? Forget herself?

Was her own reaction all she was feeling? Or had Mark been part of it, too? Was she feeling his feelings? Or just losing her mind?

"I'm not sure how to do that," she told him, a little shakily.

"It would appear that we have two options."

She spun around when he spoke. His voice had come from just behind her. She hadn't known he'd left the table.

She sucked in her breath. "Which are?"

"Either we fight fire with fire and go to the paper with your kids' test scores, your evaluations, with character references from all over the city…"

Only inches separated them, but Meredith couldn't move again. "Or?"

"Or we do the opposite. We act like it's a nuisance, like we aren't the least bit concerned. We keep it in perspective. Carry on with our jobs, business as usual."

That felt right.

She motioned toward the newspaper on the table behind him. "People are bound to talk after this."

"That doesn't mean we have to engage in dialogue

with them." He sounded so sure, all of a sudden, and Meredith actually believed she could go to work and do her job. "If your resignation would imply your guilt, then the fact that you aren't resigning should have the opposite effect."

In a perfect world.

"I think we should say something to the kids," she told him quietly. "At least the ones in my class. And probably to their parents, too. They're getting the other side, and it's only fair that they hear our reassurances."

"I'm not opposed to that."

"I think you should be the one to do it."

He watched her for long seconds. "Let me think about it."

He hadn't said no.

"If I do call some kind of meeting, you should be there, too."

"Okay."

"I can downplay Barnett's spin on this," he continued slowly, frowning as he looked at her. "His public attack on you is inexcusable. But…" He paused and Meredith knew she wasn't going to like what was coming. Mark's nearness was starting to suffocate her. His approval meant so much—she was beginning to recognize that it meant more than it should—and his disapproval was hard to take.

Her awareness of him was also tricky. Barnett's threats would be moot if she suddenly developed a hankering for her boss. District policy on sexual relationships between colleagues at the same school was perfectly clear and completely unflexible.

"I'm not sure how I explain your initial action. We

both know what I think about that. I'm pretty much on Barnett's side there."

"So I'll do that part," she said quickly, before everything began to go backward. "I did fine on the news. You said so yourself."

"It'll need to be soon."

"I agree."

"I'll see if I can set up something with the parents tomorrow morning before school."

"Fine."

"Seven-thirty work for you?"

"Yes."

He nodded, then glanced at his watch. "We need to head out or we're going to be late." He didn't move.

She stared back at him.

"You're a lot of trouble, Meredith Foster."

The words *I'm worth it* popped into her head and she kept them there.

"I have to go with my conscience, but I'll do what I can to help you."

"Thank you."

He lifted a hand toward her face—stopped midway and let it drop. "Don't thank me yet," he told her, turning away and reaching in his pocket for his car keys. "It might not be enough."

Those words were his farewell.

Standing alone in her kitchen, Meredith heard them again in her mind. There was a limit to what he would do. And it might not be enough.

For now it was all she had.

She'd have to do a lot of right living to make sure that what she had was enough.

AT SEVEN-THIRTY Thursday morning, parents repre-
senting twenty-nine students showed up in Ms. Foster's
third-grade classroom. Mark was at the door, welcoming them and watching as Meredith stood at the front
of the room, greeting everyone with reassuring smiles.
Their sons and daughters were enjoying doughnuts and
juice, compliments of Mark, in the gymnasium with
Macy Leonard. While he might have doubts about the
advisability of hiring Meredith Foster, in the past five
seconds he'd understood without a doubt that he'd
made an excellent choice in his secretary.

"How's it going?" Susan, dressed in a sleek black
pantsuit with a red silk blouse, came up beside him. She
looked great.

"So far, so good," he told her quietly, resisting the
urge to kiss her. She was a great woman, a great friend
and he was lucky to have found her.

Or rather, lucky that Meredith Foster had introduced them.

"Everyone showed up."

"I was afraid I wouldn't get here in time," she told
him, her gaze gliding over the sea of adults sitting in
miniature chairs. He'd grown used to the sight of small
desks and low toilets in his workday life, but to
someone like Susan he guessed it might seem pretty
unusual. "I've never done my rounds so efficiently."

"I'm glad you're here," he said, giving parents a
chance to greet each other, put themselves at ease,
before he called the gathering to order.

"Did you tell her I'd be coming?" Susan motioned
toward Meredith, who was over by the wall talking

to a group of parents about various pieces of artwork on display.

"No." From the moment he'd first seen Ms. Foster that morning, he'd been all business. He had a job to do. He couldn't lose sight of that fact—or lose focus, either. He wasn't going to be swayed by the fact that Meredith Foster was the best friend of the woman he intended to marry. "Let's get this show on the road," he added, moving into the classroom.

"Ladies and gentlemen, thank you all for coming."

The room, which had been buzzing, grew still as Mark stood with his back to Meredith's desk—and to the two women standing behind it. He'd seen them hug, and that had been enough.

"Is there anyone here who has not seen or heard about the article in the paper regarding Larry Barnett and Ms. Foster?"

Some heads nodded. No hands were raised.

"That's what I figured. I asked you here to reassure you that we have everything under control at Lincoln Elementary. I wanted to give you a more complete version of the truth, answer any questions you might have and offer you the opportunity to move your children to another third-grade class if you so choose."

He heard the gasp behind him, felt a pang, even though he knew he'd been under no obligation to tell Meredith his plan to give parents of her students the possibility of moving their children out. He'd had a call from the president of the school board that morning and had obtained the man's reluctant consent to handle the situation his way for now, assuming he at least gave the parents a choice.

More than two dozen faces stared back at him. Some of the adults out so early were dressed professionally, probably going straight to work from the grade school. Some looked as though they'd barely rolled out of bed. They were dressed in everything from sweats and overalls to three-piece suits. And every single one of them looked concerned.

"Before I say more, I'd like to give Ms. Foster a chance to speak with you." He stepped aside, watched Meredith make eye contact with the parents of her students as she came forward.

Her conservative navy slacks, white blouse with its bow at the neck and her understated navy earrings and bracelet were carefully chosen, he was sure. He had to give her credit for doing even that job well. She'd worn her hair down, too, giving her a softer look.

Not that his approval mattered. How she wore her hair had nothing to do with him. He'd always preferred short hair on a woman, anyway.

"I'm glad you came," Meredith started. "I take my job very seriously. I come to work every day aware that I will be spending the next six or seven hours of my day caring for your children, not just teaching them how to add and write and read, but teaching them how to get along with each other, how to thrive in society. How to be kind. And I hope I teach them that there are good people in the world, that there are people outside their homes who care about them, people they can trust. I hope that I show them they can trust me, as it's only with utmost trust that they will lend me their minds, be willing to receive knowledge from me."

She was good. Mark's skin tightened and a chill

spread through him. She really meant what she was saying. And this was what made Meredith Foster the best teacher he'd ever had in his employ.

"I would never, ever do anything to hurt any of your children," she continued without missing a beat, her gaze moving over the room, connecting every single person there. "On the contrary, I tend to stick my neck out in an attempt to help them. Which is what I did for Tommy Barnett. I believed that he was having problems at home and I would not have been able to live with myself, had I not said something to his mother about my belief. I can't honestly tell any of you that I wouldn't do it again. Nor will I tell you that I wouldn't do the same for your child. Because I know that I would. That is the promise you have from me. I will be here, I will be focused and attentive, and if I ever suspect that any one of your children is struggling in any way, I will come straight to you."

Meredith paused. Heads nodded.

"That's all I have to say. Thank you." She turned to him. "Thank you, Mr. Shepherd."

Mark cleared his throat. He was on. And he didn't have a thing to add that would be better than what she'd just said.

CHAPTER NINE

THE HALLS WERE EMPTY of children, quiet and yet very much alive as Meredith walked from her classroom to Mark's office late that afternoon. The day's energy resonated, filling the space with innocence, frustration, fear and joviality.

She shifted the black M&M bag to her other shoulder. Tired as she was, she could pick up on all the various emotions that were lingering—or perhaps she was so tired she was simply imagining they must be there. Either way, she couldn't fathom not walking these halls, next to lockers and doorways that had been witness to thousands of secrets over the years. She couldn't fathom not being aware of the children.

Panic churned in her stomach and she forced herself not to give in to it. She hated feeling powerless. Her destiny was out of her hands at the moment, but she understood enough about life's process to know that it was only temporary.

So why wasn't that helping?

The outer door to the principal's office was open, which was how Macy left it when she went home if Mark was still here. He'd said he'd wait for her.

And he was talking to someone. She'd thought

they'd discuss the results of the morning's meeting alone—it would be hard enough to hear how many parents had opted out of her classroom without having to hear it in front of an audience.

She went in anyway.

"Oh, Kelsey. Hi, honey!" The little girl was sitting in her father's chair behind his desk, her feet far above the ground. "I didn't know you'd be here."

Mark rose from one of the two task chairs in front of his desk. "Kelsey heard some kids talking today and decided to come and see me rather than going home with Josie."

"There's a problem with Josie?" Meredith asked, glancing at the child, wanting so badly to protect her from life's hurts—big and small. Her eyes bright and dark above a pouting mouth, Kelsey was definitely upset about something.

"The talk was about you."

"Josie says you're messed up." Kelsey stared at the top of Mark's desk and chewed on a paper clip.

"Messed up," Meredith said, switching gears, trying to assess.

"You know," the little girl added. "Weird."

Meredith dropped to the chair next to the one Mark had vacated. "Because of what was in the newspaper?" She focused solely on Kelsey.

"Because of what you did. Some of the kids were talking about it today 'cause their parents asked them if they knew you and they didn't, but since I know you a lot they talked to Josie and me and some of the other kids who had you last year."

"And this is all because I talked to Tommy's mom?"

Kelsey shrugged, the straps of her pink corduroy overalls growing taut and then loosening again.

Mark reclaimed his seat, his legs stretched out in front of him, hands on the arms of the chair. Usually those hands represented some kind of security to her. Today they could crush her job, her way of life.

"Kelsey's trying to understand how you could know what was wrong with Tommy when he didn't tell you."

I see. And her father, an unbeliever, was supposed to enlighten her?

Ignoring him, she sat forward. "Hey, Kelse, remember when Rock Hudson tricked Doris Day into thinking he was a naive scientist, when he was really the playboy ad executive who was trying to ruin her?"

The little girl glanced up. "Yeah."

"How'd you feel?"

"I dunno." She looked away and then back. "Mad."

"Why?"

"I dunno."

Meredith waited.

"Because he was a jerk."

"Yeah, but not to you."

Kelsey dropped the paper clip, put both hands on the arms of her father's chair, giving Meredith a piercing look. The likeness between Kelsey and her father grabbed at Meredith's heart. These were special people.

"You felt what the Doris Day character felt, didn't you?"

Kelsey frowned. "I guess, but..."

"I know, it was just a movie and you were supposed to feel that way," Meredith said, having to concentrate in order not to be undone by the child's skeptical father sitting next to her.

At least Mark was letting her handle this; she appreciated that.

"The movie people made it easy for you to feel that way," she explained. "But you could feel that way in real life, too, if you paid really close attention to what was going on in another person's life. You knew all about what was happening to Doris Day because you were completely focused on the movie and the director showed you all the important stuff about her without you having to look for it. They did the work for you."

Kelsey was quiet, but she appeared to be considering what Meredith had said. Meredith knew all the signs of boredom and a wandering mind, and Kelsey wasn't fidgeting, her gaze was steady and she wasn't yawning.

"Just as most of us have the ability to watch a movie and feel what the characters are feeling, we can watch other people, sometimes even just in our minds, and we can feel some of what they're feeling. It's just a matter of paying attention to the right things."

Kelsey closed her eyes, her brows drawn tight. And then she opened them. "I can't feel what you're feeling. Or Daddy, either."

"I know, honey. It's hard for most people, because we aren't aware we have that ability and as we grow up we lose it."

"But you didn't lose it." It was half question, half statement.

"No."

"Why not? Did your mom teach you?"

"No." Meredith sat up straight, waiting for words to come, praying that they would. "I don't know why," she said, afraid the answer was too lame. "Some of us just are more emotional than others, I guess, so we're more aware of the emotions that other people feel."

"What am I feeling?"

You didn't test the gift. Ever. But you used it for the good of others.

Meredith took a deep breath, closed her eyes briefly, waited for the calm and then looking Kelsey in the eye said, "You're a little mad at me. You want to believe what I'm saying, but you aren't sure you do. And you feel like I've let you down. I embarrassed you in front of your friends. You aren't sure you can trust me. You're worried that Josie's going to think you're weird, too. You feel uneasy. And you're hungry."

The room was completely silent. She couldn't even hear Mark breathing beside her.

"How'd I do?" she asked.

Kelsey didn't say a word.

"And now you're scared," Meredith added.

Still watching her, Kelsey nodded. A child she adored was afraid of her. How *had* she done?

"THAT WENT WELL," Meredith said to Mark as soon as Kelsey was settled at Macy's desk with her homework and he'd closed the door between the two offices.

Taking the chair his daughter had vacated, Mark pulled a folder from the end of his desk.

The one with the names of all of those students who wouldn't be in her class the next day? Or were there so many she wouldn't have a class?

"You made a good argument just now," he finally said. Which was something, coming from him.

"You did this morning, as well."

"Thank you." Platitudes were nice. Even if they weren't going to keep her job for her. "I lost my audience when Mr. Larson asked me if I really believed I could feel other people's emotions, like I was nuts or something—although those folders you passed out with my reviews and letters from grateful parents were great. So was your idea to have Susan there. To listen to her, you'd think I was a saint. And still I lost them." She hadn't felt so low in a long time.

If ever. Losing Frank at the altar hadn't been as bad as the prospect of losing her life's work. She tried not to hate Mark Shepherd for calling the question like this, without warning. Without giving her the time to play this one out, to see if Barnett would hang himself, figuratively speaking—or give up. The day before, she'd thought Mark had agreed to give her a chance.

"Actually, you didn't," he said, his brow raised. "Lose them, that is." His eyes were bloodshot, his hair a bit more disorderly than normal. Mark hadn't had an easy day, either. "Just as with the television interview, you conducted yourself with such confidence that you instilled it in others."

She tried not to get excited, couldn't afford to feel too much at the moment in case she fell apart in her boss's office. "How many others?"

"Twenty-nine."

She couldn't believe it. "No one chose to move his child?"

"Not one parent."

Meredith burst out laughing. Not a quiet, amused chuckle, not an appreciative, humorous expression, but a loud, boisterous eruption she couldn't seem to prevent.

Mark was polite, serious, but kind, as he escorted her to the door.

And Kelsey said a mumbled goodbye as she left.

Feeling like a beggar who'd just been given a gift, Meredith took what she could get—from both of them.

"HI, SWEETIE. Good news!" Mom held the car door open for Kelsey on Friday, a smile spreading over her face.

"What?" Kelsey asked, pulling hard so the door would shut behind her. She had good news, too. Josie was her best friend again.

"I talked to an attorney and he says he's going to help us, so we can see each other without hiding."

"Really?" She wanted that so bad it almost hurt to let herself believe it.

Her mom brushed at the hairs on Kelsey's forehead. "Really." Her eyes looked so sure that Kelsey thought she must be right.

"Thank you," she said, nearly crying as she gave her mother a hug. Life had been weird lately, but maybe not anymore.

"You don't need to thank me, baby," her mom said, sounding like she was crying a little, too. "You're my daughter. You're supposed to be with me."

That was what Kelsey thought, too. Stuff got messed up, but it was getting better now and that was all that counted.

"Listen, I need to make a couple of stops," her mom said when they finally stopped hugging. "My allergies have been bothering me and I'm all out of medicine."

"'Kay." Kelsey didn't care if they shopped, as long they were together. And her dad didn't find out.

The store took a while to get to, since they had to drive for a while to be sure Kelsey didn't see anyone she knew. And then they wouldn't let her mother buy as many boxes of allergy medicine as she wanted, even after Mom explained that she lived far away and didn't have a lot of money for gas. So then they had to go to another store. Mom's allergies were really bad and her neighbor was reacting to whatever had bloomed, too, so Mom was picking some up for her.

As they drove, Kelsey told her about Ms. Foster. Mom had seen her on TV and wondered if Kelsey knew her. Kelsey told her mom about Josie and that they were best friends again. Mom listened to every word she said and that was right.

Kelsey didn't like keeping secrets from her dad, but how could she be wrong when she was with her mom who loved her and was working it out so Kelsey wouldn't have to lie?

"We've got half an hour before I take you back to the corner," Mom said when they'd finished with the third store, which gave her more boxes of pills than the other two had. "Would you mind terribly if we go by my house so I can get this stuff to my friend? She was really feeling bad earlier."

Kelsey didn't want to go there. Mom's house was dirty and boring, and Don was there. But she wanted to be with her, so she shook her head. "I don't mind," she said.

Mom smiled and turned the car in the direction of her neighborhood. Meredith would have known she didn't mean it about not minding. Her mom didn't get it at all.

Kelsey wasn't sure which way she liked better.

SHE STOOD in the living room alone while Mom went out through the garage to the house next door. She was supposed to be sitting and she could turn on the television, but she didn't feel like doing either. Don wasn't out on the road with his truck like she'd hoped. And Kelsey didn't want to see him.

"You gotta get used to it," she whispered, because she needed to hear someone talk before she got too scared and just ran away. She loved her mom so much. She'd learn to like her house. And be okay with Don, too.

Her mom was.

The garage door opened. "Hey, squirt."

"Hi." Kelsey looked down. The man's teeth were just too gross. It had to be more than coffee that did that to them. One was even broken.

"Your mom told me you were in here. She'll be back in a second."

Wondering what her dad would say if he could see her right then, Kelsey nodded.

"I'm just going out to my truck to get some flares," he said, heading toward the back door beyond which there was a big cement pad where Mom said he kept his truck when he wasn't driving.

Don owned his own rig, but drove for only one company. Mom acted like that was a big deal.

He was back before Mom, his arms full of red dynamite-looking things like she'd sometimes see on the highway with Dad when there'd been a bad accident. "Truck drivers always have lots of these," he said, smiling at her. Kelsey wished he wouldn't. His beard went in his mouth when he did that and it showed his teeth.

She made herself smile as much as she could. And let go of a big breath when he disappeared again through the garage door. At least he seemed happy. That was a good thing. Wasn't it?

There was a box open on the wood table by the couch and Kelsey wondered what was in it. And where most of the junk around the room came from. Mom had never had little glass rabbits like the ones that were all over the top of the television and the fake flowers in the window were more dusty than pretty. Her head jerked back around to stare at the floor when the garage door opened again.

"Sorry that took so long, honey." Mom was back.

Kelsey glanced up to tell her it was okay, and saw that Don had come back in, too.

"Let's all three sit down and talk for a few minutes, shall we?" Mom said like someone from a TV show and not like her mom at all.

Kelsey took the chair that didn't have a big brown spot in the middle of it. Mom and Don sat on the couch and Kelsey looked away when he put his arm around her. It was just too…weird.

They asked her about school. Or Don did. Mom already knew most of that stuff, anyway. Kelsey always told her about school.

"So you're pretty popular, I'll bet," Don said. His voice was nice. He still gave her the creeps.

"I dunno," she said.

"Of course she is!" Mom said kind of excitedly. "Look at her. She's beautiful. And she's smart. And besides, she's my kid!"

And her dad was the principal.

"How many friends you think you have?"

"I dunno." Her stomach was starting to hurt. Probably because it was close to dinnertime. She had to leave soon to get to Josie's before her dad got there.

Mom laughed kind of funny. "He's asking because we wanted to have a little party for you," she said. "It's to celebrate, when I get to have partial custody of you again, and we need to know how many people will be here so we have enough food."

"Uh, I don't really have parties," Kelsey said. The backs of her legs were itching through her jeans.

"We don't have to wait to have a party," Don said. "We'd like you to feel free to invite your friends over anytime you want. Treat this place like your own."

She nodded. And tried to picture this being her home.

"Why don't we arrange something soon?" he said. "Like next week? You could bring a friend with you when you come."

"I can't."

"Why not?" Don's eyes looked kind of like her dad's when he was talking to someone who broke a school rule.

"My dad would find out."

And she didn't want her friends to come there. The

thought made Kelsey feel ashamed. But it was still true. She had to get used to loving her mom here first. Besides, all her things were at her house.

"Well, as soon as your mom has everything worked out with the lawyer…"

Kelsey didn't say anything.

"You can bring over all your girlfriends for a pizza party."

She wondered what she and Dad were having for dinner. And if Susan was coming over.

"Let's cross that bridge when we come to it," Mom said, rubbing her hand on Don's leg.

Mom saved her, just like moms were supposed to. Meredith had done that before, too, when Susan was asking dumb questions. But her friendship with Meredith was messed up now.

Thank goodness she was getting her mom for real.

"We'd better be going," Mom said then, standing up. Don put a hand on her butt and she leaned down and gave him a kiss. "I don't want Kelsey to get in trouble."

"Hey," Don said, "I just thought of something." Mom and Don looked at each other. "Your mother says you go to Lincoln Elementary."

"Uh-huh." Kelsey was at the door already.

"I have a friend whose son goes to the junior high next door and his dad's not allowed to see him, but he wanted to give him a letter and some new crystals for his rock collection. Maybe you could deliver them for us."

She'd already said no about her friends coming over.

"That would be nice, wouldn't it, Kelsey?" Mom said. "Kind of like your friend Josie helping us see each other."

It was. Kind of. It made her feel safer to know there was a boy in the school right next door to hers who was going through the same thing she was.

"Do I have to keep it secret?"

Mom looked kind of sad for a minute. "Yeah, just for now, honey," she said. "It's like you and me. They're working on being allowed to see each other for real."

"How heavy are the crystals?"

"Light," Don said, punching her lightly on the shoulder. "I wouldn't ask you to carry anything heavy, squirt! They're really more like shards of glass, except you can't cut yourself on them. My friend says they look cool when you hold them up to different lights. I guess his son uses them for art class."

"How many? 'Cause I don't want my dad to figure it out."

"We'll split them up and do them a little bit at a time, how's that?"

Kelsey couldn't think of any more excuses. And if she didn't go soon she was going to be in trouble, for sure.

"Will you do it for us, honey?" Mom asked, running her fingers through Kelsey's ponytail.

"I guess, but us kids at Lincoln aren't allowed to go over to the junior high, and besides, I don't know who he is."

"I'll have his dad tell him to come and find you," Don said. He left the room and Kelsey thought they were done, but her mom stood there without leaving until Don came back, carrying a little brown paper bag that would fit in the side pocket of Kelsey's backpack.

"Here it is," he said. "The boy's name is Kenny and

I'll have him meet you right after school on Monday where you always meet your mom, okay?"

"'Kay." She took the bag, glad to be almost out of there and spun toward the door.

"Wait, Kelsey, I have to ask just one thing."

She turned back. "What?"

"It's private stuff, between a dad and his son. So don't open the letter, okay?"

She hadn't been going to anyway. "I'm not a snoop," she said and walked outside, hoping that her mom would be right behind her.

CHAPTER TEN

"HEY, MER, you dressed?"

Meredith rolled over on her bed the second Saturday in April, squinting to read the digital 7:06 that was almost too faded to see in the light of the setting sun. And then she glanced down at the sweatpants and T-shirt she'd put on after her shower around noon that day.

"Sort of."

"Well, get dressed. I'm coming to get you."

She took a bite of popcorn from the bowl next to her, pushing aside a couple of books in order to sit up. "No, you aren't. I'm journaling."

And there was a movie on the bed, somewhere, waiting to be watched. She'd rented it.

"Your mother called."

Damn. She hated it when her mother called Susan.

"I'm fine."

"She said you haven't been out of your house except to go to school since a week ago Thursday."

"I told her I'm on a vision quest." As much as one could be on a soul-searching mission in the middle of a school year when one was a teacher.

"Mark told me Kelsey was a little hard on you last Thursday in his office."

Momentarily, the comment sent a shot of fear through her. "Kids are honest," she said as the feeling passed. "She had reason to be confused. I'm glad she talked to me."

"And I hear she hasn't spoken with you since."

"No, but she's got her best friend back." She'd noticed the two hanging out together at lunch and recess all week. And she'd been thankful for that. Kelsey needed a best friend more than just about anything else, to help stabilize her through the changes that were coming to her life.

"And you canceled your handball game."

"I had a lot of papers to grade."

"You didn't go to yoga."

"The vision-quest thing." Her mother and Susan should understand that. They'd been the ones who'd talked her into going on the two-week spiritual hiatus that had helped her come to terms with her gift one summer during college.

"It's not flying, Mer." Susan's voice was dry. "A legitimate vision quest I would support completely. This 'excuse' of one to camouflage the fact that you're hiding, I'm not buying. Get dressed. Mark and Kelsey are expecting us in half an hour."

"I can't." She heard the change in her voice, the weakness, and hated that it was there. She hated popcorn, too. Meredith dumped the stuff, plastic bowl and all, in the waste basket in the corner of her room.

"Yes, you can."

"Not until I figure out some things." Over by the window, she scanned the familiar branches and leaves covering half of her garage. Watched the clouds change color as the sun slid behind them.

"What things?"

"What's real about me and what isn't."

Susan's determination was stronger than her own. But then, Susan was stronger than she was. "What does that mean?"

She sighed. Closed her eyes. But everything was the same when she blocked out the world.

"Do I really feel what other people feel, Suze—or do I just think I do? Am I nuts? Because I gotta tell you, if this gift is for real I'm wondering why more people don't accept it. Wouldn't you think people would recognize the truth?"

"So you're saying that because people are skeptical it can't be true?"

Maybe. That could be just what she was saying.

"I'm saying I'm keeping to myself for a while, staying away from other people and their feelings so I can clear my head."

"You're hiding because you felt Kelsey's fear and it scares you. The gift scares you."

"How do you know that?"

"Your mother told me."

That was a low blow. The one person who was always spot on when Meredith struggled was her mother.

"Why didn't she tell me herself?"

"Because she's in Florida. And worried about you."

"I'll be fine."

"I know you will. And in the meantime, I'm coming to get you. We now have twenty-five minutes. Don't waste any more time arguing, Mer. I promised your mom, and that's all there is to it. I have a key to your house, remember? If I have to bring the party to you, I will."

Meredith stood at her closet, unable to settle on an outfit. What kind of night would this be? Professional? Earth mother? Vampy? She didn't feel like anything but sweats.

"Why Mark and Kelsey?"

"Because you need to be around that child."

"My mother told you that, too?"

"No, I figured that one out on my own."

Meredith smiled. And it felt good.

"And because Kelsey's been acting stranger than ever around me and Mark, and I need your help."

She didn't want them in her house. Didn't want to have their energy here, mixing with hers, after they were gone. And Susan needed her.

She stared at her jeans. Tight ones. Loose ones. Beaded ones. And her skirts. Long colorful cotton. Short and black. "Where are we going?"

"Mark's."

"To do what?"

"Grill hamburgers out on his fire pit and roast marshmallows."

She pulled out a pair of tight beaded jeans and a form-fitting purple sweater. Purple for peace. Beads for Kelsey. Tight because she liked her jeans best that way. And then she glanced in a mirror. "I need more than twenty-five minutes."

"I've got the fire log in my back seat."

"You go ahead and I'll meet you there," she said, feeling better about that idea. She could leave when and if she had to, that way.

"If you don't show, I'm coming over there—with boyfriend, his daughter and hamburgers in tow."

She had no doubt Susan would deliver on the threat. "I'll be there within the hour."

SOMETHING WAS WRONG with Kelsey. Meredith's fear escalated hugely the moment she walked out to Mark's backyard and came face to face with the little girl. Wearing a zip-up hooded sweater and jeans, Kelsey sat by herself on one of the two swings attached to a wooden set off in a corner of the yard.

With a quick greeting to Mark and a hug for Susan, Meredith made a beeline for that second swing. Sat. Pushed off slowly.

"Hey, Kelse."

Meredith decided that the mumbled reply was hello.

"You got new jeans."

They had beaded butterflies down both legs.

"Yeah."

"I like them."

"Thanks."

Kelsey wasn't so much rude as she was just plain absent.

"You still mad at me?"

"I guess not."

Susan was right. Meredith needed to see the child. Someplace where speaking with Kelsey wouldn't jeopardize the little girl's relationship with her friends at school.

"We still friends?"

Kelsey shrugged. "I guess so."

The child's expression was hidden in shadows,

despite the flickering light of the fire pit and the porch lamp on the house.

"Susan says you picked hamburgers."

"Mmm-hmm."

"Grilled hamburgers have always been my favorite, too." Too pacifying. Not of interest to Kelsey at the moment.

The little girl said nothing.

"You want to tell me what's wrong?"

Kelsey pushed off harder, swinging away from Meredith. "Nothing."

Grabbing the chain of the child's swing, Meredith slowed her down, careful not to tip her out as she did so. "I don't like to be lied to any more than you do."

The words were harsh. She hadn't meant to be harsh. But they'd come out that way, all the same.

Kelsey stared at her and Meredith could have sworn there were tears glinting in her eyes.

"I'm not lying to you," she said after a lengthy pause.

But Meredith knew she was. And that, if she pushed, Kelsey would continue to lie.

"Okay, I'm glad. You're my date tonight, you know, so if anything does start to bother you, you'll let me know, right?"

Kelsey shrugged, her small shoulders rubbing against the swing's chain. "Sure."

And that was the best Meredith could do.

DINNER WAS GOOD, and surprisingly fun. Mark entertained them all with some of the wild and crazy stories he'd heard from kids as excuses for misbehavior during his five years as a principal. Meredith laughed so hard she had tears streaming down her cheeks.

And Kelsey, sitting beside her at the picnic table, was laughing just as hard.

They roasted marshmallows, and laughed again as more of the melting white confections fell into the fire than stayed on their sticks. Susan talked about the s'mores she'd had for the first time the previous year at a hospital picnic, astonished that roasted marshmallows, chocolate squares and graham crackers could be so good together. And Meredith sipped a glass of wine and told herself not to think about anything but the moment.

Kelsey was smiling. Susan looked content, her face peaceful in the firelight. And Mark was...Mark. Solid. Strong. Sure.

And gorgeous in jeans and a beige sweater that almost exactly matched his hair. His face was lined, as though he'd had a hard day—or week—but when he looked at Susan or Kelsey, he smiled.

He didn't look at Meredith.

And for that she was thankful.

"It's time for bed, sport," he announced when every single one of the marshmallows had either fallen into the ashes or been eaten. "Get your teeth brushed, and then I thought it would be nice if Susan came in to hear your prayers."

With one foot over the bench, Kelsey froze, her eyes like glass as she stared at her father. "No!"

Meredith fell into a pool of feeling so intense she couldn't begin to identify it.

"Excuse me?"

"I don't want her in my room."

"This is my house, young lady. My friends are welcome wherever I say they are." Clearly Mark was shocked. And not at his best.

"I won't say my prayers if she's there, and you can't make me do that. They're between me and God."

"Kelsey Elizabeth!"

"No, Mark, it's okay," Susan said, placing a hand on Mark's arm as he rose.

"It's not okay," Mark reached for his daughter, hauling her around the table with a hand on her upper arm. "You apologize at once."

"No."

"Kelsey, I said apologize."

His grip wasn't firm enough to hold the child if she attempted to pull away. But his voice could have stopped a grown woman in her tracks.

"No. They're my prayers and you have no right to give them to anyone."

"You, young lady, have no right to speak disrespectfully to me or to anyone else I bring into this house."

Kelsey stood resolute, her chin puckered with displeasure.

"I asked you to apologize."

"No."

"Kelsey, Susan has been nothing but kind to you, taking you shopping for clothes, cooking for you, offering to help make your Easter dress. Inviting you to tea."

"She's trying to be like my mother."

Susan shrank and Meredith's heart ached for her friend. But her entire body was filled with Kelsey's misery and she had no idea how to make any of it stop.

"She's not trying to be like your mother at all, Kelsey," Mark said. "But she is trying to help, when your mother isn't here to do so."

"I don't need her help."

"Kelsey! I will not stand for this rudeness."

Kelsey stomped her foot. "And I won't stand for you trying to make her into my mother!" she screamed. "She's not my mother! She's not! I hate her!" With one quick glance at Susan, accompanied by a sob, the little girl tore out of her father's grasp and ran for the house.

"Kelsey!" Mark started after her.

"I'm going to go," Susan said at the same time.

"No, wait," Mark turned back and then looked toward the house, his brows drawn.

Meredith stood. "Mark, you stay with Susan. You're too angry to give Kelsey what she needs right now. I'll go to her."

His clenched lips relaxed after a long moment and he nodded, his shoulders dropping. "I don't know what to do with her," he said. "I never would have believed she could behave that way."

"She's hurt," Meredith said, worried about both Kelsey and her friend. Susan's eyes were filled with tears. "And she's scared."

And she might kick me out of her room, as well, Meredith thought as she headed into the house alone.

MARK WAS SITTING by himself in the living room when Meredith came out of Kelsey's room almost an hour later.

"Where's Susan?"

"Gone. She didn't want to be here if Kelsey came out. She said to have you call her in the morning."

Meredith couldn't remember where she'd left her bag. "Did she go home?"

He shook his head. "She was going to the hospital… Said something about a surgery she did today that she wanted to check on."

Work was Susan's way of making sense out of life. Meredith understood that. And knew that her friend was exactly where she needed to be at the moment.

"How is she?" He nodded toward an archway leading to the stairs.

"Asleep."

Mark nodded and looked, she thought, relieved. Because his daughter was no longer suffering, or because it meant that he didn't have to deal with her? Maybe a little of both.

Meredith had to go—she was overwhelmed, exhausted, and not trusting herself to think clearly. But Mark looked so shaken and lost that she sat down on the edge of the chair opposite him. Just for a minute.

"What did she say?"

"Not much."

His eyes were weary as he looked at her, his body slouched in the corner of the couch. She wondered how long he'd been sitting there, doing nothing.

"You were in there for almost an hour."

"I rubbed her back while she cried, and tried to get her to talk to me. She agreed to put on her pajamas and brush her teeth. It took us ten minutes to find Gilda. I listened to her prayers and sat with her until she fell asleep."

She hadn't been able to leave the child until she was peaceful. And she'd wanted to give Susan and Mark some time alone.

He shook his head. "I just don't get it."

"She's scared, Mark. I don't know a lot about your wife, but my guess is that Kelsey suffered more at her hands than she lets on. The idea of introducing another woman into her life, aside from the fact that she has to share you, has got to be causing her some serious misgivings."

He nodded thoughtfully.

"Barbie never raised a hand to her, if that's what you're thinking."

"I didn't think she had," Meredith said, choosing her words carefully. "But I wasn't sure."

"What has Susan told you about her?"

"Only that you came home from work one day and she was gone. And that Kelsey had afternoon kindergarten and was with you when you came in and found her missing."

"Barbie adored Kelsey," he said, staring off into the middle of the room. "From the moment she found out she was pregnant, that child was the light in her life. She was more peaceful with Kelsey than I'd ever known her to be."

"She hadn't been before?"

"Barbie's a sensitive woman—always was—which made her life kind of turbulent at times. Sometimes she'd get upset about the most inconsequential things. She'd storm and fume and then it would be over and she'd be fine. On the other side, however, even the smallest things could make her happy."

"How long were you married before she got pregnant?"

"Four years."

"Did she have a career?"

"She has a degree in journalism, and before Kelsey she was working at the *Tulsa Times*. She was still at a pretty junior level, writing obits and covering local events, but she'd had a couple of impressive bylines and was on her way up."

"Did she keep working after Kelsey was born?"

"No." He shook his head. "She'd intended to, but when the time came she couldn't bear to leave the baby with a sitter."

"How did you feel about that?"

He glanced over at her as though he'd just realized who she was—and that she was asking some fairly personal questions. Meredith was ready to leave.

"I encouraged her to stay home," he said then, with a discouraged shake of the head. "I was pretty much head over heels in love with the kid myself and wasn't any more eager than Barbie was to hand her off to strangers when she was still too little to tell us how she was being treated."

"Did your wife miss journalism?"

"That's the damnedest part," Mark said, sitting forward, rubbing his hands together. "She didn't seem to at all. Those first four years with Kelsey she seemed so happy. Now that I look back on it, I can see signs that she struggled, too. I know I should've encouraged her to go back to work, but I sure didn't see it at the time."

"Change is hard. She'd have struggled going back to work, Mark, even if that had been the right choice. But it doesn't sound like it would have been."

"You don't need to spare my feelings," he said with a sad grin.

"I'm not."

Mark watched her for a long minute and suddenly Meredith knew that something had changed. In him. In her. She had no idea. Was too emotionally drained to figure it out.

"So what went wrong?"

He didn't answer right away, except to shrug. And then he said, "I can't pinpoint anything that was wrong between us. I've tried until I drive myself crazy with it, but I can't figure it out. The random outbursts grew more and more frequent and over the most innocuous stuff, and she just wasn't happy anymore. With me, with herself, the house, this town… Anything."

"Except Kelsey."

"Except Kelsey. Until she started school. Then even Kelsey seemed to bring her sadness. Kelsey was off with others, didn't need her as much. I think she felt abandoned."

"Most women go through something like that when their firstborn starts school."

"I know." Mark grinned at her for real. "I'm in the business, too."

She'd forgotten. For a second there he'd just been a person. Not her boss.

"But with Barbie it was more than that. She couldn't seem to be happy on her own, although she desperately wanted to be. She started to worry all the time—about everything. Getting sick and not being able to care for Kelsey. Kelsey getting sick. Me being in a car accident."

"Sounds like a serious case of depression."

Mark agreed. "I begged her to go see someone, even told her I'd go, too. But she said she didn't want psychological help, because she wanted the chance to control her own mind. She said that she had the power to do it and knew if she gave up she'd never get herself back. She also worried about the side effects of medications. She'd already seen her doctor and he couldn't find anything physically wrong with her, though he did suggest antidepressants. She wouldn't take them."

"She sounds like a strong and determined woman."

With his head bent toward his hands, Mark glanced up at her and back down. "She was sleeping quite a bit and she knew that wasn't good, so she started drinking caffeinated beverages. Said it made her feel good— gave her a pick-me-up. In a few months, she had a soda or cup of coffee by her side all the time. She was up to almost a twelve-pack of cola a day. Which eventually made her more jittery, and then she needed something to bring back the good feeling. That also brought about more unpredictable mood swings."

"A vicious cycle," Meredith said, feeling a whole lot more than she wanted to, yet oddly welcoming the information. Knowing about Mark's ex-wife brought her closer to the daughter Barbie had borne.

"I tried to get her to exercise. The endorphins helped her mood swings and the physical activity calmed the jitters. But that lasted less than a month. She took up quilting, photography and Web design, all of which she began enthusiastically and ended in short order the first time she got frustrated."

"Is that why she left?" Meredith asked after a bit. "To try something else new?"

"She left the day I found out the secret she'd been

keeping from me and told her it had to stop immediately."

"She was having an affair?"

"She was addicted to meth."

CHAPTER ELEVEN

"SHE CHOSE methamphetamines over you and Kelsey?"

Mark, having fought for three years the pain and self-doubt associated with desertion, with not being enough, took comfort from Meredith's shock at Barbie's choice.

"The drug is lethally addictive," he said. "It's a disease worse than cancer, spreading across this country in higher numbers than any other single illness. And Barbie was dissolving it in her first cup of coffee every morning and I didn't even know it." He stopped, remembered back to that final day. He'd been dreaming about Barbie, had gotten out of bed early to come and find her, to tell her how much he loved her, and he'd seen her take a little jewelry-sized plastic bag from the velvet pouch in which she kept the electric knife blades.

"Until the day I saw her do it."

Meredith sat back in her chair, her eyes filled with compassion, concern, disbelief. The woman was always so...full of emotion. It was overwhelming. And compelling.

"How long had she been using?"

"She wouldn't say." She'd done nothing but lie that day and he'd been left wondering how many months, even years, before that had also been filled with lies. "But based on the chunks of money I found missing from a savings account of ours, I'd say it had been at least six months. At close to two thousand dollars every two weeks. You'd think I'd have noticed, wouldn't you?"

"From what I hear about meth, from the training we get at school, one of the reasons it's so popular is because it's hard to tell someone's a user—until you see the yellowing skin or weight loss. Apparently other than having a lot of energy, people can act pretty normal under the influence."

Yeah, he had the facts, too. "It gives them the feeling of being in complete control, while the whole time it's controlling them."

"It's what we all want, isn't it?" Meredith asked quietly, her expression sad. "To be in control."

Looking at her, Mark found understanding. He found himself unable to turn away. In the midst of this awful night he found a human compassion in her that made it all bearable—an acknowledgment of suffering and tragedy, yet also an affirmation of the worth of going on.

Which was ridiculous considering she hadn't said anything of the sort.

"What do you want to control?" he asked, honestly curious. She seemed so intent on helping others take control. Mark. Kelsey. Susan. Her students. Their parents.

Her hair spread over the chair behind her as she laid back her head. "Me," she said, still watching him. "Just me."

"Control what you say?" Did she feel more shame about the recent upheaval at school than she'd let on? That would make a hell of lot more sense than her stalwart and unrelenting defense of her position.

She shook her head. "Control what I feel."

Her eyes were troubled and he found himself watching her lips—wanting them to smile.

"That's not as hard as it might seem," he said, glad that he had at least one answer for this woman who seemed to have them all. "Just use your head, take the time to think instead of react. Logic will never steer you wrong."

She did smile, then. With what appeared to be genuine humor. And perhaps a bit of pity mixed in. "Oh, Mark," she said. "You don't really believe that, do you? Deep down inside?"

"Of course I do," he answered without even needing to check deep down inside. This was something he knew.

"The mind is a fabulous thing. But you were given a heart, too, for a very good reason. Your mind is your connection to the world around you. Your heart is your connection to your soul."

He wasn't into the woo-woo stuff, but he certainly respected her right to be.

"My wife listened to her heart and look where it got her."

"That's not fair, Mark. Your wife used her head—we all do. We all have to. But she used it to make bad choices."

Maybe. He didn't think so, though.

"What I know is that Barbie was always an emotional person. Her sensitivity is what drew me to her to begin with. I grew up in a family that was undemonstrative at best. We love each other and express that love with Christmas cards and pictures sent once a year. When I first met Barbie and she wrapped her intensity around me, it was as if I'd finally come alive."

"Yes," Meredith said. It seemed as if her entire body nodded in affirmation. "You moved from your head to your heart."

"And I got wrapped up in an uncontrollable mass that ate itself alive." He wasn't going to convince her. He had to speak, all the same. "I don't trust feelings." If they were ever going to find a way to work together peacefully, Meredith had to understand and accept this. "With Barbie the emotions took over her life, and while she was happy in the beginning, she was also upset a lot. She couldn't ever just *be*."

"It doesn't have to be that way."

He wasn't finished. "And in my own case, I allowed my love for her to blind me to things my mind should have realized. I believed in her, made excuses for her. She was having an emotional breakdown right before my eyes, she wouldn't listen to reason, and all I could do was watch our lives fall apart."

"You think if you'd loved her less you could have saved her?"

"I think that I believe in logic, what I can see, what makes sense to my mind. I trust things that are proven to be true—and the people in whom I can see a steady track record of trustworthiness."

"You base trust solely on logic?"

"That's correct." She was getting it. There was some satisfaction in that.

"Trust comes from the heart."

He almost got frustrated with her again. She didn't give up.

Neither did he. He didn't want to be frustrated with Meredith tonight. In the first place, she'd brought some peace to a turbulent evening. And in the second, if he gave up she'd leave and there'd be nowhere else for them to go, no common ground upon which they could meet. They'd have nothing more to say to each other. Ever. He didn't really have a definition for their relationship. It was more than boss/employee but not quite as intimate as friendship. But whatever it was, he didn't want it to be over.

She was almost family to the woman he intended to marry.

"I don't know how to listen to my heart," he said.

"You know. You just don't realize that you know."

Which made perfect Meredith sense—and was nonsense to him.

"You listen to your heart every time you do things for Kelsey that aren't guided strictly by logic."

He thought for a minute. "I have a reason for everything I do for her."

"What about those butterfly jeans I saw her wearing tonight? Those weren't a logical purchase. Last I heard, the sequins could come off in the wash."

He stared at her hard. "And last I heard, they don't."

"Still, they cost twice as much as other jeans, which would have served the same purpose."

If the purpose had been to keep his daughter clothed and warm. "I can see where you're going with this," he said. "You know darned well that I gave in and bought those jeans so Kelsey would feel good about herself."

"And about you."

"In part, yeah, I guess."

"So it was about feeling, Mark. And that comes from the heart."

"I still made a conscious choice—weighing both sides, I chose to make a financially illogical purchase for other gain."

"And that's a prime example of living fully," she said, sitting forward as her voice took on new energy. "Barbie let her emotions rule her. You let yourself be ruled by logic. In an ideal life, neither one rules but you use both."

The woman was an idealist, pure and simple. And in an ideal life his love for Barbie would have been enough to guide him, not blind him.

"So how do you explain the fact that as much as Barbie loved Kelsey, she didn't even try to see her, let alone get partial custody of her?"

"You had an uncontested divorce?"

"Completely. She wanted out that badly. I gave her the things she wanted, her clothes, jewelry, half the bank account, and she left me the house, the child and most of the furniture."

"She probably knew, with her drug addiction, that she'd never be granted custody of Kelsey."

"No one knew about her drug addiction. Not the courts. Not the lawyers. I told her that if she got counseling, got cleaned up, I wouldn't make an issue of it if she wanted to see Kelsey. I wasn't out to get her. I wanted to help her. And I wanted to help my daughter, too. Kelsey adored Barbie. She needed her."

"She needs you, too, Mark," Meredith said, leaning forward. The scoop neck of her sweater fell open and

Mark looked away. "Kelsey needs all of you, not just your head."

"My daughter needs me to use my head to make the best decisions possible regarding anything that affects her life," he said, keeping his gaze steadily on Meredith's. "Thanks to you, I've met a wonderful woman. I'm attracted to her. I love her. And because she's the exact opposite of Barbie, she's perfect for both Kelsey and me. Where Barbie would react, cry, scream and run, Susan will think. I've never even heard her raise her voice."

"I'm really sorry to hear that." Meredith's gaze darkened.

"What?"

"Susan's got a great set of lungs," she said. "And if she's not using them, she's not quite as alive as I'd hoped."

God, she was infuriating. "Life doesn't always have to be about conflict."

"I agree," she said, her voice soft, almost as if she was speaking to Kelsey or one of her students. "But if it doesn't have any at all, it also can't have its opposite and counterpart—pure joy."

Just speaking the word seemed to bring a spark to Meredith's face. Her lips curved upward, as if she had a special secret, and damn, he wanted to know it, too. He was tired. Had been fighting alone a long time. It was late. He'd just heard his daughter speak to him in a way he'd never believed possible— seen her go to bed without telling him good night for the first time in her life.

Though he instructed his eyes to do so, he couldn't pull his gaze from Meredith's lips.

"I have to go." She stood up.

So did he.

"Do you know where I put my bag?" She fidgeted, glancing around the room. And then back at him, as if she couldn't do anything else, either.

"I think it's in the kitchen," he said. "Susan brought it in from outside."

There, he'd mentioned the woman he loved. The woman they both loved. They were on track again. Safe.

Meredith started to speak and then cleared her throat. Was her throat as dry as his?

"I'll just go get it."

Without taking his eyes from hers, he moved aside. She took a step. And then another.

"I'll say good night now," she half whispered, pausing as she passed him. "My car's out back."

"Thanks for…everything."

Her head turned as she took another step. She was still watching him. "Of course. I'm always here if you need me." She blinked, breaking the contact. And then met his eyes again. "If Kelsey does, I mean."

He'd known what she meant. He started to tell her. She was so close. He nodded. Held out a hand as though to shake hers—to somehow solidify his gratitude. His fingers bumped her wrist.

And Meredith's eyes clouded with pain.

"What's wrong?" He stepped closer. "Did I hurt you?" He'd barely touched her.

She shook her head, her eyes glistening as though she might cry. He'd never seen her cry. Had hardly seen her lose her composure at all.

"I…" Meredith tilted her head, gazing up at him. Her eyes seemed to beseech him to understand what she couldn't say.

He could have been in a wind tunnel, as clearly as he could hear at the moment. He didn't seem to know much of anything. Except that he hadn't meant to hurt her. In any way. At any time.

"You're a very special woman, you know that?"

Trembling lips, a tremulous smile, were her only answers.

"I'm sorry."

"For what?" The words were almost hoarse.

He didn't know. The past. Their differences. The trouble his daughter was causing.

"This," he said. And bent to touch his lips to hers. It wasn't sexual. Wasn't a come on or meant to be in any way disrespectful. It simply was.

Meredith's soft, sweet mouth surprised him. She pressed gently, filling him with warmth. He would pull back now, probably should never have leaned forward to begin with. But he wasn't ready to let go. To be alone. To send her out into the night with whatever demons were lurking behind those expressive eyes— demons she faced alone.

She was mystery and woman and friend. And he opened his mouth. She opened hers, too. Tilting her head slowly to fit him more securely. He shared the connection with her, a moment that made no sense— and made perfect sense. Until his tongue took them into something else.

Something powerful. Compelling. And dangerous.

"I HAVE TO GO." Meredith yanked away from Mark's lips, aghast. What in the hell had she done? Whose feelings had she been experiencing right then? Please let them be Susan's.

Mark nodded, looking none too pleased himself.

With awkward movements she got to the kitchen, found her bag. Mark was behind her.

"That never happened," she said to the wall, afraid of looking at him again.

"And that's no way to handle this."

She turned around against her better judgment. Searching for meaning in the eyes that had led her to betray her best friend. Something she'd thought she'd never do.

"If we pretend, hide, run, we give it power."

He was right. She had nothing to add.

"It won't happen again." He sounded sure about that.

"Of course not." She didn't feel sure at all. About anything. Who was this woman who'd taken possession of her, and how would she find peace again? Was it even still there?

"Look, it's been a long night, Meredith. We've been through a lot, both in real time and in reliving other times."

She nodded.

"We had some pretty heavy-duty conversation. Unusual conversation."

Agreed.

"It gave us a sense of…momentary closeness."

Okay.

"And with that came a natural inclination to make a physical connection."

She could go with this. "It wasn't sexual," she said.

"No sexual intent whatsoever."

Fine, then. She wanted to ask him if he found her sexually unattractive, but the question was ludicrous.

"We haven't just jeopardized our jobs."

"Absolutely not."

"Or been disloyal to Susan."

"Not in the least."

His peace didn't make her feel peaceful. "Are you going to tell her or am I?"

He was quiet for a moment. And then shrugged. "Tell her if you need to." The response was completely unsatisfying.

"Don't you think we owe it to her?"

"If it was sexual, we would. But it wasn't. And who, except for the people who were here, would understand that?"

He was right. No one would get it. She wasn't even sure she did.

She reached for the door handle. "It will never, ever happen again."

"I know."

"We will not even get close to this happening again."

He'd stayed by the counter. "Not even close."

It hurt to look at him.

"Okay, then. Good night, Mark."

She opened the door and ran.

"HEY, KENNY."

"Hey."

"Here's your bag." Standing on the far side of the bushes that surrounded Lincoln Elementary, Kelsey unzipped the side pocket of her backpack. "Sorry it's so crumpled," she said. "I had to fit parts of my volcano project in here, too."

Kenny grinned and that made Kelsey feel good. She'd told Josie how cute he was, but she hadn't told her friend that Kenny's smile made her feel weird stuff in her stomach. She was really starting to like the way his hair was so long that he looked like he needed it cut all the time.

"No problem," he said. "It's really lame that you even have to do this."

"I don't have to," she told him, wishing she was in junior high, too. "I mean, last week, before I knew you, I kinda felt like I had to. But not this time. I told Don on Friday that I'm happy to help."

"Why would you be?" he asked, completely serious as he took the bag and stuffed it under his arm inside his jacket. "You could get in lots of trouble."

"No more than I'm already in," she told him with a groan.

Someone passed and he pushed them farther into the bushes, standing in front so whoever was there wouldn't see her. Kelsey wanted to die, thinking that an older boy as cute as Kenny would do something nice for her like that. She wished Josie could've seen it.

"Why?" he asked when the coast was clear. "What'd you do?"

"Screamed at my dad in front of his friends. Didn't apologize when he told me to."

"He's a creep, huh?"

"No…" Would he like her less, if her dad was cool? "He's just… He's got this woman I think he might marry and he wants her to be like my mom and all, and I can't let her."

Kenny put a hand on a thick stake that was tied to the bushes, leaning a little closer to her. He smelled kind of different. But good. Kelsey liked it.

"No shit," he said. "That's tough. I remember when

my old lady first started dating again. I hated it. But then I realized that because she brought other guys home it didn't mean I couldn't still have my dad be my dad. And besides, I didn't want my folks together, anyway."

He didn't? He was so grown up. "Why not?"

"Because when they were together it was like them against me a lot of the time. When they aren't, it's just me and them."

Yeah. Kelsey considered her time alone with each of her parents. He was right. "I never thought of that."

"I don't like it so much, now that I live just with my mom and can't see my dad," he said. "But that'll change."

"My mom has a lawyer to fix it all for us." She told him something she'd only ever have told Josie before she knew Kenny.

"Yeah, my dad had one, too, but they cost a lot of money. We're working on that, though."

"You're a nice boy, Kenny."

"Nah." He laughed. "I'm not."

"Yes, you are."

He got back his usual serious look. "You really think so?"

Kelsey flicked her hair back—she'd pulled out her ponytail on the way across the playground and pocketed the clastic. "I really do."

"You know." He switched hands on the stake. "No one's ever told me that before."

"Well, they should have," she said, feeling pretty smart for once. "Because it's true."

"Well, Kelsey Shepherd, I think you're nice, too."

Her whole body got that funny feeling. "You do?"

"Yeah, but I'll bet you've had lots of people tell you that."

She couldn't remember if they had. "Nope. Just you."

He looked at her for a long time, and then stood up. "Well, I gotta go. My mom's gonna be waitin'."

"'Kay, me, too," she said, wishing they didn't have to leave. It was going to be hard waiting for next Monday to come. "Bye, Kenny."

"See ya."

She watched him run all the way to the end of the bushes and around the corner to the junior high. She might be losing her dad, and stuff was all screwed up with Meredith, but she'd met Kenny and she was getting her mom back.

Life worked out funny sometimes.

CHAPTER TWELVE

"YOU'RE BEAUTIFUL, do you know that?"

Susan gave him a hug, her face buried in his chest. He was a lucky man and he was going to concentrate on that fact.

"And you're a good kisser," she said.

He'd greeted her at her door with a kiss, but he hadn't been the only one clinging. He bent to kiss her a second time.

Susan turned her head. "I didn't call you over here to do this." She sounded more emotional than he was used to. Sad almost.

He'd been a bit surprised, pleasantly so, at her Wednesday morning call, asking if he could get away for a lunch hour at her house. She'd had a patient cancel and she wanted to see him.

"So why did you ask me here?"

"I've been doing a lot of thinking since Saturday night…"

"So have I." Mark turned her in his arms so that he could see her face clearly.

"Susan, will you marry me?"

"What?" She was staring at him as if that was the last thing she'd expected him to say. After Kelsey's outburst he could understand that.

"I want to marry you," he said slowly, clearly, wanting her to know that he'd given this a lot of serious consideration. That his mind was firmly made up. He hadn't expected to pop the question standing in her foyer, but… "You're everything I want in a woman. I think about you a lot." He brushed her breast lightly with the back of his hand. "I'm obviously attracted to you," he said with a chuckle. "You're smart. Kind. Loyal…."

"Stop." She backed up a step, frowning. Mark wasn't all that upset by the reaction. She'd consider all aspects, as he had. A passionate reaction to his proposal would not have been like her. Would not have been the response he'd look for in the woman he'd choose to marry the second time around.

This time he had to get it right. He couldn't put his daughter—or himself—through a second failure.

"I'm going to ask you something and I want a completely honest answer, no matter how hard it might be to give," she said.

That sounded ominous, but he was willing to try if it meant that much to her. He nodded.

"I mean it, Mark. I don't want you sparing my feelings—or your own pride, either, for that matter."

"Fine." He reached for her hand. She intertwined her fingers with his.

"When we make love do you think of me?"

"Of course."

She looked him straight in the eye. "Only of me?"

Mark started to say yes, but her eyes demanded complete honesty. And he owed her complete honesty. He looked away.

"Hey." With a finger on his cheek, she turned his

head back to her. "It's okay." She was smiling—and she had tears in her eyes. "Because I do it, too," she admitted.

He wanted to know who else she'd been thinking about. And he would never tell her who had infiltrated his thoughts. It didn't mean anything. And the other night in his kitchen had been one of those quirky moments when life is askew, when nothing makes sense. An overtired mind getting confused.

"Every single time we've made love, Bud's been there with me," Susan continued softly. "I've been telling myself that's natural..."

"I'm sure it is." It was logical.

"You're the first man I've made love to since he died."

Mark was moved by the confession. "I wish you'd told me."

She squeezed his hand. "I think the fact that I didn't is part of all this," she said.

He still wasn't sure what "this" was.

"I don't think we should see each other anymore, Mark."

Everything suddenly changed. He still held her hand, but it was all different.

"Why?" he asked, taking a time-out to analyze what she was saying.

"Because it's all too *practical*." That was the last response he'd expected to hear from her.

"You've been talking to Meredith."

"No." She smiled gently. "But I probably should have. I expect I could have spared us both several months of trying to make something fit that wasn't ever going to. Kelsey knew it wasn't right. Kids always get these things, you know."

"Of course it could fit! We enjoy each other's company. We don't fight. We make…" He'd been about to say "great love," but then he stopped himself.

"I don't want to spend the rest of my life thinking about someone who's dead when I make love." Her eyes filled with tears again, and that touched him more than anything else that had come before.

"It'll pass, Suze," he said, using his free hand to brush her hair from her forehead.

"I know it will," she said, sniffling, blinking and smiling. "When I find a man who makes me forget him."

"What if you never do?"

"Then I'll spend the rest of my life looking and waiting, which is a better choice than giving up."

"Which is what you'd be doing if you married me?"

"Wouldn't you say so?"

He mulled over what she'd said. He didn't like any of it.

"Are you angry?"

"No!" He squeezed her hand, let it go. "Of course not."

"You sure?"

He nodded, surprised to find that he didn't feel a bit annoyed, even though he'd just been rejected—for the second time in his life.

"Hurt?" she pressed, when he really wished she'd just say a quiet goodbye.

Not that he couldn't just turn his back and leave. But something held him there, as if he owed her this.

"I'm…" He didn't know what. "Confused…" he finally said. "Sad, I think."

She nodded, smiling in a sorrowful kind of way. "And if you were in love with me, you'd be hurt."

He stared at her, and even as he held her gaze he felt himself softening. She was right. Absolutely, completely right. Damn it.

"YOU SURE you don't want to consider a marriage that would be pretty much guaranteed to be peaceful, amiable and interesting?" Mark turned at Susan's door, not completely ready to walk out of her life.

She held on to the door, revealing both strength and vulnerability as she leaned there in her navy suit, every strand of her short hair in place. "I've spent the past five years half-alive, Mark," she said softly. "Being with you brought me back, and now that I'm here I want it all."

He cupped her face. Kissed her softly. "Good for you."

"It's time for you to start living again, too, you know."

People wanted different things out of life. "I'm not sure what that means," he said. "I'd decided marriage to you *was* 'having it all.'"

"It wasn't."

He nodded. He should be depressed. He wasn't.

"You're going to have to risk it again, you know."

He frowned and glanced at his watch, although he knew he could take whatever time he needed. He'd told Macy not to expect him back. "Risk what?"

"The grand passion."

It must be a woman thing, this need they had to make everything emotional. Even Susan, as it turned out.

"I don't want to spend the rest of my life alone," he told her—and himself. "I also don't think I have what it takes to put up with another Barbie."

"Emotions and Barbie aren't interchangeable," Susan said. "I'm a doctor, Mark, and if you get nothing else from me, get this. Barbie was intensely sensitive. By all accounts you're right about that. But that wasn't her downfall. Her downfall was her character—which is what drove her to make the choices she made. That was what kept her from seeking medical help when things got unmanageable, and that allowed her to give in to illegal comfort."

"I'm going to miss you." He took her hand.

She nodded.

"What do you plan to do now?"

"I don't know for sure," she said, head tilted as she rested it against the door. "Be open and wait and see, I guess."

"Any prospects?" He cared, but he wasn't even all that jealous.

"Maybe." She grinned. "There's this administrator at the hospital. I can't seem to get away from him, yet I always dismissed him because he's nothing at all like me. Far too impractical. He flies planes in his spare time. Do you have any idea how dangerous that is?"

He smiled back. She was an extraordinary woman. "I have a feeling you're about to find out."

She shuddered. "I don't know."

"Well, if you need me to check him out for you, you let me know." He was only half joking. "If you ever need anything, you let me know," he added, this time not joking at all.

"Thanks."

And then, as he contemplated getting back to school, another thought occurred to him. "Who's going to tell Meredith?"

"She's my friend, so I guess I will," Susan said, as though she didn't even consider it an issue. "Unless you want to."

He dropped her hand, stepped outside. "It's just that I'll probably see her before you do and it might be awkward to lie to her."

Susan gazed at him so thoroughly it made him uncomfortable. "And there's Kelsey to consider, too," was all she said. "They do seem to have formed quite a special attachment. Perhaps you should be the one to tell her."

He nodded. He was the logical choice.

She agreed. Gave him one last quick kiss on the cheek, grabbed her purse and walked him to his car. Mark watched her pull out of her drive behind him, and didn't miss the tears she wiped from her cheeks.

It was only as Mark arrived back at school that it occurred to him that Meredith might well blame him for the breakup with Susan. Notwithstanding the fact that she'd done the breaking up, he could still be judged as the one at fault for not giving Susan what she needed, for not making her happy. He started to regret not agreeing with Susan when she'd suggested that she be the one to tell Meredith.

Kelsey, on the other hand, would be pleased. For once. Their relationship had been painfully stilted since his daughter's outburst four nights before. She hadn't been in to watch him shave once since then. Maybe that would change now it was just the two of them again.

And if he ever did hook up with someone else, he'd do it differently where Kelsey was concerned. His daughter would have to be the one to instigate any relationship she might or might not have with any woman he chose to be his future wife. She'd been correct about one thing on Saturday. He didn't have the right to choose whom she invited into her inner world.

"There's a message for you from Angela Liddy, that reporter from KNLD in Tulsa who interviewed Ms. Foster three weeks ago," Macy said as Mark pushed into the outer office of the principal's quarters at Lincoln Elementary.

"Thanks. Anything else?"

"Just the new music teacher wanting permission to have the piano tuned."

"She has it." He closed his door behind him.

Two minutes later he opened it again.

"Macy, see that Ms. Foster stops in before she leaves for home this afternoon."

"Will do, sir."

He nodded, shut his door and thought about a gallon of caramel chocolate fudge ice cream with raspberry swirl. Everything else that came to mind made his neck muscles ache.

"DO YOU WANT the bad news or the worse news?"

What Meredith wanted was to go home. She hadn't seen Mark since Saturday night and she'd had a particularly trying day. Her students' parents might have chosen to keep their kids in her class, but the kids were not the same children she'd had before Barnett had started his slur campaign against her.

They argued with her more. Ignored her more. And that afternoon Jeremy had asked her to predict what grade he was going to get on the spelling test she'd been about to administer.

If the class had laughed, she might have been able to shrug the whole thing off, laugh with them, make some pithy comment in return. But though there'd been a few loud guffaws, most of the kids had looked embarrassed, uncomfortable—unsure of her.

And that hurt.

"Meredith?"

She sat down, her narrow denim skirt sliding halfway up her calves. "I'm sorry. I'll take the worst."

"Barnett's going to be on talk radio Saturday morning."

What had she done to bring this upon herself? "Who told you?"

"Angela Liddy. The station is a subsidiary of KNLD."

"So what more can he say?"

"He's got some experts who are going to be appearing with him."

"What kind of experts?"

"A psychologist, for one."

She could feel herself turning pale. "And let me guess," she said. "A psychic."

"So I'm told."

"What time?" Maybe she, and everyone she knew, would be out for the day.

"7:00 a.m."

When everyone she knew—and members of the school board—would be just waking up, possibly listening.

"He's attempting to blow my credibility in the community."

"You knew he wasn't going to go away."

She glanced up at him and caught him staring at her. Oddly. Differently. Probably because of what had happened Saturday night. She'd known *it* wouldn't disappear, either.

"Has anyone heard from Ruth Barnett?" she asked. "Or anything about how Tommy's doing?"

Mark shook his head.

"So what's the bad news?" she asked, almost afraid to hear.

"Susan and I have decided not to see each other anymore."

She sat straight up, her heart pounding. "What?" She hadn't felt anything strong from Susan since they'd spoken on Sunday. "When?"

"This afternoon."

Meredith's eyes narrowed as she watched him. And she started to feel sick. "Why?" If Saturday had anything to do with this, she was leaving town. She wasn't good for people. As hard as she tried, she just wasn't good.

"Because Susan realized that we were more about convenience than love, and she wants the real thing."

"*Susan* broke up with *you?*"

"Yep," he said, moving to stand behind his desk. "Right after I asked her to marry me."

"So it didn't have anything to do with Saturday night?"

"Of course not," Mark answered immediately, but he was sorting envelopes on his desk rather than meeting her gaze. On the surface he'd told her the truth, but somewhere deeper down there was no "of course" about it.

She had no idea what that meant.

And at the moment, she didn't want to know.

ON FRIDAY, Kelsey didn't argue when her mother suggested that they go straight to her house from school. They'd been spending time there and Kelsey was getting a little more used to the place. Besides, she'd have to go there when things got worked out and she could see Mom out in the open. They wouldn't be able to hang out in her car forever. And they sure couldn't go to Kelsey's house.

"Dad's not dating that woman anymore," she said, even though she knew Mom didn't like to hear about him. Just in case she was only with Don because she knew Dad was taken—which Kelsey had told her to try to make her jealous and come home.

"Mmm," Mom said, as if she didn't even hear her. Kelsey looked over at her, a little worried about the next couple of hours.

"I'm really glad."

She glanced over, not sure her mother had heard. "It's not that she was bad or anything," she added for some reason. "I mean, I didn't hate her, she just wasn't, you know…"

You, she wanted to say. But Mom wasn't listening. She was driving, staring out the front window, but her mouth was open a bit and her eyes stayed closed too long when she blinked.

"So how's Don been?" Kelsey asked, making her voice as cheerful as she could. She only got to be with her mom once a week, except that one Thursday that Mom called her away from Josie—and that couldn't happen anymore because Kelsey didn't have enough good excuses to keep Josie's mom from telling Dad that she was gone.

And with only this one day, she didn't want Mom to be in one of her scary moods. She wanted her to be happy. Kelsey used to be able to make her happy all the time.

She wanted her to stay awake and not wreck the car.

"Mom?" she asked more sharply. "How's Don been?"

"On the road most of the week."

"He's gone now?" She was glad about that, except that she'd wanted to ask him some questions about his friend—Kenny's father. Kenny might like it if, when she saw him on Monday to take him more crystals for his art, she could tell him about his dad.

And maybe, someday soon, he'd show her some of his art.

"Did you say something?" her mother asked, her eyes tired-looking as she glanced over.

They were almost at the house.

"Is Don gone now?"

"No, he got back this morning."

"Are you feeling sick?"

"What?" Mom glanced over at her again, really starting to scare her. Something wasn't right. "Oh, no," she said, without Kelsey having to repeat what she'd said this time. "I'm just tired, honey. I'll be fine when we get back to the house. Don's making me a cup of coffee. He makes the best coffee."

Well, okay, then. If she was just tired, and wasn't going to start yelling at her or throwing up or anything. She needed a ride back to Josie's before Dad came to get her.

THEY WERE ONLY at the house for a couple of minutes before Mom disappeared through the garage door. At first Kelsey just looked around. The place was messier than usual, with dirty dishes, even a cereal bowl with gross milk in the bottom of it on the table by the couch, and papers and books and stuff lying where usually they sat.

When her legs got tired, she pushed some of the stuff aside and sat on the rocker, and from there she could see the garage door. A lot of time had passed and Mom still hadn't come back. Kelsey figured she'd gone out to tell Don they were home, but she didn't know that for sure. He might be in some other part of the house. Maybe taking a nap.

He could get up and find Kelsey there. She didn't want to be caught in his living room alone without her mom.

She looked at the garage door again. Maybe she should just go and get her to come back in.

And why was Mom taking so long when they only had a little time together? She said she wanted to see Kelsey as much as Kelsey wanted to see her. That was why she was paying a lawyer.

What if she wasn't just tired but she was sick and she didn't want to make Kelsey worry?

Kelsey stood up. Then sat back down, staring at the garage door. She wished Josie was there and that she could ask her what to do.

Something that sounded like a click came from somewhere else in the house. A door opening? She couldn't be sitting there if Don came out. What if he walked around the house in his underwear, like Josie said her dad sometimes did?

Gross. She did not want to see Don in his underwear. That would be worse than his teeth.

That did it. Kelsey stood up and went to the edge of the kitchen where the garage door was. Maybe she'd just stand there with her hand on the knob, in case Don came out. Maybe she'd hear her mom in there talking to someone.

She didn't hear anything. Even when she held her ear to the door. She'd never been in any other part of the house, never even as far in as she was now, and she wished she still hadn't been. The kitchen was worse than the living room. The floor had pieces missing, one of the counters was cracked, and there were dishes and boxes and trash and empty bottles everywhere. And a hot plate, as if Mom never cooked on a real stove. But there was one of those, too, and it looked like someone had spilled junk on it a long time ago and never cleaned it up.

She didn't want to be there anymore, even if she could hear about Kenny's father. She wanted to go home. Right then. She'd tell her mom she didn't feel good—which was mostly true.

When another sound came from the house, Kelsey pulled on the garage door. She had to find her mom, had to get out of there. She was sweating and her hand slid off the door handle, but she grabbed it again and pulled harder.

And then, staring into the glaring light coming from the garage ceiling, she started to shake.

CHAPTER THIRTEEN

"KELSEY! What are you doing out here? You shouldn't have opened that door!"

Don was sitting on a stool at a counter and Mom was on his lap, with her shirt partly undone and Don's fingers on her boobs. She had a cup of coffee in one hand and Don's head in the other, and all around them it looked like a science lab with beakers and hot pads and vials and things. In one corner was a huge pile of flares, like the ones she'd seen Don bring through the house that day from his truck.

"What is this place?" She felt like she had on Saturday night, when no matter how mad Dad got, she couldn't give in.

"It's my lab, sweetheart," Don said, his hand slowly sliding from her mom's chest. He pulled the edges of Mom's blouse together. "Just a little hobby of mine."

"What does it make?" she asked, scared to death and wondering how she was going to get out of there.

"It doesn't make anything, sweetie," Mom said, standing up slowly. She buttoned her shirt, and grabbing a broom, she started sweeping up red dust from the garage floor. "It's just experiments to see what different stuff does, like scientists do when they're looking for cures."

Kelsey didn't move. Mom seemed to be feeling a lot better, which was good. "Where are the microscopes?"

Mom glanced up at her. "For what?"

"Everyone knows scientists use microscopes."

Don stood behind her mom, pulling her back against him, his hands on her hips. "She's right, you know, love," he said, with his face on the side of Mom's neck.

"Don!" Kelsey had never heard her mom talk to Don in her mean voice. She started to shake again, afraid of what the big man would do to her mother.

Mom dropped the broom and it fell to the ground with a crack that made Kelsey jump. "Come on, Kelsey, let's go."

She wanted to run away and never come back, but just like on Saturday night she stood her ground. "What does it make?" she asked, looking straight at Don. She didn't know why she did that, but she just wanted to make sure her mom was safe. That she was safe.

She couldn't come back, if she didn't know that.

"What do you think it makes?" he asked, coming closer.

Mom pulled at her elbow and said to Don, "Leave her out of this."

Out of what?

Scared to death, Kelsey glanced at her mom—who was staring at Don. She looked at him, too, and then back at Mom, and neither one of them looked at her at all.

"She's already in it up to her neck," Don said. The words were soft, but he sounded mad and his broken yellow teeth were showing a lot.

"No, she's not."

"Who's in it?" Kelsey asked, confused. Her legs were shaking and she had to go to the bathroom.

"No one," Mom said, putting an arm around Kelsey, who felt like she might start crying.

"You are," Don said. And then looking at her mom again, he said, "Telling her is the only choice, Barbie. She's seen it. If she says anything, it's over."

Mom's fingers got so tight on Kelsey's shoulder that tears did come to her eyes. She was afraid to move.

"She's just a baby."

"Who's been delivering goods," Don said. "She'll keep quiet about it if she knows she could go to jail."

Jail? Kelsey felt a little bit of potty slip out. Did they even have jail for kids? Kelsey'd never seen that on TV.

"I didn't do anything," she said trying to feel the way she had on Saturday when Dad wanted her to let Susan in her prayers. She crossed her legs tight.

"That's where you're wrong, kid," Don said, coming a little closer. Kelsey's whole body started to shake.

"Stop it, Don," Mom said sounding really mean. "You're scaring her."

Don stopped. Kelsey was kind of surprised by that.

"I'm sorry, Barbie," he said. "I don't want anyone to get hurt, certainly not her." He nodded toward Kelsey. "And the only way to guarantee that is to make sure she doesn't say anything she shouldn't. She has to know what she can't say."

"Don't tell anyone you saw this garage or anything in it, Kelse, okay?" Mom asked, leaning low to look Kelsey in the eye.

She nodded. She wanted to go home.

"Not good enough," Don said. He turned to Kelsey.

"When you took that stuff to Kenny, it was against the law," he said. "If you say a word about any of this to anyone—your father, even your friends—you'll get arrested and they'll put you in jail."

A little more potty trickled out. She could feel it on her leg inside her jeans.

"Mommy?" She glanced at her mom and wanted to die when, after a minute of watching Don, her mother nodded.

She was going to jail. Kelsey couldn't believe it. She *couldn't* go there. Daddy wouldn't be able to see her or take care of her.

"Are kid jails the same as big-people jails?" she asked, starting to cry.

"Now see what you've done," Mom said, pulling Kelsey into her arms and hugging her hard. Kelsey was glad about that. If her mom held her tight enough, they'd never be able to do anything bad to her. "No, sweetie, they aren't the same," she said. "But you aren't going there."

Don came closer, Kelsey could hear his feet on the garage floor, and she could smell him, too. "You don't have to be afraid of anything," he said, his voice soft and gentle. He knelt down and turned Kelsey around so she had to see him.

She might throw up *and* wet her pants the rest of the way, too.

"Your mom and I know what to do," he told Kelsey. "We're good at this, and we'll make sure you don't get in trouble or get hurt," he said. "But you have to promise you won't say a word about any of this to anyone, because we don't know who else we can trust. Okay?"

Kelsey nodded, squeezing her legs harder.

"Promise?"

"Do you promise I won't get in trouble?"

"I swear it," he said, crossing his heart.

"Okay. Now can I go home?"

"You want a snack first?" Mom asked.

MEREDITH LEFT SCHOOL almost as soon as her students were gone on Friday afternoon. She had an errand to run. She'd told herself she wouldn't. Had decided to lie low, ignore her intuition for once. She had her job. As far as she knew, Mark had no intention of starting procedures to terminate her. She'd been served with no written statement to that effect.

She'd worn black and white again, to remind herself to stay away from the shades of gray that dominated her life—leaving no room for what-ifs.

And black slacks, white blouse, black-and-white pumps and all, here she was in her Mustang, heading toward the secluded neighborhood of expensive custom-built homes where Ruth Barnett lived.

The heavy maroon-colored door opened a crack after her first ring of the doorbell.

"Mrs. Barnett?"

"Ms. Foster?" The woman sounded more frightened than pleased to see her.

"May I come in? Just for a second."

"I…uh…don't think that's a good idea."

"I know. I don't, either," Meredith said honestly. "But I'm here anyway. No one was behind me as I pulled in, and I parked my car around back. I'd really like just a couple of minutes with you."

Another second passed and then the door opened enough to let her in. Ruth Barnett locked the dead bolt behind her.

"Is Tommy here?"

"Upstairs," his mother said, giving a jerky nod over her shoulder. "In his room playing a computer game. He's allowed to play them all he wants on Fridays."

"But not during the week, huh?" Meredith followed the woman through a formal living room to a much more comfortable-feeling room decorated in shades of soft rose.

"Not until his homework's done."

It was a good plan. One Meredith wished more of her parents would implement.

"This is lovely," she said, taking a seat on the edge of the sofa.

"Thanks." Ruth Barnett's smile was more genuine as she looked over her surroundings. "I'm hoping to open my own business soon."

"You do interior decorating?"

The woman nodded, her burgundy slacks and jacket a perfect complement to the chair on which she sat. "I got my degree last year, but Larry wouldn't hear of me going to work. He thought it made him look bad."

"Was that before or after he filed for divorce?"

"He didn't file," she said softly, glancing down. "I did."

That wasn't as much of a surprise as it could have been. She waited, hoping the woman would say more. But when she didn't, Meredith said, "According to the papers, he did."

"He wanted it that way."

Of course he did. Couldn't have people thinking he was the one who'd been left behind. An object of pity. Or a bad husband.

"Why did you allow it?"

"Because I wanted my freedom enough to let him spin the details however he wanted."

Meredith had said she was only going to stay a minute. "How are you?" she asked, her voice warm and compassionate. In another life, another time, she and Ruth Barnett might have been friends.

"Trying to concentrate on the future."

Mrs. Barnett was prevaricating.

"You know about tomorrow's show, don't you?"

The woman nodded, her hair as stylish as her clothes.

"But you aren't going to do anything about it."

"What can I do?" she asked. "Larry quit listening to my pleas long ago."

"You could call the station, tell them the truth."

Ruth Barnett paled. "No, I can't do that."

She hadn't expected her to. Not really. But she'd had to try.

"He hit you, didn't he, Ruth?"

The woman glanced out the window.

"Often?"

She shook her head.

"Enough to scare you."

"Not really," the woman said, her eyes moist, yet brimming with strength as she glanced back at Meredith. "Though I'm sure he thinks so."

"Then why don't you say something? Do something? Why do you let him hold you prisoner to his lies?"

"Do you have any idea what it's like to be married to a lawyer?" she asked.

Meredith paused, waited for calm. "No," she said, then.

"He's not only a master debater, but he can take the smallest piece of truth and twist it around so that it's completely unrecognizable, but still prove that it isn't a lie."

Meredith's stomach tightened. She felt trapped and panicky. She understood what Tommy's mother was saying.

"Add to that the fact that he's well known around here and has a great deal of influence..."

"So no matter what you say, he'll distort facts until they point right back at you," Meredith finished.

"Yes."

"Why don't you leave?"

Meredith knew the answer as soon as she asked. "Tommy," she said in chorus with his mother.

Ruth Barnett's mouth was distorted with bitterness. "There's no way I'll be able to convince any judge in this county to give me full custody of my boy. And while I might not be afraid of Larry's attempts to hurt me, I am scared to death of what he'll do to our son."

"Of what he *is* doing to your son," Meredith said now, completely certain of what she said.

"I still hope you're wrong," Ruth said, her gaze forthright. "But in my heart I know that you aren't. I also know that if I don't play along with Larry, if I try to fight him at this point, Tommy will be the one who'll lose. At least while I play dumb and stay quiet, I have access to his home and when Tommy's there I can see and speak with Tommy whenever I choose."

"I hope that will be enough," Meredith replied, fairly certain that it wouldn't be.

"I do, too." The other woman's eyes watered. "You have no idea how grateful I am to you for what you did," she said, the words no louder than a whisper. "And I can't tell you how guilty I feel, every single day, for what he's doing to you because of it."

"I only did my job."

Mrs. Barnett shook her head, and her tears ran slowly down her cheeks. "Teachers don't stick their noses out like that. They go to the school administration if they suspect something, maybe. But more than that, no other teacher at Lincoln Elementary was even aware that Tommy was having problems—including the school counselor. I'd really hoped she'd be able to help us."

"So you knew before I came to you."

"I knew he was unhappy. At first, like everyone else, I was hoping it was an adjustment period and it would pass, but it'd been a year and didn't seem to be getting any better. I talked to Tommy several times about his father and me, asked him about his visits, his unhappiness, but he won't ever tell me anything. I didn't know what to think. You changed that. I'm taking Tommy privately to see a counselor now, so if there is a problem hopefully it will be brought to light. You're a special woman, Ms. Foster. I don't know how you knew about Tommy, but I thank God every day that you did."

As Meredith had thanked him for her gift. These days she'd made a tentative truce with herself to let it come if it would. "I wish I could've done more," she told the other woman.

"You've put Larry Barnett on warning. And because of his own quick temper and inability to back down or let go, it's become a very public warning. Even if everyone believes him now and not you, if Tommy shows up with bruises or shows signs of emotional damage there are going to be doubts. You could very well have saved my son's life."

"For now."

The woman nodded. "And for that, your life is being turned upside down."

Meredith stood. "I still have my job," she said. "My home, my friends." Friend. Though she had yet to connect with Susan since her breakup with Mark on Wednesday, except through voice mail.

Ruth Barnett, walking with her toward the door, reached for Meredith's hand and pulled her to a halt just inside the living room. "You know that he won't be stopped, don't you? The news, the paper, the call for your resignation, didn't work, so he's moving on to talk radio. If that doesn't do you in, he'll still keep trying. If there's one thing I know for certain about my ex-husband, Ms. Foster, it's that he will not lose."

"He's never fought with me before." Meredith didn't plan the words. They just slid out. With complete calm.

She hoped to God she knew what she was talking about.

Ruth Barnett looked at her for a moment longer, nodded and started to smile. "I hope you're right."

"For Tommy's sake, so do I."

"You could've gone at the house," her mom said when Kelsey climbed back in the car after using the restroom at the first gas station they came to. Her panties were wet and her jeans, too, a little bit, but she'd managed to hold most of it in.

"I know," Kelsey told her. "I didn't want to be late and I was sure I could hold it."

Her mom glanced over at her and Kelsey was afraid she would figure out she was lying, but she didn't say anything. Her eyes were a lot better now, wide awake.

Even when Meredith was half-asleep, she could tell if Kelsey was hiding something.

But Kelsey didn't want to think about Meredith. Dad said they wouldn't be seeing as much of her, anyway, since he and Susan had broken up.

They got to the bushes where Kelsey had to get out. She undid her seat belt as soon as they turned the corner so she could leave quick, but when her mom slowed down by the curb she grabbed Kelsey's arm.

"You still want to see me, Kelse?"

Kelsey nodded. She did. A lot. She loved her mom. She'd get over being scared, just like she had when Mom left. And when she lost her teddy bear, Bangles, and had to go to sleep without him.

Mom smiled and it looked like she might cry. "I'm glad," she said, her lips kind of shaky and she touched Kelsey's face, making her feel even better than going to the bathroom had. "Because you're the most important person in the world to me. You know that, don't you?"

Kelsey wanted to know it. Worse than just about anything. "Yeah."

She hoped her mom was going to hug her, but she reached under the car seat, instead, and brought out a little brown bag like the other two Kelsey had given to Kenny.

Kelsey drew back, staring at that bag.

"I need you to take this to Kenny on Monday, honey," she said.

She couldn't stop looking at that bag. She didn't mind seeing Kenny. To tell him he might be in trouble. She shook her head—hard.

"I really need you to," Mom said, her voice still soft and not mad.

Kelsey couldn't touch that bag. She wasn't putting it in her backpack or carrying it home. It would be there all weekend and she could go to jail because of it.

She might need to throw up instead of eat. What would kid jail be like? She wished she could talk to Josie about this, but she was afraid. Don said no one.

"What's that stuff in the garage for?" She didn't care, but she had a feeling it had to do with all of this.

"It's just like we said, honey," Mom smiled at her. "Don likes to do experiments. He was really into science when he was in school, but his parents couldn't afford to send him to college so he became a truck driver."

"Then why can't I tell about it?"

"Because he uses some stuff for his experiments that you aren't supposed to bring inside houses. You're only supposed to use them in labs, but since he's not in school and didn't go to college he's not allowed in one of those. Now take this and run before you're late."

Kelsey stared at the bag again.

"I don't want to get in trouble."

"The only way that will happen is if you don't take this bag," Mom said. "I know it sounds bad, Kelse, but it really isn't. Don's a good guy and so are his friends. It's just like you and me seeing each other right now—

sometimes you have to do things backward, but they're still good things."

She wasn't taking that bag.

"There's no way anyone will know what you're doing unless you tell them."

"What if Dad finds it?"

"Does your father go through your backpack?" Mom asked, sounding like she might get mad.

"No!" Kelsey quickly assured her. She didn't want Mom and Dad to fight.

"Then just make sure that you don't take it out of there and it'll be safe."

Yes, but...

"You trust me, don't you, Kelse?"

Kelsey nodded.

"You see, if you don't take this to Kenny, he might be so upset he'd tell on you, and then you *would* get found out."

How could he tell on her unless he told on himself, too? Unless he just said that he'd seen her on the junior high side of the bushes and that she'd talked to him. That would get her in trouble without anyone even knowing about the bag.

But Kenny wouldn't do that to her. Would he?

It was all so hard and confusing. And she was going to be in big trouble if she was late.

"There's another problem," Mom said, running her fingers through Kelsey's ponytail. "If Kenny tells, I might get in trouble, too. Only my trouble would be much, much worse than yours."

Kelsey stared at her mom, shocked. She wasn't the only one in trouble?

194 A CHILD'S WISH

"Why?"

"Because I gave the bag to you and I'm an adult. I could go to real jail and then there's no way we'd be able to see each other—not even on Fridays like we are now."

Frowning, Kelsey wanted to just take the bag and go. She also wanted not to take the bag and then go.

"Why is it breaking the law to take Kenny his crystals?" she asked. "Is his dad so bad that he can't have anything to do with him?"

"Sort of," Mom said. "Now just do as I told you," she added, handing Kelsey the bag. "Put this in your backpack, take it to Kenny and don't say a word."

Kelsey looked at her mom a long time. Even with her hair a mess and no makeup she was pretty. Kelsey loved her so much.

Her stomach didn't feel good, but she grabbed the bag, shoved it in the side pocket of her backpack, kissed her mom goodbye and got out.

If nothing else, at least she'd be seeing Kenny again.

CHAPTER FOURTEEN

THE ANSWERING MACHINE picked up and Meredith disconnected the call, hanging the phone back in its holder on the wall. She was tired of speaking with her friend through answering machines. Susan wasn't at the hospital—she knew, she'd called there, too. And her office had been closed for a couple of hours.

She turned off the kitchen light and wandered through the house. Seven o'clock on a Friday evening and she was at a loss.

Standing at the desk in her spare-bedroom office, she dialed again. And when the machine picked up, on a hunch, she hung up and hit redial. On the fourth try, she was rewarded with a click.

"Hello." Susan's greeting wasn't friendly.

"It's me."

"I know." Her friend's voice softened with guilt. "I saw you on caller ID."

"So you *have* been avoiding me."

"Not really."

Meredith waited.

"Okay, maybe a little, but not entirely. I've had one hell of a week. Almost lost a patient last night—a little girl with a simple adenoid surgery who reacted to the anesthetic."

"Oh, Suze, I'm so sorry." And then, after a moment, "She's okay, though, right?"

"Yeah."

"But you aren't."

"I just need a little time to trust myself again," Susan said. "It scares me how close I came to saying yes when Mark asked me to marry him, simply because it was safe."

Meredith dropped down on her white quilt. "I thought you loved him."

"I think I do." Susan sounded surprised. "Mark's a wonderful guy. I'm just not *in* love with him."

She lay back on the bed, staring at the pattern of swirls on the ceiling. "Susan Gardner, you aren't going to convince me the man didn't turn you on."

"I'm not even going to try. How could he not? He's gorgeous."

Right. Any woman would notice that. "So?"

"Sexual attraction is physical," Susan said slowly. "For me, it doesn't last much past the first kiss or two. To be in love, there has to be that added spark, you know? The feeling that lasts after the orgasm is over, making the moment, the lovemaking, go on and on and on."

"The kind that makes your heart leap every time the person walks in the room, even after you've been married for fifty years," Meredith said. It was a theory that her head "knew," but her heart had never "felt."

The only time her heart had leapt at the sight of another person had been when Mark Shepherd had shown up in her classroom to yell at her—and love had been the furthest thing from her mind.

"It's what you felt with Bud, huh?"

"Yep."

"You're sure you just didn't give Mark—and yourself—enough time?"

"No." Susan's reply was so baldly honest Meredith's eyes teared over.

"Then call him."

"No."

"Why not?" *Come on, tune in.* Let me feel her. Meredith was experiencing spurts of emotion from Susan, but couldn't get the calm feeling long enough to distinguish them clearly from her own—or to decipher them.

"Because. It's not right."

"Why not? He loved you, Suze. He asked you to marry him. I'm sure he'd love to have you call him back and say you've changed your mind. He's not the type to hold grudges or…"

"I haven't changed my mind."

"Suze, if this is fear, I'm going to come over there and throttle you."

The long silence that followed almost had her hanging up and getting her keys.

"He's not in love with me."

Meredith couldn't listen to that. "Of course he is. Any fool could see that he adored you…."

"When we made love, he had someone else on his mind, too."

Meredith's nerves weakened with panic and her chest filled with guilt.

No. Absolutely not.

"Who?"

"I didn't ask."

"Then how do you know…?"

"I did ask that much."

"Why?"

"Because I wasn't thinking about him, either."

Her heart was beating faster than it should be. "Who were you thinking about?" she asked, at the same time wondering how anyone could be in the middle of making love with Mark Shepherd and have any ability to think at all.

"Bud."

Her breathing slowed. "Oh, Suze, that's natural. Mark's the first."

"Like I said, he wasn't thinking about me, either, Mer."

"So, he was married a long time, too. Besides, guys' minds wander, don't they? They fantasize a lot more than we do."

Susan laughed. "I don't know about that."

"Yeah, me, neither," Meredith admitted, grinning. But she sobered quickly. "I'm worried about you."

"Me, too, a little." Susan's despondency worried her. "But I've learned an important lesson these past months."

"What's that?"

"I don't want to live my life half-alive."

"I love you, Suze."

"I know. I love you, too."

Meredith couldn't hang up. "You sure about that?"

"Completely."

"No matter what?"

"No matter what."

The swirls on the ceiling were making her dizzy. Meredith closed her eyes. "I kissed him."

An excruciating pause followed.

"When?"

"Last Saturday night. After that whole Kelsey episode." When visions of Mark's eyes, his mouth coming closer swam behind her eyelids, Meredith opened them. Getting dizzy staring at the ceiling was better.

"Did you sleep with him?"

"Of course not! He's yours. He loves you and you love him. Or maybe you do. I don't know," Meredith turned onto her side, curled into a fetal position. "I've been dying inside ever since, Suze. I'd never, ever be disloyal to you. Not ever."

"I know."

"But I was. It was only one kiss. I didn't mean it to happen. He didn't, either, for that matter. I know it sounds crazy, but it really was an accident."

"Where were you?"

"In the kitchen. I was leaving." She began to squeeze the tension out of the back of her neck.

"What happened afterward?"

"We both admitted it wasn't sexual and swore it would never happen again. I don't know what was wrong with me, Suze." She paused and when Susan said nothing, she continued. "I've tried a time or two this week to convince myself that I was just feeling your feelings. You'd left upset, and I usually tune in to you when you're upset. But I don't know. Especially now that you've broken up with him…."

She was rambling. She could hear it. Could feel the nervous energy singe her body beneath the skin.

"I just had to tell you," she whispered. "I couldn't stand that I'd wronged you and that you didn't know. If nothing else, there has to be honesty between us. You're not only my best friend but the sister I never had. You're my family."

"It's okay, Mer," Susan finally said. "Truly. I'm almost as curious about you and Mark as I am hurt. To think of the two of you together, when I was at home trusting you to be taking care of Kelsey and nothing else…."

She'd hurt Susan. Meredith could feel the tears on her face, but she didn't wipe them away. They were the penance she would always pay—inside if not out.

"And I think that's just further confirmation that I'm not in love with him," Susan continued slowly.

"Or maybe it's just that you've been my friend too long to hate me, so you're trying not to."

"Meredith." Susan's tone was sharper. "It's okay." She sighed. "I really mean that. Even if you'd slept with him and I'd been madly in love with him, it would be okay, because I know you. I know your heart and your intentions and I know without a doubt that you would never consciously or willingly do anything to hurt me. Whatever happened between you and Mark was because it was meant to happen. It was stronger than you were. And I gotta tell you, woman, that's pretty strong."

"I'm so sorry." She sniffled, almost welcoming the tears.

"Let it go, Mer."

"Not until you say you forgive me."

"There's nothing to forgive."

Meredith blinked back more tears. "Yes, there is."

"No there isn't, but I forgive you anyway."

"How can you?" Her question wasn't idle. She truly didn't understand.

"I have no idea, but I do. And you'd do the same for me."

Meredith quieted. Her whole body slowed down and the tears stopped. "You're right about that," she said, feeling calm inside for the first time in a week. "I know you, too, and I know you'd never consciously hurt me, either. You do the best you can."

"Yes."

"And that's what I did, too."

"Yes."

"Thank you."

"You're welcome, now get some sleep and call me in the morning."

"Yes, doctor."

Meredith was smiling when she hung up the phone. It was a full ten minutes before she realized she hadn't told Susan about the radio talk show. At the moment, Larry Barnett's negativity didn't seem important.

Susan knew the worst and still loved her.

"HEY, DADDY."

Shaving cream on his face, Mark glanced up in the bathroom mirror to see his daughter, still in her Care Bear pajamas.

"Morning, Kelse."

She climbed up onto the vanity, watching as Mark rinsed his razor, her foot kicking the cupboard. It felt good to have her back.

"What'cha doing today?"

"You and I are cleaning house, going to the grocery store and then it's your choice," he said. It was what they did most every Saturday—other than when he'd had preset plans with Susan.

She nodded, and Mark could see that her little face was unusually serious.

"What's wrong?"

"Nothing." She answered too quickly. And her voice was a little high. His radar signaled trouble.

Razor midway to his face, Mark stopped. Studied her. He'd thought, with Susan out of the picture, Kelsey would be back to normal. Unless she knew he'd talked with Mr. Brown yesterday. Kelsey's teacher had given him the troubling news that his daughter's grades had dropped considerably over the previous two weeks. Mark had assured Rod Brown that the problem had been attended to.

"Mr. Brown came to see me yesterday."

Kelsey's foot stopped swinging.

"He says you've been having some problems with math and spelling."

She shrugged. "It's dumb stuff."

Shaving with some difficulty, since he needed to give his daughter a serious stare, Mark said, "No, madam, it is not, and I believe you know that."

He caught her chin, which was dropping toward her chest. "Are you having problems with it?" he asked. "Do you and I need to spend some extra evening time on homework?"

"No."

"You're sure?"

Her gaze met his. "Yes." Mark's heart melted at that sweet glance. He finished shaving. Wiped his face. And leaned against the sink.

"I think I might be partially to blame for this, Kelse," he said. "I was so busy trying to get you to accept Susan, for your own good, that I wasn't paying attention to how you were actually feeling."

She looked confused, but continued to peer up at him. He wasn't sure how to help her grasp what he didn't completely understand himself.

"Anyway," he said when nothing else came to him. "I suspect your grades falling had to do with Susan and me. What do you think?"

She glanced away. Nodded. And Mark lifted her up. Cradling her in his arms as he had when she was much younger, he kissed the tip of her nose. "I'm sorry, pumpkin."

"I'm sorry, too, Daddy. I won't ever yell at you like that again."

"I'm glad to hear that," he said. "I don't ever want to be that angry with you again. I didn't like it at all."

"Me, either."

She still looked forlorn and Mark figured it would probably take more words and more than a few days to get fully past the misunderstanding. In the meantime, he had a radio show to listen to.

That was another problem. One he suspected it would be just as difficult to solve.

"CAN YOU TELL US, Doctor, how many patients you've treated who think they have psychic ability?"

Meredith stood in her kitchen, coffee cup in hand,

listening to the portable radio on her counter. She'd been there fifteen minutes and had yet to fill the cup.

"I'm sorry, I can't."

Thank God. The psychologist had an impressive list of credentials. In Oklahoma and beyond. Apparently he'd written several books that were used in psychology classrooms at many of the nation's top universities.

"Because the number is far too large to count," he added, and weight dropped like lead in Meredith's stomach. "Many of the psychosomatic illnesses I treat, as well as various psychoses, cause delusions of psychic ability. It's common for people suffering from mental illness to claim psychic counsel as a motivation for their actions. Many, many crimes are committed in the course of such delusion."

"What happens to these people?" Talk show host Delilah White had just the right amount of concern in her voice.

"Many of them, if they're brought to trial, are found not guilty on grounds of diminished capacity and are committed to psychiatric confinement."

The cup in Meredith's hand slipped, shattering on the floor at her feet and spraying her ankles with tiny shards of porcelain. She bent to clean up the mess. Picked up the biggest pieces before going for the broom. Her ankles had dots of blood on them now. She'd deal with them later.

Clever of Barnett, really. Implying through his expert witness that there were many like her and that her "kind" needed to be committed, because they were a danger to society. Clever, too, in that he hadn't really come out and said so. Because that would be slanderous.

The show went on painfully. Larry Barnett had given his spiel at the beginning. Nothing new or original there. And after Delilah White had thanked each guest, Barnett added his own sickening bits of humble gratitude.

First was the book-writing therapist, then a child psychologist to talk about what a vulnerable age eight was and how a child's perception of his parent could be permanently damaged if the evidence was strong enough to sway him; and about how kids thought of their teachers as godlike, often believing that everything they said was true.

The psychic was the worst. She admitted that she made a good living predicting futures over the telephone—and that it was all in good fun. That she didn't think anyone really believed what she told them.

A brain surgeon followed, talking about the fact there was no proof that humans possessed any kind of psychic ability. He lost Meredith, and she supposed most of his audience, with his talk of monitored brain waves and neural reactors, but his doubt about anyone who claimed to find truth without tangible, measurable input was crystal-clear.

Meredith's phone rang, but she didn't answer it. Instead she went for the broom. Couldn't find it. Cleaned up the powdery remains of the cup with a paper towel. And then, with the towel still in her hand, sat down on the floor.

Delilah White invited listeners to call in. One after another, citizens expressed their outrage at young children being exposed to psychic teachings in the classroom. At the shocking fact that young children were being taught by someone who wasn't stable. There were the usual diatribes about society and what it had come to. Open-ended questions about where it would all lead.

And as was common with radio talk shows, there were other people who supported Meredith's right to believe what she believed, and to speak of what she believed as long as she didn't teach it as part of the curriculum, as long as she didn't hurt anyone.

"Not hurt anyone?" Larry Barnett piped up. "How can an accusation of abuse not be harmful?"

"I'm sorry, listeners, but I agree with Mr. Barnett on that one. Clearly harm has been done here. The question is, what is the Bartlesville public school system going to do about it?"

Clearly harm had been done. Only one side had been heard. There'd been no trial. But judgment had been made. Meredith jumped up. Grabbed the phone. Dialed the number that Delilah White had been repeating ad nauseum.

She had to try six times to get through, and then she was asked to hold. But only until she said her name.

"We have Ms. Meredith Foster on the line, ladies and gentlemen. Ms. Foster, I'm sure our listeners are eager to hear what you have to say."

"I am a teacher of children," Meredith spoke slowly, quietly, with great effort. "I teach the board-approved curriculum—and only that. For the past four years, my students have scored significantly higher on aptitude tests than any other third-grade class in Bartlesville. As a teacher of young children, I am often exposed to emotional outbursts or withdrawals, as children this age haven't yet learned to filter or control their feelings. Because of this, I'm often aware when they're struggling. Any time unusual behavior occurs, I go straight to the parents. My only other option is to remain silent, and I believe there are more parents out there who care enough to want to know what could potentially be going on in their child's life than those who don't want me to speak of anything but ABC's."

"But, Ms. Foster, in the most recent incident, I'm told the student didn't give you any information. That, in fact, you inferred that there might be a problem and on evidence as flimsy as a sense of…knowing…you went to the boy's mother with claims of child abuse."

"I'd like to ask Mr. Barnett, why, if he's so concerned about his son, he's making a public issue of the fact that I thought the boy was unhappy. It seems to me that all this attention would be more damaging to a child than anything I said in private to his mother."

"My son is used to living in the public eye, Ms. Foster." Barnett's tone remained placidly, warm, congenial. "And he's the reason I'm pursuing this matter. I want Thomas to know that I have nothing to hide. Emotional abuse is insidious. By its very nature, one cannot be sure one is suffering from it. That being the case, once the claim was made I had to do everything in my power to assure the boy that he was not a victim."

The man was good. Which was why he was a D.A. Why on earth had she dared take him on? How could she possibly have believed she might win?

"Ms. Foster? Do you deny that you claim to use some kind of psychic ability in your work with your students?" Delilah White again.

"I am no psychic." Meredith stared at the paper towel in her hand. If she squeezed it, she'd cut her hand. Bleed. She should throw it away. "I have no abilities that every single one of you doesn't also have. I am merely perceptive. An opportunity we all have."

"So you *perceived* that Mr. Barnett, a man whose actions have been thoroughly scrutinized over the years as he rose to important positions within the state, was abusing his son?"

"I believed that the father of one of my students—"

"Former students…" Barnett interjected.

"—was causing emotional distress to his son."

"Based on your perception," the interviewer said.

"Yes."

"The child never said a word to you about it."

She took a deep breath. Closed her eyes. "That's correct."

"Uh-huh, well, thank you for calling, Ms. Foster. We have other listeners on the line…"

She heard a click. And a dial tone. She'd just helped Larry Barnett tighten the noose around her neck.

The show had another half hour to go.

Meredith tossed the paper towel in the trash.

CHAPTER FIFTEEN

THE HOUSE WAS CLEAN enough by the time Delilah White's morning show ended.

"I did all the dusting, Daddy," Kelsey said, coming up behind him in her bathroom. Brush in hand, he turned from the toilet bowl to see a reasonably dirty rag in her hand. She'd gotten some dust from somewhere.

"Great, sweetheart," he said, flushing the blue out of the toilet bowl. "As soon as I wash my hands and change my shirt, we can head for the grocery store."

"They weren't very nice to Ms. Foster, were they?" Kelsey asked, her dark hair hanging down around her shoulders—the way he liked it best. She was frowning as she followed him into his room.

"No, they weren't." The bed wasn't made. He'd intended to wash the sheets, but that could wait for another day. Pulling off his T-shirt, he grabbed a pale-green polo shirt and dropped it over his head.

"Do you think they hurt her feelings?" Kelsey was right behind him as he stopped in the kitchen for the grocery list held by a magnet on the refrigerator door.

"I hope not." His sneaker made a small catching sound as he stepped away from the fridge. Kelsey had spilled cranberry juice there earlier in the week. He hadn't scrubbed the floor this morning, either.

"But do you think they did?" his daughter persisted.

He stopped, gazed at the girl who, in her butterfly jeans and short-sleeved pink T-shirt, looked like a mini-version of the teacher she'd talked about nonstop the year before—the friend she'd avoided since Meredith's run-in with Larry Barnett had caused her distress at school.

"Yes, Kelse, I think they did."

"Then we should go see her, Daddy."

His small companion with the big heart was back. Thank God.

"She's not going to want to see us right now, honey."

"She'll want to see me," Kelsey said, all nine-year-old innocence and confidence. "I know she will. And you'll just have to be nice to her for once."

She grinned at him and he fell in love with her all over again. "We'll see."

MARK STILL FELT more trepidation than assurance as they drove down Meredith's street several hours later, groceries purchased, taken home and put away.

"Promise you won't yell at her," Kelsey said, her leg bobbing on the seat as she stared out the window toward Meredith Foster's house.

"Jeez, Kelse, you make me sound like an ogre. I don't yell."

"Just be nice, okay? She's had a hard day." Kelsey's expression was earnest.

"I'm a nice guy, sweetheart."

"Daddy!" There was exasperation mixed with warning in the word.

"I promise."

"Thank you."

Mark grinned at his offspring, wondering how he'd managed to raise such an opinionated imp.

DRESSED IN A LONG DENIM SKIRT, white blouse and sparkling beads, her long golden-red hair loose down her back, Meredith looked ready to meet the world when she opened her door. She wasn't home, depressed, needing visitors. Mark felt like an idiot standing on her front porch, a dripping banana-pie ice-cream treat in one hand.

"Hi, my dad isn't mad at you," Kelsey said before he could excuse their intrusion and hightail it out of there.

"Kelsey!" Meredith's pleasure sounded genuine. "Come on in!"

So much for a rapid departure. They were inside. With a perfectly fine woman who did not appear to need any cheering up at all.

"We brought you a treat," Kelsey said. "Didn't we, Daddy?"

"Uh, yes," he finally spoke, handing her the bag, but avoiding her eyes.

"We got some for us, too," Kelsey said, leading the way to the kitchen where she took a seat at Meredith's round table. His daughter had spent the night there once and acted like she owned the place. Mental note: Teach Kelsey some more manners.

"Banana pie!" Meredith said. "And cookie dough for you." She put a lidded and sweating cup in front of Kelsey.

"Daddy got banana pie, too." Kelsey told her, dripping ice cream on the place mat as she removed her lid.

"I see that." Meredith put his cup in front of one of the remaining chairs. Glanced up. And looked him straight in the eye. Her gaze was full of questions he couldn't answer. He wasn't sure what they were.

"The people on the radio were jerks," Kelsey said, around a mouthful of ice cream. "Daddy even said so. Didn't you, Daddy?"

Meredith was still watching him. "Yep."

His employee's shoulders relaxed visibly.

And, ironically, so did Mark's.

"YOU WANT TO GO to Osage Hills with us?" Kelsey asked as she licked the last of her ice cream off the plastic spoon. "We're going on the trail to the waterfall, and then Daddy and I are going to play Frisbee."

Hiking. Playing. It sounded wonderful.

"I'm sure Meredith has plenty to do this afternoon, Kelse." Mark intervened before Meredith could reply. "She's obviously ready to go out. We're probably holding her up."

Kelsey looked at her. "Are we?"

"No." Meredith smiled. Kelsey was trying too hard; she wasn't as happy as she'd have them believe, but Meredith was soaking up the genuine warmth that emanated from the little girl. She'd missed her. A lot. "But I'm sure your father has other plans for the afternoon, honey."

She couldn't look at Mark again. There was danger there. Something she didn't understand.

And there was guilt. She'd kissed him, after her friend had trusted them alone together. No matter that

Susan had subsequently broken up with him. Susan might have made a mistake. She loved him.

"Nope," Kelsey was saying, her feet swinging under the table, knocking against the chair leg. "Today's my choice."

Oh. "Well, I'm sure you don't want me barging in on your twosome."

"Yes, we do," Kelsey said. "Don't we, Daddy?"

If she hadn't been so uncomfortable herself, Meredith would have laughed at the strained expression on Mark's face. "Yes," was all he said.

And because Meredith had been climbing the walls there by herself, because she adored Kelsey and couldn't bear to have the little girl disappointed in her again so soon, because Susan was at the hospital seeing patients, Meredith accepted their invitation.

THEY HIKED. They laughed. They played three-way Frisbee. And somehow they ended up back at Meredith's house with takeout Chinese food for dinner, followed by Kelsey's favorite movie, *The Reluctant Astronaut.* The little girl seemed happy, contented. But anytime Meredith focused on Kelsey, her stomach grew tight and uneasy. Just like it had that Friday night of the spring dance, when she thought she'd eaten something bad.

Maybe it was ice cream followed by Chinese food.

At nine-thirty, halfway through Meredith's favorite, *The Truman Show,* which Mark had never seen before, Kelsey fell asleep.

"I should go," Mark said when Meredith noticed

the child's head hanging awkwardly off the side of the armchair and paused the movie.

She should let him. But after Kelsey's brief mention of it, they'd done a marvelous job of avoiding all mention of the radio show that morning and Meredith needed to know what he thought—where she stood— without having his daughter intervene on her behalf. "You could put her on the bed in my guest room," she said. "Just until we finish the movie."

He glanced at her. Looked like he was going to refuse. And then nodded.

Meredith led him down the hall, past her room to one across the hall, and helped him settle his daughter under the covers.

Someday she wanted a life like that.

"GOOD AFTERNOON. Good evening. And good night." Meredith felt like cheering when Jim Carrey delivered his last line and walked through the movie set that had been the boundary of his life since the day he was born.

Mark was watching the credits roll.

"What did you think?"

He glanced at her, sat forward and reached for the remote control. "It was good."

"That's all? Good?" The movie had hit a chord so deep within her, the first time she'd seen it at a theater, that she'd gone back twice more that same weekend.

The television went dark. Leaving them only with the soft light from a lamp on the table by the window. "It's a bit discomfiting to realize that one can be so completely manipulated," he said now. "They kept him trapped in that set for decades and he never even knew it wasn't real."

"You're deeper than you want to believe, Shepherd," she said, telling herself that the extent of her pleasure was ridiculous.

"I'm just me," he said. "And right now, that's ready for bed."

His words, innocently intended, she was sure, hung between them. Only because it was late. And the lighting was soft. And she'd had a hard day.

She sat forward in the chair she'd been lounging in all evening. "Before you go, can you tell me what you really thought about the radio show this morning?"

"He was prepared, thorough."

"And?"

"I think he made headway."

She'd known that. But to hear him say it brought a stab of fear to her chest.

"How much headway?"

Mark glanced at her, his eyes glistening in the dim light. "You don't want to get into this tonight, do you?" he asked softly. "Today was supposed to be about forgetting."

"And the problem with that—" she tried for a chuckle and failed "—is that you always get your memory back and it's like finding things out all over again. You come down with a thud."

"Monday morning is soon enough. Give yourself the weekend, at least."

"Mark, if you know anything, please tell me. The rest of the weekend will be little more than a torture chamber of waiting and wondering and worrying. I'd much rather just know what I'm dealing with."

He sighed, rubbed his hands together and then sat

back, facing her. "I had a call from the superintendent today. He intends to recommend you be dismissed."

Her stomach dropped, but she tried to rally.

"On what grounds?"

He leaned closer, his expression compassionate. "It doesn't matter tonight, Meredith. Get some sleep and we'll talk about this on Monday."

"On what grounds?"

"Mental abuse of a child, for one."

She couldn't believe it. Couldn't breathe. The room was warm and yet her skin felt frozen. "My entire life is about helping children."

"I know. I told you we should do this later."

She stared at him. "How is later going to make this any different?" she asked him, her throat raw. "I'd never, *ever* abuse a child. That's ludicrous. I spoke with Tommy's mother. Period. I never went near him, never talked to him about any of this. If he's suffering, it's because of what his parents did with the information I gave them."

"I know," he said again, and she couldn't tell if he was attempting to placate her or not.

"Don't humor me, Mark." She heard the edge in her voice and was relieved to know she had some fight left. She felt completely lethargic, beaten, and she wasn't sure she'd have the energy she required if she tried to stand.

"I'm not." His tone, the straightforward look in his eye, convinced her. "And I don't think that charge will stick," he added. "But the second one might."

"And it is?"

"Moral turpitude."

Tears sprang to her eyes and Meredith blinked them away. "What base act did I commit?"

"Making false statements."

"They were true."

"According to Larry Barnett, they're false."

"I said that I *felt* his son was being abused. How can he, or anyone else, stand in judgment about what I feel?"

"You told his wife that Tommy was suffering from emotional abuse," Mark said. "You have no proof that that statement is true."

She had said that. Because she knew it was true.

"The superintendent's in a tough place, Meredith," Mark said, and she tried to listen to him, although she didn't give a damn about the man's predicament at the moment. "He's under a lot of pressure to make a decision here and all he has to base that decision on are the facts he has before him. He thinks the facts show you making false statements."

"That means that if enough members of the school board agree with him, I'll be getting a letter to that effect." She'd read the statutes when she'd been hired as a teacher. And again that afternoon.

"You'll have no less than twenty days before a hearing is called, at which time you'll be free to present your reasons for nondismissal."

"And then the board votes."

He nodded.

She'd wanted to know. For the life of her, she couldn't figure out why.

"It's completely out of your hands." Not that it

mattered. He'd agreed with Barnett from the beginning.

"Not entirely." Mark's speech was slow, drawn out. "I'll put together a folder similar to the one I handed out at the parents' meeting, with the more sensitive material included as well, and I'll see that it gets to every member of the board."

"What kind of more sensitive material?"

"Amber McDonald," he said. "Amber Walker now."

She'd just had a letter from the little girl's mother a couple of weeks before. Amber had gone to a slumber party—had had a great time—and had called her stepfather to come get her the next day. It was the first time she'd allowed herself to be alone with him—with any man—since her abuse and she'd acted as though it happened every day. Her mother was very hopeful.

Meredith was, too.

"Obviously we can't speak about her publicly," Mark was saying. "But we can include the information in a confidential packet."

"What do you think about that episode?" Meredith asked, too tired to figure it out on her own. Tired physically. And tired of feeling ostracized. She could keep her feelings to herself. They didn't mark her in any way. Didn't show. No one would know they were there and she could be normal, just like everyone else.

In another town. And if she was fired for moral turpitude, in another career.

"I think you saved a little girl's life."

"So why is this time any different?"

"You didn't get lucky."

He thought the previous time had involved luck. As

if she'd just guessed that little Amber was being molested. As if she played some kind of Russian roulette with children's lives. Meredith wasn't surprised by his words, but she was shocked by how much they hurt her.

She stood. "You'd better go."

Reaching for her wrist, Mark pulled her down beside him on the couch. "Meredith, listen, I'm on your side."

She couldn't look at him. "How can you say that? You don't believe I know what I'm talking about."

"I believe you think you do," he said, the softness of his words compelling her to listen. "And if a wrong is unintentional, it's not moral turpitude."

Peering at him, Meredith tried to focus, to allow the bit of relief teasing her heart to flower into something powerful enough to heal the panic.

"They don't have to prove that I intended to hurt Tommy, only that I intended to speak a false statement in an effort to help him."

"All you have to do is convince the school board that you believe what you say you do."

"How do I do that?"

He shrugged, gave her a soft grin. "I have no idea how you do it, but I know it's true," he told her. "You've certainly convinced me that you believe in yourself."

Well, that was something. Especially since she wasn't sure anymore that she even knew who she was, knew where she stopped and other people started.

His hands were on his thighs. Strong hands. Capable. Gentle. And she was in them. He didn't believe in her gift. But he believed that she did.

He seemed to think that might be enough.

"HERE'S YOUR BAG." Kelsey shoved the brown paper package at Kenny, hardly looking at him. She'd run as fast as she could across the playground, checking behind her the whole time. She looked behind her again, scared to death that someone would be there, seeing her do this.

"Thanks," Kenny said. "How you been?"

"Fine."

"Oh."

"Well, 'bye." She bent to push her way back through the bushes and climb over the fence.

"Hey, wait." Kenny stepped forward. She could see the ratty bottoms of his jeans just above his black tennis shoes.

"What?" She'd worn her butterfly jeans again today, just because she was seeing him, even though they were a day dirty. They were her best jeans and she'd wanted him to notice her. Now she just felt stupid. It wasn't fun seeing Kenny, when she knew she could go to jail.

"What's the matter with you?"

"Nothing."

"Yeah, there is. You mad at me?"

She kicked a clod of dirt on the ground with her toe. "No."

"Then what?"

He sounded like he might start to cry if he were a girl. Kelsey turned her head to check and she was right. His face was sad and not at all laughing at her like it usually was.

She hated when people were sad. Especially if it was her fault. "I'm sorry, Kenny."

He didn't say it was okay. He just stared at her a minute. And then said, "What's wrong?"

She'd promised not to tell. But maybe Kenny didn't count, since he was part of it.

"Do you know how much trouble we could get in?"

He shrugged. "Not if we don't get caught."

He wasn't too worried and Kelsey figured he didn't know about the jail part.

"But Kenny, what if we do?"

"How can we? We're just kids."

Should she say it? Could she let him get in that much trouble without telling him? "They have kid jail."

His eyes got narrow like he was thinking, but he was looking at her.

"You know?"

She nodded.

"How'd you find out?"

"Don has a lab in his garage," she told Kenny. It felt so good to finally say the words out loud, instead of just in her head. And maybe together, she and Kenny could figure a way out of this. "I accidentally walked into it on Friday and he and my mom freaked out. Don said I had to keep quiet about you and the lab, too, 'cause he does experiments you're only supposed to do in real labs and not at home…"

She couldn't say the words fast enough there were so many of them. But she stopped when Kenny started shaking his head.

"What?" she asked him.

"You're such a baby, you know that?"

"I am not." She hadn't been a baby for a long time. And now she could go to jail.

"That wasn't a science experiment, Kelsey," Kenny said, sounding like a know-it-all. But nice, too. "It's a meth lab."

CHAPTER SIXTEEN

KELSEY TILTED HER HEAD against the sun's glare. "What's a meth lab?"

"You know, where they make tweek…glass… crank…"

He was acting like she knew what he was talking about.

"Ice, Kelsey," he said, hiking his jeans up over the boxers on his hips and letting his long blue T-shirt fall back over them. "Crystal. It's all the same thing."

Kelsey brightened fractionally. "He makes those crystals?" She pointed to the bag. "I thought they were rocks from the ground." Hadn't Don said so? She couldn't remember.

"Of course he makes them," Kenny said. "And I sell them to kids at school."

"No you don't." She shook her head. "You use them for your art."

"Hey." Kenny stepped back. "I don't use them at all. I'd never touch that stuff. It could kill you."

"How can crystals kill you?"

"It's drugs, Kelsey. You know, methamphetamine. People snort them or dissolve them in coffee or smoke them, and they get high."

How did people suck rocks up their noses? Kelsey didn't want to know.

"Real drugs?" she asked. "Like on TV?"

He nodded.

"Like they tell us to stay away from?"

"Yeah."

"Drugs are pills. Or needles."

"They used to be," Kenny said, sounding important again. He sure knew a lot. "But now there's this stuff and it makes you feel really happy and energized and you can make it in your own house."

"Like Don does."

"Right. Except my dad says he does it different than most people around here. He does a 'pseudo' method, using cold pills, instead of Nazi, which used batteries or something because cold pills are watched now. Anyway, the cops aren't used to that around here, which is why we won't ever get caught."

She didn't get half of that. And didn't care. "Do kids take them?"

He nodded. "You'll learn all about them in fifth grade."

"So I've been bringing you drugs." She just couldn't believe it. Couldn't believe her mother would let her do something like that. Which meant that her mom must not know.

"Right," Kenny was saying. "Don makes them. You deliver them. And I sell them to make money for a lawyer, so I can go live with my dad." He sounded pretty pleased about the whole thing.

"I'm a *drug dealer?*" She'd seen shows on TV about that. The dealers were always horrible, dirty people who killed other people and then died.

"No, goof," Kenny punched her arm lightly. "You're a kid who don't know no better. You're safe. Trust me."

She didn't feel safe. She felt sick—and scummy. And like she couldn't live with her dad at all anymore or some of her dirt would rub off on him.

"I gotta go," she said, pushing through the bushes and scrambling over the fence so fast she scraped her arm. On the other side, Kelsey ran, as fast and as far as she could. And when she got too tired to do that, she lay on the ground and cried.

Until it was time to go to Josie's to meet Dad and go home for dinner.

THE LETTER FROM the superintendent came on Wednesday. Mark hand-delivered it to Meredith's room after school. And invited her to follow him home for dinner so they could talk strategy. She suspected he was also feeling sorry for her, but she went anyway. If she had any hope of surviving this intact, she needed his help.

She'd talked to Susan and her mother on Sunday, and both had adamantly insisted that she wasn't crazy and that her only course was to listen to her intuition and her heart and to do what they told her. It had sounded so simple then.

"How's Kelsey been?" she asked as they walked together out to the parking lot.

She wasn't surprised when he frowned. "Odd," he told her. "I think she got in a fight on Monday."

"A fight?" Meredith stopped. That didn't sound right at all. "With who? About what?"

"I don't know." He squinted against the sun as he faced her. "She wouldn't say."

"But she admitted to fighting?"

"No, she didn't. But her clothes were dirty like she'd been rolling on the ground, she had a scratch on her arm and she'd been crying."

Meredith tried to clear her mind, her inner self. Her own problems were minor, if Kelsey was in trouble. She'd sensed something the other night and ignored it. And this afternoon she couldn't get through her own muck to find the little girl. Frustrated, she asked Mark, "How did she explain the state she was in?"

"Said she fell on the playground on the way to Josie's."

"Wouldn't Josie's mother have cleaned her up?"

"That's what I asked. She said they played at school until it was almost time for me to come pick her up."

"Do they do that often?"

"Often enough."

So it could be true.

But Meredith knew it wasn't.

MARK WOULDN'T LET Meredith help with dinner. He was making his specialty—a boxed meal, for which all he had to do was add hamburger and water—and there weren't enough jobs for two. She couldn't help with the table, either, because it was Kelsey's job and he didn't think it was healthy for the girl not to follow through on her responsibility.

She insisted on helping with the dishes and by then he'd run out of excuses. She was too close, the situation too intimately domestic without Susan there. Meredith might be a friend, but she was also an employee. He was her boss. They should have gone out to eat.

As soon as Kelsey went to her room to do her

homework, Mark got down to business. "The hearing is set for twenty days from today," he said. "That's Tuesday, May 9. It's the soonest possible date according to Oklahoma statutes."

She dried her hands and hung the kitchen towel on the rack Mark had installed inside the cupboard door. Kelsey had picked out that particular towel, and it had butterflies all over it.

"I intend to spend most of the next couple of weeks contacting individual parents and board members, making sure that anyone who doesn't know about you and your work has an opportunity to do so. It would help if you'd give me a list of all the parents you can think of to whom you've given nonacademic advice over the years."

She nodded.

"Susan said something a few weeks back about your track record—wanting to know the number of times you'd advised parents according to your hunches and ultimately been proven correct. I think she's on to something. A chart like that would be solid proof of your ability to figure out the truth in some difficult situations."

"Makes you feel good, doesn't it, Mark?" she asked him, her eyes clouded as she reached for her bag. "The idea of having that proof in your hand before you stand up for me?"

And just like that she'd pissed him off again. The woman was intent on making his life hell. "Do you want to beat this thing or not?"

"Of course I do," she acknowledged. And as he watched her deflate, he wished he hadn't caused her pain.

"Do you think you could collect any information to refute Barnett's experts from the other day?"

"I'm sure I can. My spare bedroom is full of it."

"Twenty days isn't very long."

"I'll be ready," she said calmly. Mark couldn't figure out how she did it—remaining steadfast in the midst of so much turmoil. He made his decisions based on fact, on what he could prove, and he often doubted himself. Had he been in her shoes, he might be tempted to cut his losses.

"You're really okay with all of this, then?"

"No." She glanced up surprised, her bag over her shoulder. "I have no idea how I'm going to get through the next three weeks."

He wasn't certain, but he thought her lower lip trembled.

"I'm going in to tell Kelsey goodbye," she said.

He played it safe and let her go.

ON FRIDAY, Susan called Meredith to say she had a date. The man was an administrator from the hospital. He flew planes, and they were going to Dallas for dinner.

"You sound different, Suze," Meredith told her friend, staring out the window of her classroom during planning period as she spoke on her cell phone. Susan felt different, too.

"I... Steve's been bugging me to go out with him for a couple of months," she admitted, "but I wouldn't even consider it."

"Because of Mark."

"That. And Steve's so different from me. He lives

life by the seat of his pants, Mer, while I plan every holiday a year in advance."

Meredith chuckled. "You do not."

"I live pretty rigidly."

"You didn't used to."

"I know."

"He makes you spark, huh?" A picture of Mark's face swam before her mind's eye. Susan might have married him.

"Yeah, I think he does."

Hallelujah.

"Now, tell me about Kelsey. Your message said you were worried."

"Something's up with her," Meredith said. "But I'm so depleted I can't get a fix on what it is."

"How sure are you about this?"

"Ninety-five."

"Okay." Susan's take-charge voice kicked in. "You have to find a way to spend some time with her. You know once you're with her, you'll be able to get through the noise and figure out what's going on."

Meredith did know that. And still she hadn't made any attempt to see the little girl—not even on the playground or in the cafeteria. "What would I do with the information if I got it?" she asked. "Tell Mark his daughter's in trouble? That she needs help? He'll never believe me."

"And now's not a good time for that, huh?"

Mark was just about her only hope of getting through the Barnett thing. And it was a slim hope at that.

"If I thought I could be of any use to Kelsey, I'd do it anyway." At least the old Meredith would have.

"How do you know you can't be, until you know

what kind of trouble she's in? You might be able to help her without anyone being the wiser."

It wasn't her way. She always went to the parents. These children were not hers.

But until she knew...

"I'll see what I can do," she said, feeling marginally better.

"And in the meantime, you can spend some time with her father and figure out what's going on there."

Meredith glanced toward her classroom door, as if someone could have overheard her friend's absurd statement.

"There is nothing going on between me and Mark," she said in an urgent whisper.

"Then there should be."

"Susan, just because you've found someone, doesn't mean that everyone has to."

"I'm a doctor, Mer, not an idiot."

"Then stop talking nonsense."

"You spent Saturday with him."

"Kelsey felt sorry for me."

"And that's why Mark gave up his whole day?"

"Saturday was Kelsey's choice and she chose me."

"And that's why you spent the entire afternoon and evening with Mark Shepherd? Watched a movie with him after his daughter fell asleep? Because Kelsey chose you?"

That was what she got for blabbing to her best friend.

"You were gone and I'd just listened to that horrible radio show. I'd have gone out with an alligator if it had asked."

"And dinner on Wednesday?"

"To talk about the hearing."

"What do you feel when you look at him?"

"Attracted." She heard her answer and stopped. Susan always had been better at twenty questions than she had. Her friend would have made a bang-up lawyer. "He's an attractive man," she added. "A woman would have to be dead not to notice."

"And what about when you think of him?"

"I think I'm still feeling your feelings."

"Like when you think about kissing him? Or try not to picture him in bed?"

"Yeah. See? It's all you."

"I never thought of Mark like that unless I was looking at him. In my thoughts it was always Bud. Or occasionally Steve."

Then...

"It can't be me who's feeling that way, Suze. He'll break my heart."

"No, he won't."

Meredith heard voices in the hallway, reminding her that she was sitting in a third-grade class that would be filling up with third-grade children in another fifteen minutes. She closed her door, embarrassed that her heart was beating so fast.

"One of us would have to quit our job."

Susan sighed. "I know. And I'm still stumped there. You both love what you do and you're great at it. I haven't figured that part out."

She couldn't afford to be disappointed. Her life was already enough of a mess without adding even the possibility of unrequited romance. "Because there's nothing to figure out," she said dryly.

"It's not like you not to be honest with yourself."

That stung. Smacked of moral turpitude. Enough so, that she calmed down and took a look at what might be lurking inside her. And started to panic.

"I have a class to teach in ten minutes," she said.

"Do you want him to kiss you again?"

No. Absolutely not!

But this was Susan. Demanding honesty. "If things were different, maybe."

"That's what I thought," Susan said. "And you know what else? I'd bet a year's salary that he feels the same way."

"You would?"

Susan wasn't empathetic. There was no reason to believe her.

"Yeah. I suspect that's part of the reason he's so mad at you all the time. You wouldn't be able to drive him crazy, if you didn't also attract him like crazy. You know how these things work, Mer. For every up there's a down. Where there's love, there's hate. Where there's joy, there's sadness. The opposites define each other."

Susan was making too much sense. Scaring her.

"I'm too intense for him," she said softly. It was something she'd known for a long time—part of the reason she couldn't ever love Mark Shepherd. "Mark's marriage was fraught with conflict because of his wife's intensity. He certainly isn't going to trust his heart to another emotional woman."

"But you *use* your emotions, Meredith. They don't completely control you the way they controlled Barbie. She wasn't healthy."

"Mark doesn't believe in my gift." And there was the

final reason she could never allow herself to consider any kind of committed relationship with Mark Shepherd, no matter what her heart and her body felt. She couldn't risk being left at the altar a second time.

The first time had almost destroyed her.

"There's no way around that one," Susan agreed. "He's just got to come around."

But Meredith knew he wouldn't.

KELSEY WAS JUST GETTING ready to slip through the fence on Friday, when she heard her name being called. Josie had already rounded the corner so she knew it wasn't her.

Turning slowly, afraid it might be the police, she just about started to cry with relief when she saw that it was Meredith.

"Hi," she said, happy to see her friend, but worried, too, that her mom would think she wasn't coming and leave without her.

"What'cha doing out here all alone?" Meredith asked. She had her denim bag today and was wearing it over her shoulder like she was on her way home.

"I'm waiting for Josie." She hated the lie. Almost as much as the drugs. "She forgot something."

Kenny said what they were doing was no big deal. Kelsey sure hoped he was right. More, she wished with all her might for a way out—a way to love her mother and have everything else be okay.

"Okay," Meredith said, glancing around. Kelsey wanted to make sure that she couldn't see her mom's car through the bushes, but she was afraid that would make Meredith peer over there, too. "You sure you're okay?"

"Yeah, I'm sure." Another lie. If she had to keep telling them, she hoped she'd get a lot better at it. As good as Kenny. She wondered if he'd ever gotten so scared he almost wet his pants. "What're you doing way out here?" she asked, trying to sound bored and normal.

"I was thinking about you…"

Kelsey froze, remembering Meredith's secret powers. Josie promised her they weren't true, but she'd never seen her teacher this far out in the field before and…

"And I saw you heading this way from the cafeteria door and followed you."

Oh, good. No powers. Oh, bad. "Why?"

"I was worried about you."

Kelsey tried her hardest to stand still and hope that Meredith wouldn't wait for Josie to get back before she left. "How come?" *Please, Mommy, don't leave.*

"I don't know," Meredith said, staring at her like Josie's mom looked at Josie sometimes when Josie had a problem and she was trying to help. "But if you're all right, then I guess I'll go."

"I am." Kelsey nodded, relieved. Mom should still be there. She hoped. 'Course now she had to wait until Meredith was back at the school before she dared climb over the fence and slip through the bushes.

"You're *sure* there's no one bothering you?" She looked toward the bushes and Kelsey started to sweat.

"Positive."

"Because you know, whatever might happen, if you talk to your dad or me or anyone else here at school, we can help. Teachers and parents are kind of like Santa Claus sometimes, the way they can get things for kids that kids don't believe they can get."

Kelsey nodded. She had to go.

"Even if there's an older kid from next door trying to bully you." She nodded toward the junior high and Kelsey's stomach started to hurt. Did Meredith know?

"There's no one."

Meredith wrapped her arms around her middle. "Promise me something."

"Sure." Kelsey's backpack was getting really heavy.

"If you ever do feel you're in trouble and you can't go to your dad, come to me, okay? I promise, no matter what, I'll help you."

Kelsey thought about running up and throwing both arms around Meredith and begging Meredith to take her away. But Mom was waiting. Loving her. Trusting Kelsey not to get any of them in trouble.

She'd feel horrible if she screwed up and her mother had to go to jail, even if Meredith could keep Kelsey out of it.

"I will," Kelsey finally said. And with one more look at her, Meredith walked across the field. Kelsey watched her the whole way and Meredith never turned back to look. She couldn't know or she wouldn't have left Kelsey alone to go with Mom and get more drugs.

Kelsey brushed away some stupid tears and climbed through the bush.

CHAPTER SEVENTEEN

"HI, IT'S MEREDITH."

"I know." Mark held the phone in the dark, the covers down at his waist, leaving his chest naked to the night air. He was hot as hell. "I recognized your voice."

He'd just gone to bed—at an embarrassingly early nine-thirty on a Saturday night. But Kelsey was asleep and there wasn't much else for him to do except fold laundry. He'd scrubbed all the floors during the morning cleaning session.

"Is this a bad time?"

"No." He'd been thinking about her.

"I was just calling to see if you'd like some time to yourself tomorrow. I have a hankering for Doris Day and cookies, and wondered if Kelsey would want to join me."

What a coincidence. "She asked me to call and see if you wanted to come over for breakfast." He semi-issued the invitation he'd just about talked himself out of. "We're going to try making crepes and she seems to think we need a woman around to supervise."

"Have you ever made them before?"

"No, but I make killer pancakes, and it can't be too much different."

She kind of laughed. "That's what I thought the first time I tried them. How is she, by the way?"

"Fine. I haven't seen any grades yet, but she was my little pal all day—followed me around chattering the whole time while I took care of the house. And she did her chores, and didn't grumble a bit when I lugged her off to the hardware store."

"I take it she doesn't like to shop there?"

"She hates it. Says it's 'boring enough to die.'" It felt good to be talking to Meredith—probably because she was older than nine.

"So how'd you get from hardware to crepes?"

"They learned about French food in school this week and one of the mothers had made some for the kids to try. Apparently they had powdered sugar."

"I make mine with fruit. She might not like the healthy kind."

"We already bought the strawberries." He lay back against the pillows. "So you'll come?"

"Sure, I spent the day gathering the information you asked for," she said. "I'll bring it along."

"Great."

They were working. And taking care of Kelsey. They were friends. He was okay with that.

THE FOLLOWING FRIDAY Kelsey was invited to a slumber party, and she and Josie were going to leave together from Josie's house. Mark finished up the last of the pending business in his office, made a couple more calls on Meredith's behalf and headed down the hall to see if she'd left for the day.

With her back to the room, she was wiping a wet

cloth along the blackboard. She had on one of her long cotton patchwork skirts with all the colors and a violet top that, when she lifted her arm, showed just a sliver of the skin at her waist.

Not that he really noticed.

Mark looked away. "You got plans this evening?"

"Oh!" She swung around. "Mark! You scared me."

"Sorry." He was. That had been dumb. Not like him at all. "Do you?"

"Have plans?" she asked, back at her desk, putting papers in a folder. "Just this." She held up the folder. "Grading papers."

Working. He had plans to do the same. Compiling the chart he planned to distribute to the members of the Bartlesville public school board. With Meredith's help—as well as help from a surprising number of parents of previous students—he had compiled much more data then he'd expected to have. And he was kind of anxious to see the results. For her sake.

Susan had predicted a percentage in the nineties, in terms of correct assumptions from Meredith. He'd be glad to get fifty—a fair guessing average.

"Did you need something?" She was staring at him.

"Just wondered if you wanted to get some dinner."

"Kelsey's gone."

"I know that, but how did you?"

"I've been making a point of seeing her every day, just saying hello. She mentioned the slumber party— seemed to be looking forward to it."

"It's only her second one." But he wasn't thinking about children's parties. "Why have you been specifi- cally looking for her?" The idea was pleasing—and made him uncomfortable at the same time. He'd spent part of the afternoon reading accounts of all the times she'd sensed troubled kids in the past four years. He didn't want to be one of her statistics.

"No reason." She turned for her bag. "I've grown fond of her."

She said she'd made a point of finding her. As though for a specific reason. He watched her load her bag, wanting to push.

She glanced up. "What?"

"Nothing." But he couldn't let it go. "You sure there's no other reason you're seeing my daughter?"

She shrugged and his mood dipped a bit. She could feel people's fears all she wanted, so long as she kept his daughter out of it.

"I was concerned about that nonfight she was in," she told him. "I just wanted to keep an eye out, to make sure no one was bullying her."

Mark relaxed. Felt like a damn fool. And smiled. "Thank you." He wasn't used to sharing Kelsey's care. It was nice.

"So how about dinner?" he said. She was coming toward him, her bag over her shoulder. It was bright pink with orange-and-green trim around the pockets. Only Meredith could pull off carrying a bag like that— wearing an outfit like that—and appear completely mature and professional at the same time.

"Okay. Your place or mine? I have eggs. Or chicken in the freezer."

"I thought we'd go out."

She gave him a sideways glance as they stepped out into the late afternoon sunshine. "Not a good idea."

"Why not? We're working, for heaven's sake," he said, thinking about the portfolio they had to discuss. "And there's nothing in policy that prevents us from being friends. Happens all the time."

"I wasn't talking about us, Shepherd," she said. "I'm just not up to the stares and whispers tonight."

"What stares and whispers?"

"The ones I've been getting every time I go out anywhere since Delilah White's program. The parents of my students know what's going on, or at least they're giving me the benefit of the doubt because they know me, but everyone else in town seems to think I'm a witch or something."

She'd pissed him off again. On her behalf, this time. People didn't have to believe her, but they damn sure should live and let live.

"I have steaks in the freezer. And a new propane tank on the grill."

"Sounds good to me."

BARBIE DIDN'T TAKE Kelsey to her house after she picked her up from school on Friday. She didn't want Don to hear what they were going to talk about. But she worried about it anyway. Don was good to her, the best. He understood her. She couldn't lose him. She wouldn't.

She just had to have her daughter, too.

"How about some chocolate ice cream?" They used to have ice cream as a family every night before bed. Mark had been a freak about the flavors. Kelsey would only eat chocolate.

"Okay," Kelsey said, her little hands resting on her

thighs. She used to look at those hands sometimes and wonder how she could possibly expect them to handle all the jobs she gave them. "But cookie dough would be better," she added.

Cookie dough? Resentment flared in Barbie's chest. *She* hadn't introduced her daughter to cookie dough ice cream. Someone else had done that. And bought the overalls Kelsey was wearing, too. And the little pink top. And put her hair in a ponytail.

Barbie reached for the meth pipe under her seat. And then pulled her hand back. Ice cream was just around the corner, and she liked ice cream.

"I saw my lawyer this week," she said, forcing herself to concentrate. "He showed me the paperwork for filing a motion for joint custody and he's going to do it as soon as I have the money for his retainer and the filing fees."

"What's joint custody?"

"You live primarily in one place, but your dad and I share all the decisions about your life."

Kelsey glanced over as Barbie pulled into the parking lot of the ice-cream store. "Do I get to see you, then?"

God, she loved this child. How could she ever have left her? Barbie almost started to cry at the thought. She'd lost so much that she'd never be able to regain.

"Mom?"

"Yes," Barbie said, thinking about that pipe. If she could just have a second to take care of business, life would be so good. "Yes, you will, honey, that's the whole idea."

Keep your mind on memories or activities that make

you happy, that was what Don told her to do when she was feeling low. But when the dark thoughts came, nothing felt good. Except maybe ice cream. And Kelsey. If she didn't feel so bad about how hard it all was. And complicated. If she didn't panic.

"You want a cup or a cone?" She pushed open her door, feeling for the bills in her back pocket. One step at a time.

"A cone." Kelsey followed her into the store.

Barbie hadn't had a say about those cute blue-and-pink tennis shoes, either.

"THERE'S ANOTHER KIND of custody," Barbie said, feeling better as, back in the driver's seat, she licked her scoop of chocolate ice cream. She really should do something about her hair. She wanted to be pretty when she was out with Kelsey and ran into her daughter's friends. She didn't want to embarrass her. Barbie remembered what it was like to be a kid.

"What kind?" Kelsey asked, and for a second there Barbie wasn't sure what she was talking about. And then remembered.

"Sole," she said. "It's where your father has you all the time and makes all the decisions, but I get to visit you." Her lawyer had suggested that as her beginning option. And then later put in for another change of custody to ask for joint. Barbie didn't have the money for two of these procedures.

"So I'd still get to see you," Kelsey said.

Barbie bit back a sharp retort. "Yes, but I'm your mother, Kelsey. I should be consulted about the choices being made for you."

Kelsey licked her ice cream. She didn't seem to get it. But then, she was only nine. Maybe Barbie was expecting too much. And she needed more. Her ice cream was a bother because if she didn't keep licking, it would drip. And Barbie didn't want to lick right then.

"If your father fights this, you might be asked some questions," Barbie said. "And we need to be very careful about what answers you give."

There were moral issues. Her lawyer had been very specific about them. If she exposed her daughter to drug users in her home, she would not be granted custody of any kind. No one understood that she and Don weren't really drug users. They were just getting by the best they could, coping with what life handed them.

"'Kay," Kelsey said, watching as a car pulled up next to them.

Barbie reached for the little girl's wrist as she raised her cone to her mouth. "This is important, Kelsey, or we won't get to see each other."

Kelsey stared at her. "Do I have to lie some more?"

"No!" Barbie hated the confusion of it all. "Lying is bad," she said. "We just have to be careful not to talk about Don's lab in the garage."

"The drugs, you mean." The child's voice was harder then Barbie had ever heard it.

"What do you mean? There aren't any drugs."

"Kenny told me."

Damn it! She was going to kill him. She'd told Don they couldn't trust a kid. But the money was good. And they needed the money. Don had just been accused of stealing from the company he'd been driving for and even though he'd said he hadn't been, they'd fired him. He'd get loads of work other places, even with another trucking company. He always did. But in the meantime, there were payments to make on his rig, and rent and court costs. And she had to get her hair done and…

"I won't say anything about the drugs," Kelsey said. "But you're going to stop them just as soon as all this gets done, right?"

Ohmygod. Harder and harder. "Right."

"'Kay, 'cause I really, really hate it."

Yeah, Barbie did, too.

MEREDITH AND MARK DID discuss the upcoming hearing over a glass of wine while the steaks were cooking. Meredith made sure of it. She felt safer that way. As long as they were working, she didn't have to worry about being there alone with him. Until Mark dropped his piece of news.

"What does the governing board want with *you?*" She walked around behind him to the other side of the grill, the light from the porch bathing the darkness that surrounded them. And then strode back. "It's because of me, isn't it? If you speak up for me, your job is in jeopardy."

"You don't know that."

"No, I don't." She slowed down. Took a sip of wine. "I mean, what can they get you for? There's nothing in the Due Process Act about dismissal for supporting an employee."

"No, but there is willful neglect of duty. If they perceive my duty to be supporting the governing board."

She stopped pacing, stared at the back of his head. "So they *are* after you because of me."

"I have no idea what they want," Mark said. "I just got the summons today, and it said nothing except that they had a matter to discuss with me. I'm meeting with the superintendent next week."

Before her hearing. Coincidence? Or design?

"I'm cooked if you aren't there."

He turned, fork in hand. "I'll be there."

His intention meant a lot. Probably more than it should. But she didn't kid herself into thinking that intention would automatically become action. Particularly if it came down to her job or his.

"Mark, this is serious. I won't have you losing your job because of me. I'll quit first. You're great at what you do."

He turned, his eyes clear and sure in the dim light. "So are you."

"The kids need you."

"And they don't need you?"

"You have a daughter to support."

He watched her for another long moment, and she drew in a deep breath. She had him, but took no satisfaction in the victory. The thought of facing the school board without him there was too much to contemplate at the moment.

Turning back to the steaks, he said, "I'll be there."

"I SHOULD GO." How many times had she said that to this man?

"You've got work to do, and so do I," Mark said, standing with her in his kitchen. They'd just finished the dishes. Or rather, she'd done them while he shut down the grill, put away the candles and wiped the table on the porch. Together but separate.

"Let me know when you get the graph done." Meredith pulled a strand of hair over her shoulder, ran her fingers down its length. And again. Two months ago, she wouldn't have doubted the answers he was going to find. Today, she was nervous even thinking about them. "Funny, but I never thought all those times you called me into your office would come in handy." The meetings, while not in her official employee file since he'd never issued formal warnings, had been noted in his own ledger. They'd used them to follow up on each incident.

And when he compiled the results, she might see that she was nothing but a fake with a fantastic imagination.

"Have fun grading papers."

The door was behind her. She just had to turn around. And it would be easier if he'd look away. Set her free.

"Mark, have you heard from Susan?" The random question surprised her. She hadn't had any conscious awareness of her friend.

"No." He didn't even blink.

Meredith wrapped her hair around her fingers. "How do you feel about that?"

"You sound like a psychologist."

Her eyes narrowed at the way he'd sidestepped the question. "How do you feel?" she repeated.

Hands in his pockets, Mark gave a little shake. "Not as bad as I should, which makes me feel bad." He grinned at her. "How's that for messed up?"

Her heart was beating fast again. And it had no reason to do so. Except that Mark was scaring her. Or she was scaring herself.

"Do you love her?" The question was less audible then she'd meant it to be. And the answer was none of her business.

"I thought I did."

Butterflies swarmed in her stomach. And lower. Accompanying the nervous energy that always seemed to be flowing just beneath her skin whenever he was around.

"Do you think about her a lot?" Was she pushing for Susan's sake?

"Not as much as I think about you."

She stopped breathing. Stared at him. Certain she'd misunderstood. If she hadn't, they had a major problem here.

"Because of the hearing," he added softly, taking a step closer, his gaze still fastened on her, compelling her not to look away. "And Kelsey."

She nodded. Yes. In terms of work. And his daughter. Mostly.

Reaching out a hand toward her, Mark untangled the hair from around her fist. "I've always been a short-hair man."

Her hand dropped. "I've always had long hair."

His lips came closer and she meant to move. Wanted to move. Was afraid to move in case she went in the wrong direction. As his head lowered, she knew she was running out of time. Her mouth parted. She tried to tell him stop.

And took his lips on hers instead. Ah. The feeling.

So good—like water in the desert. She didn't have to try so hard, fight so hard.

With a hand on the back of her head, Mark cradled her, kissing her slowly, his mouth moving gently against hers until she needed to cry with the fullness of it. And then the pressure increased, seeking from her, and she opened to him, not just her mouth, but herself, all of her. Sliding her arms around his waist, she clung to him, pulling herself against him and him against her. He filled her grasp, his sides and back a perfect match to the curve of her arms, his stomach and chest warm and solid against hers.

He was a part of her. Right for her.

Kissing her again and again, Mark left no space for doubts, fears, rationalizing.

He pressed his pelvis against hers and she reveled in his hardness, wanting to laugh, to cry, to strip off her clothes and be a part of him forever. Her whole body simmered with a desire so deep she knew she'd never recover. She was going to suffer the pangs of wanting him for the rest of her life.

And then she felt his butt beneath her hands. She'd wondered so many times what it would feel like. It was firm, muscled—and this was far too intimate. She was touching Mark Shepherd's butt. Her boss's butt.

Meredith pulled away. "I'm sorry," she breathed heavily. "So sorry. I should never have done that."

His eyes were only half-open, his breathing heavy, too. Somehow that made the situation worse. And better.

"I did it," he said. "It's not your fault."

A far cry from the man who was constantly chastising her for misbehavior.

Shaking, Meredith turned, pushed the hair from her face, grabbed her bag. "Does it matter whose fault it is?" she asked, fear snaking through her, replacing the sultriness of desire. "We're in trouble, Mark. We just broke the law."

He chuckled, but didn't look any happier than she was. "We didn't break the law."

"We broke policy!" She strode to the door and back, her hands around her middle. "How can I stand up there in front of those people in eleven days and convince them that I'm not guilty of moral turpitude, while I'm lying to them?"

"Hey." He grabbed her elbows, keeping distance between them as he stopped her. "Slow down, Meredith." He just stood there, holding on to her until she glanced up at him.

"It's okay," he said.

She searched his eyes for answers she didn't have. And wasn't sure he had, either.

"Policy states that we cannot be involved in a sexual relationship. We are not. One kiss is not a relationship."

"That was the second time."

"A sexual relationship requires a lot more than kissing, Ms. Foster."

He was right about that. "But we keep doing it and…"

"We won't."

"We said that last time and—"

With a finger to her lips, he said, "Meredith, it doesn't mean anything."

He wasn't attracted to her. Why had she thought

any differently? This was Mark. She drove him crazy. Pissed him off more often than not.

"It's just because we know we can't," he continued. "It's human nature, you know. You always want what you can't have and then the minute you have it, you don't want it anymore."

He didn't want her. Good. That was as it had to be. Anything else was insanity—and she was not in a position to appear anything but perfectly sane.

"You think that's what it is?" she asked. Please God, let that be all. I don't want him. I just want what I can't have. I can live with that. Recover.

"It's what it has to be."

"So we're safe," she said, needing to pull away from him so she could start getting over him. "I won't be lying when I tell the board that I've done nothing that contravenes policy."

"You won't be lying."

Meredith nodded. Tried to smile. And left.

CHAPTER EIGHTEEN

"KENNY, I can't do this anymore." Kelsey held out the little brown paper bag and wished she'd thrown it in the trash. Except that what if someone found it there and got hurt by it? Or figured out that she'd put it there? What if they found out it was drugs and did fingerprints like on television and knew it was hers?

"You have to," Kenny said. "If you don't, someone's going to tell on you and you'll be in big trouble."

She dug the toe of her tennis shoe into the dirt. "Who's going to tell, Kenny?" Only him. Mom wouldn't. And she wouldn't let Don, either. "Besides, if you do, you'll get in trouble, too."

"Not if I just tell that I've seen you over here."

With tears starting to come, even though she was trying really hard to hold them back, Kelsey stared up at him. "Would you do that to me?"

"I wouldn't wanna," he said, and looked down. "But don't you get it, Kelsey? You get to see your mom. I don't get to see my dad at all. We need this money."

Yeah, she'd thought about that for a long time and just didn't know what to do.

"It's not a big deal, I promise," he said now, taking hold of one of her hands. She liked how that felt, a hand a little bigger then hers but not as big as an adult's so that it swallowed hers up. "For drugs, the trouble you get in depends on how much you have. And there's not much here."

"How much?"

"Only an ounce," he said. "Just over a thousand dollars' worth, and my dad says they won't do anything to us for that except maybe put us in counseling. My dad says prosecution costs the state a lot of money and they have too many bigger cases to worry about."

She didn't know about any of that stuff. And she didn't want to know.

"My dad wouldn't lie to me, Kelsey, and he wouldn't get me in trouble. Just like your mom. She wouldn't do anything to hurt you. She loves you too much."

"Do you know my mom?"

He nodded. "I met her once with my dad, before they took me away from him."

She felt a little better inside. "Did you like her?"

"'Course," Kenny said, brushing his hair away from his face. "I wish she'd been my mom."

Wow. Kelsey smiled. She was pretty special. And lucky, too. She just had to be a big girl and help them all be happy again.

And quit worrying about going to jail.

"Do they whip you in jail?" she asked Kenny. She'd thought of it last week when Timmy Dorien had to go see her dad for spitting at Mrs. Melrose and her teacher told them that in the old days principals would take a strap to a student for such behavior.

"Nah," he said. "I've been there once, when my mom thought I stole a stereo and reported me to the police."

Staring at him, Kelsey asked, "Did you?" Kenny knew so much stuff.

"'Course not. My dad gave it to me, only I wasn't supposed to be seeing him."

"Were you in kid jail?"

"Juvenile detention is what they call it."

"How long were you there?"

"Just overnight. The judge believed me about my dad, especially because he came to court and told them he bought it and showed them the receipt."

"What was jail like?"

"Not so bad," he said, but she had a feeling he wasn't telling her the whole truth about that. "The worst part was taking a shower without doors and having to wear their stupid clothes and slipper things."

"You don't get shoes?" She squirmed her toes in her tennis shoes. She loved her shoes.

"Not where I was," he said. "But I got a cot. And my own locked-in place so I felt safe."

"Were there lots of bad kids there?" She was scaring herself, but she just kept thinking about jail and she had to know.

"I dunno,'" he said, shrugging. "Don't worry, you aren't going there," he told her. "Ever."

Kelsey really wanted to believe him.

"If I ever did go, would you come visit me?"

"If I could."

She was glad. She started to feel funny standing there, looking at him.

"Well, 'bye," she said quickly and scrambled through the bushes.

If only she could be in third grade again. Things were so much better then.

MEREDITH FOUGHT with herself all the way to Mark's office. When he'd called Saturday to tell her he had the chart done, she'd had more than twelve hours to castigate herself over their kiss the night before. Twelve hours to convince herself she couldn't see him outside school again.

When she'd insisted, they'd arranged to meet on Monday as soon as Macy left for the day. She'd waited in her classroom for Mark's call, doing every relaxation technique she could think of. Breathing. Picturing a serene place. Relaxing one body part at a time. Clearing her chakras.

She rounded the corner of her hallway, heading down his.

None of her tricks worked. She couldn't calm down. Kelsey was in trouble. She couldn't get away from the feeling. She'd known it at lunch today, though the little girl explained away her cranky mood by saying she'd been yelled at by her dad that morning for forgetting to feed Gilda.

That didn't sound like Mark. Or anything that would really upset Kelsey, either.

His office door was open. She could see the light spilling out into the hall.

Ever since school let out, Meredith had been consumed with an inexplicable fear. One panic attack after another. Over innocuous decisions such as what color ink to use for the spelling papers she still had to grade from Friday's test. And whether or not she should carry her bag with her to Mark's office or come back and get it afterward.

She recognized the sensations. Breathed her way

through them. And was worried sick. She needed to talk
to Mark. And knew that if she did, he wouldn't believe
her. He'd just get pissed off again.

He'd probably refuse to attend her hearing next
week.

He was behind his desk, typing something on the
computer. He'd worn a blue short-sleeved polo shirt
today. It looked good with his hair.

Which was in disarray.

"You ready?"

He barely glanced up. Rolled from the computer
stand to his desk. "Sure, come on in."

So much for the attention she'd paid to her sedate
navy suit and pumps—not to mention the time it had
taken to get the twist in her hair. He didn't even notice
the hands-off message she was sending.

"I made a couple of copies for you." He slid a folder
across the desk. Meredith picked it up. Sat.

"You might want to look at it." The humor in his
voice drew her out of herself enough to look at him. Grin
back.

And when he said, "It's okay, Meredith, really," her
heart did a little flip-flop.

She hadn't gotten over wanting forbidden things
yet, but she was working on it. Maybe by the next time
she saw him.

Flipping open the folder, Meredith searched first
for the bottom line. The graph was nice, the color-
coordinated lines a fine touch, but...

She read the numbers in the boxes at the bottom.
And to the far right, the percentage.

Ninety. She looked again. Took the time to do the

math in her head. And then peeked up at him. He was regarding her with a mixture of anticipation, resignation and discomfort.

"I was right ninety percent of the time."

"You just better hope that Tommy Barnett's not part of the ten percent."

She'd expect something like that from him—seeing only what was right in front of his nose. Tangible. "For my job, yes," she said. "But it would sure be better for Tommy if he was."

She had to call Susan. Ninety percent. She couldn't believe it. She wasn't crazy. Or insane. She wasn't kidding herself.

Of course, her friend would just say "I told you so."

And she couldn't wait to hear the words.

She glanced up at Mark again. Surely now that he had the numbers in front of him, he'd see that she was for real.

Ninety percent. What a relief. What a gift.

What a frightening, horrible thing. Kelsey's solemn face swam before her eyes. The little girl knew she was going to be hurt. Badly. She was confused, scared, alone.

But it wasn't too late. She was still safe.

"Where'd you go?" Mark asked, calling her attention back to him. His brows were drawn as he studied her.

"Nowhere."

"What were you thinking about just then?"

He'd seen the figures. Maybe the timing wasn't a mistake. Maybe now that he knew she was for real, he'd listen. Maybe they could help Kelsey before it was too late.

"I'm not sure I should tell you."

His frown deepened. "Why not?"

"Because you don't want to hear." *Do you? Are you ready to start trusting something besides what you can see and touch? Would you be willing to try, for Kelsey's sake?*

"Tell me anyway," he said, leaning forward with his hands crossed on top of his desk. "You could be wrong and I do want to hear. There's always that ten percent."

He was playing with her. He thought this was about them. She wasn't sure of that, but figured it was a good guess.

"I'm serious, Mark."

"So am I."

"I think Kelsey's in trouble."

The words dropped baldly into the after-school quiet.

"You *think* it?" His gaze was sharp.

"I *know* it."

He turned his chair a couple of inches until he was facing the computer more than her. "You were right, I don't want to hear it."

Meredith swallowed. Took a deep breath and made a quick appeal for the appropriate words. She'd come this far; she had to try.

"Mark, please don't shut me out. Not yet."

Punching a key on his computer he said nothing.

"I've had feelings for a while that she was struggling. But they'd come and go, and there was so much else getting in the way. Susan. You. The Barnett thing." She was talking too fast, but wasn't sure how much longer he'd sit there.

"In the past couple of weeks they've gotten much more consistent—and stronger. She's in trouble, Mark, I'd bet my life on it."

"And your job, too?" His gaze swung back to her, steely now. "Would you be willing to lose your job over it?"

"Absolutely."

That seemed to give him pause. For a minute. "You don't think I mean it—about your job."

"I know you do," she said quietly, feeling more calm than she had in a long time. She was doing the right thing. She knew that now. "I also know that Kelsey's involved in something dangerous. She doesn't want to be, but she's not capable of stopping."

He stood up. "I'm not going to listen to this." Hands on his hips, he swung around to face her. "I watch my daughter like a hawk. I have dinner with her every night. Spend every evening at home. I see her at school. And after school I have her being cared for by a mother I know would tell me if she suspected anything was amiss, if she didn't know where Kelsey was. Let me repeat, I know where my daughter is every second of every day."

She stood up, too. "Do you?"

"Of course I do."

"Are you sure?"

"Absolutely."

She'd never seen him this angry—his voice vibrated with it.

And then it struck her. He was afraid. Of the possibility that she might be right. Of her.

She looked him straight in the eye. "You're wrong."

Meredith didn't stick around to hear his reply.

"MARK, LET ME GET right to the point," Superintendent Daniels said as he took a seat in the armchair opposite Mark in his office Wednesday afternoon. He pulled up the sleeve of his gray suit jacket and glanced at his watch.

"The board would like to offer you the head principal's job at Harris Junior High. Chris Blakely has decided to take early retirement."

Mark let out a slow breath, switching mental gears completely. He wished now that he'd accepted the cup of coffee Daniel's secretary had offered him when he'd arrived.

"I don't know how long it's been since you've been over there, but we've made a lot of renovations," Daniels was saying.

Harris Junior High was a good twenty-minute drive from home. Twenty-five minutes from Lincoln. From Kelsey.

Head principal at a junior high was a promotion.

"...bought the lot next door and have added—" Daniels went on to give him enrollment statistics that were impressive. And a salary increase that was substantial.

"So what do you think?" Daniels asked, smiling as he sat back, one ankle resting on his knee.

"Why now?"

Daniels threw out an arm. "I told you, Blakely's retiring."

"Then I guess I should have said, why me?"

"You've got a great career ahead of you with us," Warren Daniels said, his expression growing more serious. "Junior high is the next logical step."

It was. But generally for someone who was a little older than Mark—a little more experienced.

"You can't tell me you haven't thought about the possibility."

"I had," Mark said. "Of course. But I was thinking more along the lines of moving when Kelsey did."

"That's in what, two years?"

He nodded.

"There might not be an opening then."

And they didn't want him to go anywhere else. He understood the logic. And hell, what was his problem? He'd been offered a great promotion sooner than he'd expected. What kind of man had a problem with that?

"Tell me this doesn't have anything to do with Larry Barnett." Meredith had mentioned the coincidence in timing and damn it, he couldn't get her words out of his head. And not just the ones about this appointment.

"We were going to make the offer anyway, but when Larry suggested to me over lunch last week that he thought it would be better to make the offer now, get you away from the Foster mess before it taints your career, I thought he made good sense."

Of course he did. Larry Barnett was a master debater, convincer of juries, smooth talker. Was there anyone in this city that the man did not know?

"We're offering you a way out," Daniels said. "If you take the offer, we can have you moved by early next week, give you a few weeks with Blakely before school's out for the summer and he retires."

"Who'll cover my position?"

Daniels named a couple of possibilities. "We'll put it out for applications."

"Shouldn't both positions be posted?"

"Technically," Daniels said. "We'll post it, take apps, but yours will be one of them and since you'll be over there, helping Blakely, you'll be the obvious choice."

When one had a will, and power, there was always a way.

"I'd like a couple of days to think about it."

Nodding, Daniels didn't pressure Mark any further.

"How ARE YOU EVER going to be happy with me if you won't go to the bathroom in my house or eat any of my food?"

Kelsey had a headache. She was tired, from bad dreams, and scared. She'd told Josie about the drugs when they went to the slumber party. She'd had a nightmare and Josie had woken her up because she'd been crying in her sleep and she'd just blurted it all out. Josie told Kelsey it was bad and she had to stop, and every day she worried that Josie was going to tell her mom—or worse, quit being her friend. Kelsey had broken her word to her own mother. She was sneaking around behind her father's back. She didn't mean to do any of it, but it didn't seem to stop.

"How will the judge know I can provide for you, if you don't give me a chance to show him?" Mom was still talking about food.

Kelsey couldn't figure out how the judge was going to see her eating a snack at her mom's, anyway. "I'll eat."

"Every time I offer you a snack you say no."

The living room was cleaner, so you could see the rips in things easier. But at least there wasn't any food trash and junk like that. "'Cause it's always so close to dinner."

Mom didn't say anything, just flipped on the television and changed stations a lot. Kelsey thought about laying her head down on her mother's shoulder and taking a nap.

But Don was in the garage. She didn't think she should sleep with him there.

There was news on about a fire someplace near Tulsa. And then a woman crying about what her husband did to her. Mom didn't say anything for a long time and Kelsey got scared that she was mad.

She counted the throbs in her head. "I will next time I come here, I promise."

"Will what?" Her mom glanced over at her, not mad but not happy, either.

"Have a snack. And go to the bathroom, if I have to." Like she did right now.

The worry left her mom's eyes. She'd had her hair done, and even though it wasn't like before it was pretty. Mom was pretty today.

"What would you like?" she asked. "We can make a list and when I go to the grocery, I'll buy it all so you can have choices when you come." She smiled the smile that always made Kelsey feel good and warm inside. "I'd love to shop for you again, sweetie, and have food in my cupboards for you. I've missed it so much."

"Me, too," Kelsey said, too tired to watch every word. "I have to go with Daddy every week and help decide stuff and it's hard to know what we should have for dinner so many days away. I'm just a kid. I shouldn't have to decide what I want to eat some other day. Mostly I just know what I want *that* day."

"That's right, you shouldn't." Mom's words were loud. She pulled Kelsey over, holding her head against her shoulder. "Poor baby. We'll take care of all that soon," she said. "Then you can just be a kid again."

Being taken care of was good.

CHAPTER NINETEEN

THE SPECIAL HEARING of the Bartlesville school board was being held in the city council meeting room. Meredith arrived alone—dressed in black, a suit with a narrow knee-length skirt, and power red, her silk blouse—and took a seat on one of the wooden pews. Members of the board were filing in, sitting up on a dais in front, with the president standing behind the podium in the middle. She set her bag down on the floor, adjusted a couple of pins in her hair, and waited.

Mark came in, taking a seat in the front row. She'd never seen him in a suit and tie before. He looked impressive—and distant. Turning, he saw her a few rows behind him. Nodded. And turned back.

They hadn't spoken since she'd walked out of his office the week before. Kelsey hadn't been all that forthcoming, either. Because her father had warned her off or because the trouble was escalating, Meredith didn't know.

More people filed in. Some looked at her. Many didn't. A few greeted her effusively. No one sat with her.

She wished she hadn't told Susan not to come. Her friend had rounds that evening, but she had offered to get someone to cover for her.

"Ladies and gentlemen, let's get started, shall we?" Meredith's heart grew tight in her chest, and her skin was covered with sweat. The walls of the small room closed in around her, imprisoning her like a criminal.

And someone slid in close beside her. And then, on the other side, someone else.

"Susan?" Thank God her friend hadn't listened to her. And... "Mom?" She couldn't believe it when the familiar face beamed back at her. Dressed in a forest-green suit with matching pumps, her mom looked every bit the Phillips Petroleum executive she'd once been.

Squeezing her hand, Evelyn Foster whispered, "You didn't think we were going to let you do this alone, did you?"

She hadn't been thinking all that well lately. With her chin high and tears brimming in her eyes, she listened as the proceedings against her began.

AT FIRST the testimonies were much the same as those in the newspaper, television and radio events. Barnett's side. Her side. People represented both—some she knew, some she didn't. If not for her mother and Susan holding her hands, she didn't think she could have sat there, listening, feeling the emotions being sent in her direction. It was too much, too overwhelming.

Too draining and damaging. She wanted to go home, crawl into bed and stay there.

Barnett's experts were there. She hadn't seen them and supposed they must have come in late. They pretty much repeated what they'd said on Delilah White's radio show. Almost as if they'd been coached. Not that she'd ever be able to prove as much.

Susan let go of her hand. She wasn't surprised. She'd have let go, too. "I'd like to speak." Susan's words registered at the same time that her friend rose and went forward to the microphone that had been set up for the public—less so that those in the room could hear than to ensure that any comments would be on the official transcript of the meeting.

"My name is Susan Gardner," she said, looking impressive in her sleek black pinstriped pantsuit, her hair and makeup as chic as always. "I'm a physician on staff at Jane Phillips Medical Center. My life's work is in the science field. I've taken all the classes, participated in all the labs. I rely every day on what the test tubes and microscopes show us. I could prevent or cause deafness with one movement of my scalpel. I only act when I can clearly see the direction to take."

Members of the board were nodding, eyes open, receptive.

"You're going to be fine," her mother whispered. Meredith nodded. Of course, "fine" didn't mean you had a job.

"And what I can tell you, ladies and gentlemen of the board, is this. If I had to rely solely on my own cognitive skills, if any of my peers had to, we'd all be dead long before our time. Do you know what we, the physicians, the scientists, were talking about at lunch today? The presence of miracles in our work. The intangibles that we cannot predict, control, see, that save lives when we can't. The miracles wouldn't happen without our hands, our learning. But neither would they happen if that was *all* we had. Whether a heart beats or it doesn't is not something we can necessarily predict. It's not something we can control. We do what we can, we hope, we wait. And we cheer when the outcome is positive."

A cough in the room sounded sharply, testimony to the silence that had fallen. "I've known Meredith Foster for more than fifteen years," Susan said softly, leaning down to speak directly into the microphone. "And I'd trust her with my life. The woman is no different than any of us. And she uses nothing we don't have. You hear about women's intuition all the time. Well, men have it, too. They use it every time they listen to that little voice in their heads that warns them of danger or nags them to do something they've thought of putting off. Meredith's gift to all of us is the fact that, even if most of us ignore that voice within us, she listens to hers. And most particularly with children, the voice is loud and clear. She's more aware of others than we are because she cares enough to listen. Surely you won't penalize a person for being less selfish than you are."

It felt as if the whole room sighed when Susan sat down. Except for Meredith. She was biting her lower lip, holding back the tears.

She didn't say anything. She couldn't. But she would never forget what Susan had just done for her—or the message that she'd sent. No matter what happened, Meredith had just won.

AN HOUR AND A HALF into the hearing, Mark could sit still no longer. "I have something to say."

The president of the school board recognized him. Called on him by name, a frown on his face. Mark still hadn't given them an answer regarding the job offer. He hadn't felt that any decision would be fair until after this hearing. He hadn't known whether he'd speak or— if he did—what he'd say. And whether the board would still want him. He'd figured he'd save them the trouble of having to withdraw the offer by not accepting it.

Daniels, who'd seemed more impressed than disappointed by his non-answer, had granted him another week to make up his mind.

Avoiding even a glance at the bench where Meredith and Susan sat with a slender older woman who wore her graying hair in a bun, Mark stepped up to the microphone. He'd left Kelsey with a teenage sitter and was anxious to get back to her.

"Ladies and gentlemen." He made eye contact with each one of them before continuing. "I have been Ms. Foster's immediate supervisor for four years. I haven't always agreed with her, nor do I believe in psychic phenomena. I'm not here to discuss esoterics, philosophy or science. I want to tell you about a teacher."

He hadn't rehearsed. He'd pretty much decided not to speak at all, suspecting that, since Meredith's most recent intuition involved his daughter and he knew she was wrong, he'd hurt her more than he'd help her. Still, he opened his mouth and the words came.

"I delivered to each of you a folder containing confidential information regarding this employee's accomplishments. It would also have included any warnings and disciplinary actions had there been any. The fact that there aren't any is significant. If you were to inspect the files of most of my employees, you would see at least one suggestion for improvement in their work. I believe in managing with an eye to greater accomplishments, which means to me that no matter how good someone is, there is always room for improvement. It is my job to find that room and to help my employees see it in themselves.

"I tried to do so with Ms. Foster. But how do you improve on scores like hers? Every avenue I have for review, parental dissatisfaction, barring this one episode, student test scores, disciplinary problems in the classroom, tardiness, lesson-plan schedules—she receives top scores over and over and over again. What she believes, how she perceives, what instincts she uses or doesn't use, all seem irrelevant to me in this discussion. Her spiritual life is not an issue. Her intelligence is not in question. To us, she is a teacher and in four years' time, she has fulfilled the requirements of her job above expectation and beyond reproach. Ladies and gentlemen, what you see before you is as close to a perfect teacher as I've ever met."

Making eye contact with no one, Mark spun around and returned to his seat.

Half an hour later, Superintendent Daniels stepped up to the microphone.

"Ladies and gentlemen." He looked across the front of the room, and then turned and included the people on both sides. "I think we all know that this is a very delicate, very difficult decision to make. One that has been deliberated over a period of many weeks, and with heavy hearts. There is much to consider, much information to process and I can assure you, firsthand, that the members of this board before you have suffered a great deal as they've considered all of the information presented tonight and previously."

Cut the crap and get to the point, Mark thought. He could feel Meredith behind him. Was impressed as hell that she'd remained in the room. He didn't think he could have done so.

And more than that, he was made uncomfortable by the conviction that kept her strong. She didn't waver. Ever. He'd never met anyone like her.

He didn't know how the board was going to vote— he suspected that it would not be in Meredith's favor. What he did know was that they'd all put her through enough. The woman deserved resolution. She deserved peace.

"I think the one thing that no one has mentioned here, the one thing we must all consider is the elephant on the table before us, the big ugly thing that we are not acknowledging, but that is as real as all of us sitting in this room. Fear."

He turned again and it seemed to Mark that he looked him right in the eye before he realized that Daniels was making eye contact with as many people as he could.

"Let's face it," Daniels said, sounding like a good old boy. "We all fear the idea of someone knowing our innermost secrets. We fear the idea of anyone having the ability to know them without our telling them."

From what Mark could tell, every eye in the room was trained on the man.

"Even if Meredith Foster does not have this ability, even if she cannot know what we feel, the fact that she believes she does gives life to the possibility, and to living in constant fear when we're around her."

Mark could relate. He hated it. But he could relate.

"We are all here, without fail, to serve the children of this community. Our children have been made aware of Ms. Foster's beliefs. They know that she goes to parents when she suspects something wrong with a child. And if we, as adults with full faculties of rationalization fear her, can you imagine how the children in her care must feel? Or could grow to feel?"

The room was silent. Mark was suffocating. And burning with a need to grab Meredith and run.

"This is our bottom line, ladies and gentlemen. We are not God, or spiritual advisors, or scientists, or doctors. We are educators and our goal is to provide our children with the best education possible. The question is, will they be able to continue to open their hearts and minds and trust this woman whom they may also fear?"

Mark remembered Kelsey's reaction when she'd first heard about Meredith's trouble with Larry Barnett. She'd been outraged. Ready to do battle for Meredith Foster. Until her friends had gotten to her and filled her head with confusion, based on the opinions of their parents who didn't know Meredith. Or what they were talking about. And still, while Kelsey had played the social games and appeared to go with the crowd so she'd be accepted, the second she'd thought Meredith needed a friend, she'd insisted on being that friend.

His daughter was a very smart little girl. And this time, it wasn't a trait she got from him.

A member of the board called for a vote. Roll was called. Mark sat straight and tall, when all around him he felt the tension. He wished he could see Meredith— that he'd had the courage to sit beside her.

The board did not call for dismissal—a token gift. They voted instead for non-reemployment, which for all intents and purposes, was the same thing.

He didn't wait for the official words to conclude. He stood, needing to get to Meredith immediately.

But he was too late. The bench where she'd been sitting was empty. Meredith was gone.

"HOW SURE ARE YOU?"

Meredith peered frantically between her mother and Susan, dread weighing so heavily within her that she could barely stand in the hallway outside the board room.

"Ninety-five percent," she said, finding it so hard to breathe that the words were only a whisper. "I wasn't even thinking about her. I was sitting there listening to the trial and suddenly it didn't even matter. It's like she was calling out to me. Me, specifically. That's never happened before."

She could feel her mother and Susan exchange glances.

"I'm not crazy," she whispered. "Nor am I buckling under stress."

"Who said you were?" her mother asked. "I've been living with your uniqueness your whole life, Meredith Ann Foster. I recognize the signs."

"Me, too," Susan said softly.

That was all the encouragement she needed. "Go get Mark."

"WHAT'S GOING ON?" Meredith didn't know how much time had passed, but it was too long.

People were streaming along the hallway behind Mark, staring at her. "Is the meeting over?"

"Yes," her mother said. "Just ended."

"What's up?" Mark asked again, loosening his tie. She could feel him staring at her. And in spite of the past week, in spite of his anger and disbelief, she needed his strength if she was going to get through this.

Kelsey needed his cooperation.

She looked him straight in the eye. "Kelsey's in danger."

"What?" he said, glancing away from her to take in her mother and Susan. "You're upset about the vote, I understand that, but you can appeal. We will appeal. You have ten days to file a petition for a trial in Washington County District Court. This isn't over."

"Mark," Meredith said, bending over against the pain in her stomach. "Kelsey's in danger!"

She could feel heads turn in her direction and they didn't matter at all. Nothing mattered but the little girl calling out to her.

Mark's gaze met hers, and she calmed. "Kelsey's at home with a sitter," he said. "She's fine."

Shaking her head, Meredith tersely said, "Call." And held her stomach while Mark pulled out his cell phone and did so.

Her mother was flying back to Florida first thing the next morning. She had an appointment with her primary care physician to confirm the liver results. Meredith wanted to go home with her. To be cradled in her mother's arms.

She could hear Mark on the phone, composed at first, asking the sitter to double-check Kelsey's room and make sure she was asleep. And then more caustically demanding that she check the bathroom, if the little girl wasn't in her bed.

Two minutes later he hung up the phone, his face ashen.

"She's gone."

MARK NEEDED TO GET out of there fast. To beat up everyone in his path. He needed to scream. And to cry. Feeling more helpless than he'd ever felt in his entire life, he stood in the hallway of the city building and looked at Meredith Foster.

"Where is she?"

"I don't know."

"What do you mean you don't know?"

He wanted to grab her by the shoulders and shake her senseless. And he wanted to hold on to her until his sanity returned. His daughter, his life's blood, was missing.

Meredith had warned him.

She was his salvation. It made no sense.

Almost doubled over, leaning against the wall, Meredith grabbed his hand.

"Help me." His plea was all he had left.

"We have to find Josie," she said. "Do you know where she lives?"

"Yes, of course." Mark rattled off the address.

"Come on, I'll drive you," Evelyn said.

"And I'll go to Mark's house, in case there's any word there," Susan added. "I'll also phone the police."

"Have them meet us at Josie's house," Meredith called as she ran with Mark and her mother out the door.

"We'll be there in no time, Mark," Meredith said as

they climbed into the back of her car. Her mother already had the keys in the ignition.

"Does she know where she's going?"

"I lived here for thirty years, young man," Evelyn said. "I know these roads better than you do."

"Who is she?" Mark asked Meredith, not letting go of her hand even when she had to use it to put on her seat belt.

"My mother."

At another time, Mark might have felt uncomfortable knowing that, ashamed even. At the moment he just felt grateful to have two Foster women in his camp.

"Nice to meet you, ma'am," he said.

"You, too, son," Evelyn replied. "Now just relax. That girl of mine was put on this earth for situations like this. She'll find your little girl in time. You just wait and see."

Mark would give half his life to have that kind of faith. But for now he was going to get by on the coat-tails of a woman who should hate him for not believing in her daughter, but who was too busy helping him to do so.

Meredith groaned as her mother took another sharp corner. She wasn't sure if she was going to be ill or pass out. At the moment, she'd settle for either if it would relieve some of the pain in her stomach.

"She's sick, Mark," she said, her throat raw.

"Sick how?"

"I don't know." She hated the blank places, the missing pieces. She could feel the urgency, but couldn't get them there. "It feels like alcohol, drugs maybe. Her head is spinning. And she's scared." Meredith started to cry. "She's so scared I can barely stand it."

"Hold on, baby," Evelyn said from the front seat. "Mark, put your arms around her, hold her, give her what comfort you can."

Mark did. And Meredith's nerves settled again. The man reached her like no one else ever had. For now, she was grateful.

"WHY JOSIE?" Mark asked when Meredith's breathing slowed to a more normal pace.

"She seems to be thinking about her," she said. Even to herself, she sounded insane.

Mark didn't say a word. Just continued to hold her close, breathing with her, two hearts beating side by side.

JOSIE WAS ALREADY in bed when they arrived.

"It's a school night," her mother said, fear in her eyes as she looked at the school principal in her doorway.

The police arrived just as Josie's father came to the door wanting to know what was going on. And within two minutes Josie was standing before them in her yellow flowered nightgown, wide-eyed and obviously scared out of her wits.

"I d-d-don't kn-kn-know anything," she said, rubbing her eyes.

"Josephine Marie, if you do not start telling these people everything you know within the next five seconds you will be grounded for the rest of your life," Josie's father said, obviously overwrought.

Meredith knelt down in front of the child.

"Josie, loyalty is one of the most important things in life, but sometimes, to be loyal, you have to look like you're being disloyal," she said, her voice even. She didn't even question her sudden tranquility. "Kelsey's trying her best, Josie, but she's in over her head right now and she could be dying. She needs your help."

Josie wanted to believe her. Meredith could see it in the little girl's eyes. "She knows you're the only one who can help us find her," Meredith said. "Please don't let her down now."

"I…"

"Please, honey, she's not going to get into trouble. She *is* in trouble."

"She's with her mother."

CHAPTER TWENTY

MARK'S KNEES WEAKENED and it took everything he had to remain standing.

"What did she say?" he asked Evelyn.

"She's with her mother. Your wife?"

"Ex-wife."

"Where does your wife live, sir?" one of the two police officers asked.

"I have no idea. I haven't seen or heard from her since the divorce was final three years ago. I thought she'd left town long ago."

"She came to school right after Christmas," Josie said with a sniffle. "Me and Kelse were walking home from school and this woman hissed at us from the bushes. I wanted to run and so did Kelsey, but then she stopped and got all funny and started to cry. Her mom had come to find her."

"Since *January?*" Mark yelped. He was waiting to wake up from this nightmare, already vowing never to sleep again.

Josie nodded, looking only at Meredith as she spoke. "She said she's been trying to get back to Kelsey ever since she left. That she's missed her as much as Kelsey missed her mom. She's got a lawyer and everything and told Kelsey that she's going to have joint custody soon."

Mark absolutely could not believe anything he was hearing.

"So you think her mother kidnapped her?" the second police officer asked.

"No," Josie said, her gaze locked on Meredith. "Her mom came to school today and told Kelsey she had to come over tonight so she could take something special to Kenny. There's drugs," she whispered.

Mark couldn't just stand there anymore. Kneeling down next to Meredith, he touched his shoulder to hers, looking for strength. Joining with her.

"What kind of drugs?" he asked, working with the child, something he did instinctively. This wasn't about him. It was about the children. He wasn't going to let Kelsey down.

"I dunno," Josie said. "But they made it there in the garage and Kelsey had to take it to a boy at the junior high. His name's Kenny."

Mark almost vomited on the spot. His sweet baby girl delivering drugs? If he ever found Barbie he was going to kill her with his bare hands.

"My ex-wife had a drug problem," he said to the cops behind him. "She was addicted to methamphetamine."

"Do you know where Kelsey's mother lives?" Cop number one asked.

Josie looked at Mark. "I don't know the exact house, Mr. Shepherd, but it's on that street out by the old milk farm, you know with the gas station on the corner that has all the green lights in the window? Kelsey went to the bathroom there once when she had to go really bad.

She wouldn't ever go at that house. She doesn't like Don, the guy who lives there with her mother."

Mark's head swam. He was seeing stars. And Meredith's hand as she touched his face.

"Let's go," she said.

"I know the neighborhood," he heard cop number two say. "There are only eight houses on the block." And then to Evelyn, "Follow us, ma'am, we'll lead you in. But once we get there—" he turned to Mark and Meredith "—you'll need to wait outside in the car. We have no idea what we're in for."

"Kelsey will want her father," Meredith said.

"It's okay." Mark put an arm around her, leaning on her as much as guiding her. "I'm not leaving my daughter's life to amateurs. There's no telling what Barbie would do if she saw me. Or Kelsey, either for that matter."

He'd wait in the car. But it would be the hardest thing he'd ever done.

MEREDITH CRIED most of the way across town, and then had to fight unconsciousness. "She's getting worse," she moaned, putting her head on Mark's shoulder. "She needs to lie down."

"Goddammit, hurry," Mark bit out beneath his breath.

Meredith wished she could help him. She put a hand on his leg, but that was all she could do.

"Hold on," Evelyn said from the front seat, and Meredith started to cry again. She loved her mother so much.

The car stopped and Meredith could hardly breathe. She wasn't sure she was going to make it. Wondered what would happen if she died right then in the back seat of her own car with her mother at the wheel.

"They're at the second house," Evelyn said quietly.

"They're running to the third," Mark added, his voice urgent. "Do you think they found something out?"

Meredith's heart started to beat faster, pumping blood and air through her body.

"Most likely."

She had to hold on.

"They're going in."

Please, God, Meredith begged, *find me fast.* And then she passed out.

SUSAN MET THEM at the hospital and stood by while the team of emergency doctors worked on Kelsey. Mark, pacing with Evelyn and Meredith, kept an eye on the hallway where they'd disappeared with his daughter and waited for Susan to come out and report to them.

"How you doing?" he heard Evelyn ask Meredith and he turned to take inventory of her color. Her cheeks were rosy again—instead of the alarming white they'd been when he'd helped her in, conscious but sick to her stomach and lethargic.

"Good," she said, and Mark's heart jumped when she smiled. "Feeling more and more like myself."

He squeezed her hand. "You scared the hell out of me."

"Me, too."

"Has that ever happened before?"

"Never."

Even now that she was more herself, she held his hand.

"She's been sick before, needed to lie down to calm herself, but it's never taken control that strongly." Evelyn, as Mark had just discovered, was a scientist. She'd held an impressive position with the oil company that was Bartlesville's claim to fame.

Pulling the knot in his tie down to midchest, he looked from one to the other of the strongest women he'd ever known, and knew the past two hours, past two months, had changed him. Irrevocably.

"Is she going to be all right?" he asked Meredith.

She peered up at him, her eyes widening. "You want to know what I feel or what I think?"

"I want to know what you know."

"She's going to be fine. Physically, at least. We have some work ahead of us in the emotional department."

"How sure are you on that?" Evelyn asked.

"Ninety."

Mark frowned, feeling like a novice. "What does that mean?"

"Anything over sixty on Meredith's confidence scale has at least some truth to it," Evelyn said. "Fifty or less, she thinks it, but she doesn't feel anything at all one way or the other."

"So ninety's good."

Meredith was staring at him, tears brimming in her eyes. "Yes, very good," she said. Mark knew that she wasn't just speaking about his daughter, but any other conversation would have to wait for another time.

Which was fine by him.

Right now he just wanted to be. He was sitting in a hospital emergency room, waiting while his daughter's stomach was pumped and hoping that her blood levels and vital signs would return to normal, and felt peaceful in a way he never had before.

MEREDITH CALLED for a substitute teacher on Wednesday morning before taking her mother to airport and heading over to the hospital to sit with Kelsey. When they'd admitted the little girl, semiconscious and disoriented, Mark had insisted on staying with her. Now Meredith was going to relieve him so he could go home and shower.

He was standing in the hallway, his trousers and long-sleeved white shirt wrinkled. He'd removed his jacket and tie sometime since she'd last seen him.

"They're in with her," he said, coming to meet her. "She might get to come home this morning. They found iodine, pseudo—which comes from cold medicine—phosphorus, lantern fuel and lye in her stomach." His eyes, when he looked at her, brimmed with a pain she could only begin to understand.

"The makings of meth."

"Apparently in the final stages, the mixture is placed in a two-liter pop bottle. Barbie told Kelsey to help herself to what was in the fridge. She'd said she made lemonade, but Kelsey couldn't find anything yellow except in the bottle. She thought her mom had stored the lemonade there because she's poor and didn't have a proper pitcher. Thank God the stuff tasted so bad she didn't drink more of it."

"How's she been?"

"Quiet. Answering questions, but that's all. She slept

all night and has been in and out this morning. She's alert right now."

"And they don't foresee any residual damage?"

He shook his head, sighed, looking exhausted beyond endurance. "Like you said, she's going to need counseling, a lot of love and time, but physically they expect a complete recovery almost immediately."

An orderly passed with a gurney. Meredith leaned back against the wall out of the way, watching the door to Kelsey's room. "So why was the place cleaned out when we got there except for Kelsey unconscious on the floor?" Meredith shivered, feeling it all again.

"I talked to Detective Armes this morning. He thinks that when Barbie realized what had happened, she got scared and split."

"And left her daughter there to die?"

"Armes thinks Barbie thought there was no way to save Kelsey. So she saved herself." The bitterness in his voice was to be expected. Meredith figured he had a long road of emotional healing ahead of him, too.

"Do they have any leads on her?"

He shook his head. "They found an old car that matches the description of the one she was driving in a junkyard fifty miles out of town. The license plate was gone, but they're sure it was hers. She's probably across the state line, possibly on her way to Mexico. They figure they're going west."

"But they'll keep looking."

"For a time, at least. It was a small-time operation. The big dealers in this part of the country use what's been termed the Nazi method of producing meth since pseudo is so closely regulated. This guy used cold medicine, which is usually just seen out west."

"Which is why they think they're heading that way?"

Mark shrugged. "Apparently. They think he's from there, or at least has close ties in the area."

Adjusting the denim bag on her shoulder, Meredith crossed her arms. She'd worn her beaded jeans this morning because they were Kelsey's favorite. She wished now she'd also worn a sweater.

"What about his rig out back?"

"He was in the process of buying it. Got behind on his payments and owed more on it than it's worth. Ames thinks he's hoping the bank will repossess the truck and cut their losses."

"Charming folks." And Kelsey had been over there, with them, every Friday for the past four months. She should have known, done more sooner.

"Kenny's father, James, is nowhere to be found. The boy's with his mother, who was devastated to learn that Kenny's father had been seeing him again. They're both being scheduled for counseling. Ames believes Kenny was as much a pawn in all this as Kelsey was."

"It's a shame it doesn't take some kind of certification to become a parent," Meredith said. "To their kids they're God."

"Kelsey's going to be fine, and that's the most important thing," Mark said, almost as if he could read her mind. His chin was stiff and she knew it was taking all he had to maintain control.

Bending forward, closer to his ear, she said, "Beat your pillow to a pulp when you go home to shower."

"What on earth for?"

"They're easy to replace. And you don't go to jail for it."

He stared at her and slowly started to smile. "You are too much," he said.

"Yeah, I know, but I'm still nice to have around."

Mark brushed the hair back from her face and ran his fingers down to the bottom of the strand. "That's an understatement," he said.

Kelsey's doctor, coming from the little girl's room, interrupted, saving Meredith from throwing her arms around her soon-to-be ex-boss.

"YOU WANT A GLASS of wine?"

She should go. Again. They'd had dinner. Kelsey was asleep in her own bed with Gilda by her side.

Reaching for her bag, Meredith glanced at Mark, standing in the archway to the living room, wine bottle and two glasses in hand, and let her arm drop.

"Yeah." It had been a long two days, getting Kelsey home, Meredith going back to work on Thursday to face the sympathies of her coworkers and worries from many of her students. By voting non-reemployment instead of dismissal, the school board had agreed to let her finish out the year. She wasn't sure that had been a kind move—for anyone.

"Was today any easier than yesterday?" he asked, handing her a filled goblet.

"About the same." He sat down next to her on the

couch, something he'd never done before. Meredith's nerves responded with a leap. "Monday should be better."

"I'll be back then."

He was close and it felt good. Too good. While he was only her boss for another month or two, they were far too different to ever coexist peacefully.

"Kelsey still isn't saying much about her mother," she said, reminding herself why she was there. And why she wasn't.

They'd all been through so much. Kelsey needed her. And she needed Kelsey, too. Mark had a lot of emotional reparation to oversee—with himself and his daughter. None of them needed to deal with the complications of a doomed sexual attraction.

"She starts counseling next week."

Sipping wine, Meredith stared at the golden liquid in her glass, getting lost in the sparkle. And then set it on the table. "She blames herself."

"I was afraid of that."

"She's piled so much on her own shoulders right now, it's amazing she can even stand up."

"Because she drank something she thought was lemonade?"

"Because she exposed her mother's drug dealings, she took drugs herself, she let that boy Kenny down, getting him and his father in trouble. She let you down. She let herself down."

"She's the victim of a sick woman." Mark's jaw was tight again.

Meredith pulled a throw pillow from the other end of the couch where she'd tossed it when she sat down and passed it to him.

Taking it, Mark didn't say a word. Just squeezed until his knuckles were white.

She watched him as long as she could, and then reached over, covering his fist with her hand. "She's young, Mark. Most of her life has been secure, solid and full of love. She'll recover."

He sipped wine, then set his glass on the table beside him with careful precision. Nodded.

"I'm not so sure about you," she added softly, looking him in the eye.

He looked back and Meredith took a deep breath. The territory was different when they connected. Dangerous.

"You can't analyze this one, Mark," she told him. "Sometimes events just happen in life and we'll never know why."

"I know why—"

"Do you?" she interrupted, understanding the hardness that came over him, but hating it anyway. "Do you know why one person is battered by emotion and another has more control? You know all about a mother's love that was so desperate it convinced itself that everything was in the best interests of the child? And what about a child's love? How do you explain all the uncomfortable and frightening events Kelsey put up with just to see her mother? How do you explain loyalty? Yours to Susan, to your job, to yourself. Mine to my best friend, my job, myself and Kelsey. Kelsey's loyalty, which fell between her mother and her father and what she knew was right…"

His grin was slow in coming and more wry than humorous. "You're right, I *don't* know why."

"And that's okay."

"Is it?" His eyes searched hers. She told herself to turn her head. Safety came in looking away. And she needed to be safe. At least for a while.

"Yes."

His eyes darkened. "What's okay about it?"

"It's trust in the deepest sense," she said, surprised by how right it felt to be having this conversation with him. A week ago, she'd never have dared—recognizing the lost cause it would have been. "The not knowing."

She felt his hand slide against her thigh, taking hers.

"It's like Truman," she said, referring to the movie they'd seen together. "His only way out was to trust his heart because everything—every single bit of external stimulation, everything tangible, every person he knew, every bit of his belief system and even a lot of his knowledge, wasn't real."

Mark was silent for a long time. He sipped his wine. Glanced around the room. And the longer he sat, the edgier Meredith became. She was a friend of his. Friends didn't sit holding hands.

They didn't fantasize about those hands.

She couldn't remember a time when she hadn't noticed Mark's hands—or remember when she'd first thought of them against her skin, holding her breasts, his thumbs against her nipples, making her...

He was watching her. "What?" She tried to cover her lapse with bravado.

"Can you feel what I'm feeling right now?"

Hell, no, she was too busy dealing with her own emotions and reactions. And then, suddenly, she understood.

"You, too?"

Surprise flashed across his face and she realized what she'd inadvertently admitted. "I need to kiss you."

She nodded. Understood. Couldn't think.

And his mouth touched hers. Just once, she told herself. To say goodbye.

Closing her eyes, feeling herself slipping into him, too, she promised herself it would be quick. She was tired. Had spent two days berating herself for not tuning in to Kelsey sooner. And Mark felt so good. His desire felt so good.

"You have the most beautiful mouth I've ever seen," he whispered, his breath tickling her lips.

"It talks too much." She sucked in a breath—telling herself the kiss was over.

"Every time I look at it, I am possessed with an urge to do this to it," he groaned, and leaning over, pushed her back so that he was lying half on top of her as his lips opened hers and his tongue explored her thoroughly.

Heart beating a warning, Meredith explored back, lost in a divine moment as she tasted him—and sensed that she'd found what she'd been meant to find.

"I've needed this for so long." His voice was hoarse. He shifted, lifting his pelvis on to her thigh and Meredith raised ever so slightly, applying pressure. Her whole body ached, and buzzed, overwhelming her with sensation. She needed release, tears, love.

Her need of this was so much stronger than any reason she shouldn't have it.

When Mark's hand slid to her breast, covering it through her blouse, she cried out, pressing herself against him.

"My bedroom," Mark groaned, pulling her with him as he started to stand.

We never make love at his house. Susan's words came to her. *He won't because of Kelsey.*

"Wait." Though it sent shards of pain through her stomach, Meredith held back, stayed sitting on the couch. "We have to think."

Mark laughed, the sound completely without humor. "Woman, you are going to drive me to the loony bin," he said. "You're the one who's always saying listen to your heart and *now* you want to think?"

"Living authentically requires both," she whispered, trying to find her voice—both inside and out. "You're only going to find the way to your own happiness if you use both. If you listen to your heart, know what's there, and then apply reason, your decisions will keep you on course for true peace and joy."

"I don't know about you," he sighed, "but I was feeling pretty joyful before you started using your head."

Meredith's breasts throbbed. "Me, too."

He dropped back down beside her, finishing off his wine before setting the glass back on the table. "So what's this about?"

His patience had returned. And that was the moment that Meredith knew she was completely, irrevocably, in love with him.

"I can't go to your room with you, make love with you and then walk away."

He brushed her cheek. "Who's asking you to?"

"The issues are still there, Mark. Not the job, since I'm gone in a few short weeks, but the rest of it...."

"There's something I need to talk to you about."

"What?"

"First, we're going to appeal the board's decision," he said, repeating what she vaguely remembered him mentioning the other night. "Policy allows you a trial in the district court before an unbiased jury and you'll stand a much better chance."

"Then the job…"

"And that brings me to the second thing. Chris Blakely over at Harris Junior High is retiring. I've been offered his job. With all that's been going on with Kelsey, I was waiting for a chance to talk it over with you."

"Is that what the superintendent wanted to see you about?"

He nodded.

"And you took the job?"

"Not yet." His gaze was forthright as he turned to her. "The initial offer was somewhat motivated by an attempt to keep me away from your hearing. I couldn't agree to that. Nor could I allow them to make a deal with me before they knew how I was going to behave at that hearing. And because I didn't know myself, I couldn't make any promises."

"And since?"

"I heard from Daniels again today. The offer stands, but I didn't want to take the job without speaking with you first."

As though she should have some say in his life's plans. Pulse increasing again, Meredith reminded herself to stop jumping off cliffs and live life calmly.

"I'm intense, Mark." She laid it right out there. "I'm

always going to be intense. I like my intensity. Most of the time." She really did. Saving Kelsey had solidified a lifelong purpose that she was committed to pursuing. "It's my gift. It helps me to do what I do."

"I know."

"You don't."

"I…"

"You can't spend your whole life waiting for me to get carried away, to lose control like Barbie did."

"I…"

"And worrying that the emotions might someday be too much for me. Because I can tell you right now, they might. Look at the other night with Kelsey…"

"I did look," he said softly. "All night long…."

"Well…"

"Meredith." He put his hand over her mouth. "Let me get a word in edgewise, will you?"

She blinked. Nodded. She'd already told him she talked too much.

"You celebrated when Susan finally realized she was only half-alive and decided to date what's-his-name the pilot."

She started to say the name, but at a glance from Mark decided that wouldn't be necessary.

"You were glad that she was taking risks, because only by doing so would she find real happiness."

"Yeah."

"Did you ever stop to see that I was only half-alive, too?" His gaze was so compelling, her stomach was turning inside out with wanting him—loving him. "I let Barbie's defection stop me in my tracks, and I don't want to live the rest of my life that way. I want real happiness."

"But..."

"I'm not done yet," he said gently. "Just as you celebrated Susan's risk-taking, I celebrate your intensity."

Tears sprang to her eyes. She couldn't believe he'd just said that.

"It's not always going to be easy or calm. Nothing is guaranteed. There will be conflict, but I saw real life the other night—I saw feeling so deep that a life was saved. I felt things I'd never felt before. I don't want to go back to being half-alive."

She didn't know what to say.

"Now's the time, Meredith," he said. "All your life you've been looking inside other people, feeling what they feel, understanding. It's time to look inside yourself."

Held by his gaze, she nodded.

"What do you feel?" His words were soft, yet powerful enough to rip through her.

"I love you."

Eyes closed, he let out a deep breath. She waited for his arms to grab her up, take her to bed. Instead, his eyes opened again and he said, "What else?"

She started to tell him nothing. Slowed down enough to verify the truth of her answer. And began to shake.

"Fear." The word was difficult.

"Of what?"

"You. Kelsey. Me. What if I'm too much? What if you can't handle me? What if I embarrass her? What if..."

"I love you, Meredith Foster," Mark said. "More intensely than I ever thought possible."

Tears sprang to her eyes. Right there in front of him. And still he didn't stop.

"You talked earlier about trust in the deepest sense. You talked about Truman and how he completely trusted what his heart was telling him. I want to know what your heart is telling you."

She tried to speak. Opened her mouth to speak.

"And…" Mark added, his gaze completely serious. "I want to know if you trust yourself enough, trust me enough, to share that heart with me."

With his last words, peace fell over Meredith, a sense of tranquility so deep she couldn't fight it. And she knew.

"I do."

"How sure are you of that?"

"Ninety-nine."

The tension leaving Mark's face was visible. He smiled, but shook his head, too. "I'm an analytical sort, and I don't like the margin of error you've given us. I'd feel a whole lot better about that one percent if you'd agree to marry me to give me a small measure of security."

"Oh, Mark," she said, laughing and crying again as she threw her arms around him. "I will. Yes, I will and if you leave me at the altar I'm going to hunt you down with a license and a judge and—"

"Excuse me…"

As the childish voice reached her consciousness, Meredith jerked back, pulling at her clothes even though they were all still respectably in place.

"Kelsey?" Mark said gently, sitting forward. "Is something wrong?"

"Uh-uh." The little girl shook her head. She looked

about five standing there barefoot in white long johns with yellow butterflies all over them. "I just woke up and heard you guys. And Meredith's crying."

"Oh, sweetie." Meredith jumped up to go to the child, quickly rubbing a hand across her eyes, but Mark got there first, leading Kelsey back to sit between them on the couch.

"What's wrong?" Kelsey asked, her face sober as she glanced between them.

"Nothing!" they said in unison, and then Meredith continued. "They're happy tears, Kelsey. Your father just asked me to marry him."

Kelsey hesitated, glanced at her father, and Meredith wanted to kick herself for blurting out the news like that. Where was all her so called sensitivity?

"Does this mean that we're going to be a real family and Meredith's going to be my mom now?" Kelsey asked her father.

Meredith's heart stopped. Her chest ached. "Is that okay with you?" she asked the little girl.

Kelsey nodded slowly. "Because I figured out something in the hospital when I woke up and Daddy was sleeping there in the chair."

"What's that?" Mark asked, his arm around his daughter, holding her close against him. The little girl slid her hand beneath Meredith's.

"That my real mom is too sick or something to be a mom and she couldn't really love me if she let all that bad stuff happen to me. I was trying to make her love me and be okay, but I couldn't do it."

Meredith blinked back more tears. "You're right

about most of that, sweetie," she said. "But your mother does love you. Don't ever think she doesn't."

Kelsey didn't say anything for a minute and as soon as Meredith quieted her mind and heart, she understood.

"It's all right that you love her, too, you know," she said softly. "Children are meant to love their parents, even when moms and dads make mistakes."

Kelsey nodded. Said nothing.

"It's also okay if you're really mad at her for letting you down."

A sigh was Kelsey's only reply to that. And then, after a silence, she reached up and hugged both of them, bringing their three heads together. "I love you," she said, hanging on to their necks.

"I love you, too, Kelsey, more than anything in the world," Mark said.

Kelsey seemed to be considering that. Or something else. She peered up at Meredith. "Is it okay if I love you, too?" she asked.

"Oh, baby, of course." Meredith couldn't hold back her tears then as she gave the child another big hug. "Because I know I already love you, Kelsey, as much as if you were my very own little girl."

Kelsey nodded as though that made perfect sense to her.

"So it's all over and we're just going to be normal now, right?" she asked.

"Right," Mark and Meredith said in unison.

And just as quickly as she'd appeared, Kelsey hopped up. "I think I can sleep again now, okay?"

Mark stood. "I'll tuck you in."

"That's okay," Kelsey shook her head. "You and

Meredith can go back to what you were doing." With an impish, although exhausted grin, she turned and headed down the hall.

A couple of seconds later, holding hands while they listened for Kelsey to settle in, Mark and Meredith could hear her telling Gilda that everything was going to be fine now. They were finally getting the right mom.

Meredith's spirit soared.

"THIS IS Angela Liddy with KNLD news, with a disturbing top story tonight. Washington County district attorney Larry Barnett was arrested this afternoon after his eight-year-old son came to school with bruises all over his body. The boy claimed to have fallen down a flight of stairs until his mother called Thomas's former teacher, Meredith Foster. In a remarkable interview with the boy and police detectives, in which Ms. Foster merely sat in the room and told the boy repeatedly that it was okay to tell the truth, it was learned that Barnett had physically abused both his wife and son on numerous occasions—"

"And Ms. Foster," Mark broke in. "Or, Mrs. Shepherd for those who care to get it right, has now been offered reemployment at Lincoln Elementary School where she will be driving her adorable fifth-grade daughter to and from class every day when school resumes in the fall…"

Meredith shivered as his gravelly voice sounded in her ear. He slid his arms around her.

"What are you doing watching that crap?" he asked, pointing to the television she'd turned on in their bedroom while she waited for him to brush his teeth and come to bed. "News depresses you."

"Yeah." She leaned back against him, holding his hands. "But sometimes you just have to hear it for yourself to believe it."

"Not you, my love," Mark said, turning her around. "You've got the inside track...."

Page-turning drama...

Exotic, glamorous locations...

Intense emotion and passionate seduction...

Sheikhs, princes and billionaire tycoons...

This summer, may we suggest:

THE SHEIKH'S DISOBEDIENT BRIDE
by Jane Porter

On sale June.

AT THE GREEK TYCOON'S BIDDING
by Cathy Williams

On sale July.

THE ITALIAN MILLIONAIRE'S VIRGIN WIFE

On sale August.

With new titles to choose from every month,
discover a world of romance in our books written
by internationally bestselling authors.

**Hidden in the secrets of antiquity,
lies the unimagined truth...**

Introducing

a brand-new line filled with mystery
and suspense, action and adventure,
and a fascinating look into history.
And it all begins with DESTINY.

In a sealed crypt in
France, where the
terrifying legend of
the beast of Gevaudan
begins to unravel,
Annja Creed discovers
a stunning artifact
that will seal her destiny.

*Available every other
month starting
July 2006, wherever
you buy books.*

GOLD
EAGLE

GRA1

If you enjoyed what you just read,
then we've got an offer you can't resist!

Take 2 bestselling
love stories FREE!
Plus get a FREE surprise gift!

HARLEQUIN®

Super Romance

THE PRODIGAL'S RETURN

by *Anna DeStefano*

Prom night for Jenn Gardner and Neal Cain turned
into a tragedy that tore them apart. Eight years
later, Jenn has made a life for herself and her young
daughter. But when Neal comes home, Jenn sees that
he is still consumed with the past. Maybe she can
convince him that he's paid enough and deserves
happiness a second time around.

"Anna DeStefano's remarkable stories of the healing
power of love touch the heart with hope. One of the
genre's rising stars..."
—Gayle Wilson, two-time
RITA® Award-winning author

On sale July 2006!
Available wherever books are sold, including most
bookstores, supermarkets, discount stores and drugstores.

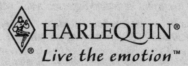

HARLEQUIN®
Live the emotion™

SPECIAL EDITION™

Welcome to Danbury Way—where nothing is as it seems...

Megan Schumacher has managed to maintain a low profile on Danbury Way by keeping the huge success of her graphics business a secret. But when a new client turns out to be a neighbor's sexy ex-husband, rumors of their developing romance quickly start to swirl.

THE RELUCTANT CINDERELLA

by CHRISTINE RIMMER

Available July 2006

Don't miss the first book from the Talk of the Neighborhood miniseries.

HARLEQUIN®

Super Romance

COMING NEXT MONTH

#1356 A BABY BETWEEN THEM • C.J. Carmichael
Return to Summer Island
Aidan Wythe is too busy running Kincaid Communications and *not* thinking about Rae Cordell to take time off. Which is why his boss banishes him to Summer Island for a forced vacation. When a very pregnant Rae also shows up on the island, he knows he's not going to get any rest or relaxation.

#1357 A FAMILY RESEMBLANCE • Margot Early
Four years have passed since Victor Knoll's death, and his wife, Sabine, can't imagine another man who could compare with him as a husband or a father. Then Joe Knoll appears in her tiny mountain town, claiming to be Victor's brother—a brother she's never heard of. He says Victor wasn't the person she thought he was. And to complicate things even more, he says he's falling in love with her....

#1358 THE PRODIGAL'S RETURN • Anna DeStefano
Prom night for Jenn Gardner and Neal Cain turned into a tragedy that tore them apart. Eight years later, Jenn has made a life for herself and her young daughter. But when Neal comes home, Jenn sees that Neal is still consumed with the past. Maybe she can convince him that he's paid enough and deserves happiness a second time around.

#1359 TELL ME NO LIES • Kathryn Shay
Dan Logan is Citizen of the Year. He has an ideal marriage and two wonderful children. What he doesn't have is the truth about his wife. But can his ideals survive the truth when Tessa's past finally, inevitably, comes out?

#1360 A TIME TO FORGIVE • Darlene Gardner
Named for her deceased uncle, abandoned by her mother, nine-year-old Jaye Smith is in need of a little TLC. Good thing she has her uncle Connor on her side. But when sparks fly for Connor and Jaye's teacher Abby Reed, it sets them on a path toward uncovering a stinging truth, which they can only overcome together....

#1361 HUSBAND AND WIFE REUNION • Linda Style
Cold Cases: L.A.
If she finishes the magazine articles she's writing, she's a dead woman. But when her ex-husband, L.A.P.D. Detective Luke Coltrane, finds out about the anonymous threats, Julianna gets more protection than she wants....